COURAGE

BLACKSTONE
BOOK 4

J.L. DRAKE

COURAGE
BLACKSTONE SERIES

Cover Design by Spellbinding Design

Editing by Lori Whitwam

CAST OF CHARACTERS

John: Blackstone member, twin sister almost died.

Sloane: …You'll just have to wait and see.

Frank: Blackstone contact for the Army, lives in Washington, DC, Mia's father.

Cole: Owner of the safe house in Montana called Shadows. Fell in love with a picture of a victim. Found, saved, and married Savannah. Leader of the Blackstone special ops team.

Savannah: Held for ransom in Tijuana, Mexico, for seven months. Saved by Blackstone, married Cole Logan, has a daughter named Olivia, lives at Shadows.

Mike: Agent at Dusk but originally from Shadows. Scary-looking teddy bear, covered head to toe in tattoos.

Catalina: Mike's wife and daughter of a cartel family. Mother of Gabriella.

Keith: Member of Blackstone. Secretive. Savannah's "big brother." Husband to Lexi and father to Brandon, Jr.

Lexi: Keith's wife, Brandon AKA B's mother.

Mark: Best friend to Cole Logan, Blackstone member. Uses humor to escape the pain from his past. Married to Mia, has twin boys.

Mia: Mark's wife, nurse, Frank's daughter, mother of twin boys (second round of kids to enter the Blackstone team).

Abigail: Mark's adopted mother, Cole's childhood nanny, and now house aide. Dating Dr. Roberts.

Dr. Roberts: House doctor, kind soul, snappy dresser, dating Abigail.

Dell: Member of Blackstone, lives at Shadows.

Davie: Member of Blackstone, specializing in diving. Lives at Shadows.

Denton Barlow: The American from *Broken* who was obsessed with Savannah, wore gold- tipped cobra boots.

KIDS

Olivia: Savannah and Cole's daughter.

Liam and Ethan: Mark and Mia's twins.

Brandon, Jr.: Keith and Lexi's son.

Gabriella: Mike and Catalina's daughter.

DEVIL'S REACH MC

Trigger: Scary as hell, president of the Devil's Reach Motorcycle Club in Santa Monica.
Tess: Trigger's old lady.
Brick: Trigger's VP of the Devil's Reach, Tess's best friend.
Rail: Member of Devil's Reach, a tad *metrosexual.*

TEAM NORTH ROCK

Steve Chamness: Team North Rock.

BLACKSTONE CODE NAMES

Cole: Raven One
Mark: Raven Two
Keith: Beta Seven
John: Fox Two
Mike: Delta Six

DEDICATION

For anyone who needs a little hope.

PROLOGUE

Location: Southern México
Coordinates: Classified

Thirteen Hours Ago

JOHN

"Raven One!" Chamness from Team North Rock screamed over the radio. "What's your ETA?"

"Drop me down in the middle," I commanded and signaled for the chopper to dive to the right and pull a quick turn. Flashes of fire lit up the gray sky as we roared toward the battle. The blades whipped the water around, which made our visual blurry. Cole's mouth was moving, but he was on a different channel, so

I moved my attention to Mark and Keith and saw they were ready to rappel when I was. Mike slapped my shoulder and signaled he was good to go. I glanced at Cole, who stood and gave a quick nod to move out.

I threaded the rope through one hand, while the other held another section behind my back. I leaned out into the air facing the chopper with the rope secured around my waist and pushed off with my feet then let gravity take control.

We plummeted toward the unknown.

The zip of the rope heightened my senses, and I was psyched as my feet hit the ground. I quickly unclipped my gun and held it to my eye to line up the scope.

One.

Two.

Three.

Four.

I counted as each of my teammates landed next to me. Once the fourth hit, we spread out like ants to our next posts. Our orders were to shoot first and ask later. Our hunt was to locate the missing rookie who had gotten separated from North Rock eight days ago. We didn't mess around when one of our own was in trouble.

"Fox Two to North Rock One," I whispered into my comms. "Landed and are in position."

Mosquitos and raindrops filled in the dead space of time while we held tight, crouched down below the thick terrain. We scanned the tree trunks to see if they'd morph into a human shape and listened carefully to try to catch even a whisper through the rainfall.

Mark held my stare as we both wondered where the other team was and how many were even left standing. Thirty more painful seconds passed, and we heard Chamness's voice.

"Follow the route as planned but come up the west side." The radio clicked off, but we froze when he clicked it again. "I've lost visual on three. Something isn't right here, boys. I feel it." Three pops in the background had us racing across the ground. The wind was wild, and the rain matched its intensity. Thankfully, we were dressed all in black, which allowed us to jet across the open field and not be seen. Most of our survival gear was stitched into the fabric of our suits. In case of captivity, it was hard to spot, often overlooked as it was in our pants, and those were normally left on.

We had no time or warning. We had gotten the call and left.

It had been called in as a level five extraction. The worst kind.

As Shadows faded into the back of my mind, thoughts of my family weighed heavily on me. Something strange passed through me as I scanned the forest, a shiver that burrowed deep down in my bones. It left an aftershock I knew would still be there days later. I had a bad feeling that this mission would be life changing.

This was a very different mission for us. We weren't

looking for a kidnapped victim. No, somehow the tables were flipped, and we now seemed to be the prey.

Cole signaled for me to move to the right as we slowed our pace and muted our steps. Once we were back under the protection of the shrubs and trees, we started to hunt our target.

"Twenty-nine red fires," Chamness commanded for us to move into formation. It was one of our many code words we used just between Blackstone and North Rock.

We formed a U shape, weapons raised as we closed in on the enemy.

Pop! Pop! I blinked back the moisture and took out two men who darted in front of me. Cole shot three, and Mike choked out another.

Six down.

Suddenly, the wind changed direction, which set the hair on my neck on end. It was almost as if Mother Nature had given us a warning that more was coming. Just like out of a nightmare, a wall of men stood up, and a rocket launcher, pointed in our direction, came into focus.

"Run!" I shouted, and we ran like hell. The blast hit hard, and I was thrown at least fifteen feet. Heat and debris smothered my body like a blanket, then…*Whack*! I hit a tree trunk and fell with a thud. Something hot licked my side, and I fought to keep my vision clear.

I rolled onto my back and began to go through my mental checklist. I slid my hand down my body, thankful that it didn't seem too bad. It hurt like a bitch, but it was just a deep graze.

I twisted hard and, with a heave, stood to locate my team. Three bullets hit a tree, and bark went flying around me. I hunched down and raced through the shrubs to where I'd spotted Cole. Mark and Mike joined us while Keith checked in a few feet away.

"Good?" Cole asked, and I gave a nod. I knew adrenaline alone would block the pain. "Good," he repeated and pulled out his map and started to give orders.

With a new plan of action, we pulled ourselves together and split up. We knew how to do this; we were Blackstone. We began using the technique we were known for and started to pluck the bastards off one by one. We ambushed each of the bastards. We were shadows in the night, unseen and deadly.

The boys disappeared into the brushes when I had to stop to reload. Suddenly, something hard hit me between the shoulder blades, and my gun was cut free from my body. My breath shot from my lungs. I swung around and blocked the next hit from one of *them*. I rammed my knee up and inward into his chest. He fell back, and I took another hit to the upper arm.

Damn! There were more of them.

Again, I whirled and blocked the next blow, but this time with my elbow. Blood and rain mixed together as my attacker's cheek split. He fell back, and another two approached. I sagged to find my footing and wondered why they were going for hand-to-hand combat and not using their weapons.

"Keep this one alive," one of them muttered. "We need to film it."

I snapped my knuckles and held my hands out, ready to fight. They both launched, and I did my best to stay alive.

I popped one in the face, twisted, and broke two ribs on his left. I got two punches to the gut while that happened, but I still had enough energy to break the asshole's arm and drive the palm of my hand in to snap his nose.

Pop! Pop! I ducked but slipped on the wet ground and fell backward down a steep cliff. I tried desperately to claw at the mud for something to hold on to, anything that would stop my race toward God knew what. I hit a rock and started to flip rather than skid. Colors blurred together with the sounds, and my head raced to keep up. Automatically, my hand went for my gun in my thigh holster. *Shit*, it was missing.

Something smacked into me hard, and I came to a screaming halt. I whipped out my calf pistol and swung around, jamming it in someone's face. I blinked as I too was staring down the barrel of a gun. A millisecond later, the fog cleared, and I focused on the face behind it.

"What the fuck are you doing here?"

ONE

JOHN

His chest rose and fell and, given his ratty look, I guessed he'd been in the woods for a while. I lowered my gun but didn't tuck it away.

My mouth flexed uncomfortably as I did a check on my body. Everything seemed to be working.

"The fall got you pretty good," he huffed.

"Yeah." I squeezed my eyes shut as a jolt of pain plowed through my skull. I sighed and forced myself to focus on him. "Wanna tell me what you are doing in the middle of the desert, Brick?"

He shrugged. "Deal went south. Just using the woods to hide until morning."

"Seems convenient."

"Could say the same about you." He tried to light a cigarette, but it was too wet. "Fuck!"

I knew there was definitely more to the story, but I left it alone.

We lowered our voices when we heard someone talking.

"We need to get moving." I checked my clip as we kept low and started to make our way around the hill. We needed to find higher ground.

The mud was thick, and Brick's sneakers were slowing him down. This painful pace wasn't going to cut it. We needed to get higher now.

I pressed my fingers to my comms. "Fox Two to Raven One." I waited for Cole to come in as Brick took a moment to stop.

A crackle broke through the earpiece. "Fox Two to Raven One. If you can hear me, click your com."

Again, static.

Shit.

"That can't be good," Brick muttered.

"We need to get up there," I said more to myself and shielded the rain from my vision to inspect the mountain. "Come on."

He grunted but followed. He slipped a few times, and I had to wait for him to continue to climb.

"Follow in my footsteps, so the mud isn't as thick."

He tried, but his Vans were filled with sludge.

Fifty-six minutes later, we made it to the top of a ridge where I could get my bearings.

"You ever think of working out more?" I smirked, and he tossed me the finger.

"I work out, just in different ways." He chuckled, but his eyes widened, and I felt the danger before I saw it. I whirled around and jammed my fist straight into the guy's nose then punched him in the throat. He fell back, and his head slammed into a rock.

Quickly, I ripped his weapon free and handed it to Brick, who admired the AR with a silent *whoop*.

The fat guy moaned, and blood drained from his nose, but it would be a while before he'd wake fully.

I cut his jacket off and tossed it out of my way. My knife had sliced his shirt too, and when I rolled the bastard over, I caught sight of some ink on his forearm.

Seven. I memorized the number and the design then went back to removing his weapons.

Taking off my watch, I flipped it over and bit the back of it off. Cole had added two different tracking devices inside the watch, one for us and one if we needed to monitor someone else.

"Watch my back," I ordered Brick, who stood and scanned the cliff.

Carefully, I removed the tiny device and used my knife to cut into the tongue of the fat bastard's sneaker and tucked it neatly inside. I patted his pockets and felt a thin wallet.

Dammit, no ID.

I improvised instead. Removing one of his credit

cards, I pressed his thumb onto the plastic and slipped the card into a baggie in my side pocket.

"Hey!" I hit Brick's shoulder to grab his attention. "Time to go."

"Yeah." He waited for my lead.

"Do you have any idea how far you'd been walking since you saw a road?"

"Maybe forty minutes." He turned around like he was finding the direction he came from. He started to climb higher to another part of the cliff. "Look, there."

I squinted through the rain that was finally tapering off, and sure as hell, there was a road.

"That's pretty good." I was impressed.

"Well," he followed me to the edge, "this ain't my first rodeo, my friend." His fake drawl made me grin.

Carefully, I dipped low and scanned the area. There was the road a few miles out, but what was more appealing was the gas station off in the distance.

"How good are your knees?"

Brick shook his head, confused. "You want, like, a zero to ten here or…"

I ignored his sarcasm and pointed to a bush.

"See that bush?"

"You mean that cactus?"

"Sure." I dropped my voice when someone shouted from behind us. Company was coming. "When I say jump, jump, and once you land—"

"You mean once my knees shoot up into my chest? That's, like, thirty feet down."

"Correct. Pull them out and run southwest and meet me at that gas station." I pointed it out to him.

"And where are you during all of this?"

"I'll be running parallel to you so if we get seen they'll have to split up." I moved closer to the edge and planned out my moves step by step.

"Ready?" I turned to Brick, who was now beside me.

"No."

"Too bad." I gave him a nudge, and he dropped off the ledge. He landed awkwardly and shot me the finger before he jumped up and scrambled across the terrain and into a gully.

I glanced back at the fat man, as his noises were getting louder.

Easing my body over the crumbly rock, I balanced my weight on my fingertips and dropped straight down. My knees absorbed the impact, and I landed without a sound. I kept low as I raced across the clearing and slipped into the tree line and blended with the brush.

I kept my eye on Brick. He was a distance ahead of me, and we both ran like cheetahs through the brush. Low ground was not my comfort zone, and we could be attacked at any moment. I constantly scanned my surroundings, mentally calculating each move. I imagined myself like a human spring ready to bend to whatever Mother Nature had in store on this run.

The road came up fast, and I waited for Brick to cross and disappear into the ditch. Once he was out of sight, I did the same, nearly taking his shoulder off as I landed next to him.

God, I missed my brothers already.

Brick's chest heaved while he patted his pocket for his smokes. He pulled them out and cursed at the damp, crushed mess.

"I blame you." He shook the box into his hand and showed me the cigarettes.

"You're welcome. They were wet, anyway," I muttered and suddenly tuned in to a new sound.

"If I was Rail, you'd be getting a mouthful right…" He trailed off when he realized I wasn't listening. "What?"

"Shh," I ordered and closed my eyes to block out all the white noise. The sound of pebbles scraping over sand made me hyperaware we were about to have company.

Static from a radio had us both frozen mid-move, and Brick motioned with his eyes that someone was approaching from behind me. He moved his weapon, but I shook my head. If there were more cartel around, we needed to stay quiet. I pulled my knife from my belt where it was hidden in the buckle. It was small, I knew, but it could be just as effective as a bullet if used correctly.

Brick spread out his hand and silently counted down to when I should make my move.

Three.

Two.

One.

I darted from the protection of the ditch and rammed my knife into someone's ribs, and when he fell,

I kneed his face then carefully lowered his heavy body down to Brick, who dug through his pockets like a grave robber. He grinned when he found a half pack of smokes.

I felt the bullet graze my cheek a hair of a second before I heard the click as the bullet left the chamber.

"Shit!" *That was close.*

Brick shot up pulled me back down and stared into my face.

"You good?"

"We need to move." Hot flames burned my face. It had been a close one, but I knew it was only a flesh wound.

We stayed low and worked our way along the ditch, but when we came to a storm drain, Brick hesitated.

"Anything could be in there," he hissed.

"But we know what's out there, so get on your knees and crawl."

"You know that came out sexual, don't you?"

I pushed his back and shot him forward just as we heard footsteps.

I tried my hardest not to think what was living inside the steel tube, considering not many of these were around the area. When we got to the other side, we raced toward the gas station, only to be greeted with more bullets.

"Jesus Christ!" Brick skidded as the bullets kicked up the dirt around him. "Plan B would be a great option right now, Black!"

"Truck!" I tossed at him. A semi-truck had just

finished at the pump. "Come on!" I picked up the pace and closed in on the trucker getting into the driver's side.

The engine roared to life, and so did Brick. He yelled he'd been hit. I reached back and grabbed his leather cut to pull him up behind me and cursed as he dropped his gun.

"The fuckers got my leg!"

I quickly glanced down and saw the blood draining from his calf.

Shit.

More bullets sprayed in our direction, which prompted the trucker to floor it, shifting gears out of the parking lot. I caught his face in the mirror and awkwardly ripped the top of my patch off to show we were Americans. I swore something passed between us, because the truck slowed slightly but then began to accelerate as I grabbed the handle to the massive back door and hauled Brick up on the small ledge with me. I looked back and saw the cartel, who now seemed to be arguing as one guy pointed in the opposite direction while another pointed at us. Why weren't they scrambling into their vehicles to follow the truck?

"You good?" I hit his shoulder to get his attention. He was drenched in sweat, and mud and leaves clung to his clothes.

"Yeah," he grunted as he tried to shift to a better spot.

The trucker took a couple of turns, which I hoped would throw the cartel off. Our fingers were white and cramped by the time we hit the next town. After a sharp turn, the truck took a side road and slowed almost to a crawl. I took it as a sign he wanted us to know this was far enough. I didn't want to push our luck, so I took hold of Brick's arm and nudged us off the step, not wanting to put the driver in any more danger. Brick stumbled, and I grabbed him before he did a face plant into the dirt.

"Jesus, warn a guy," he gasped as he tried to regain his feet.

"Sorry, man. We were lucky to get a lift this far." I pulled him to cover in some bushes until I felt the road was clear. I spotted what looked to be a run-down diner not far away, and we made our way slowly toward it.

The place had a strange vibe to it when we entered. I helped Brick to a chair as two employees quickly disappeared into the back. I kept an eye on the door as I pulled a piece of clean cloth from the supply in one of my pockets and wrapped his leg as tightly as I could.

"Yeah, that hurts," he complained, but I knew he was going to be fine.

"A bullet will do that." I stood back and examined the gash in my side. I stuck a field dressing on it then bound it in place.

"What don't you have on you?" Brick tried to laugh but coughed with a wince as he tested the leg.

"When you do the shit we do, you get lots of good stuff."

A movement caused me to whirl around at the same time as I pulled out my knife and held it ready.

"Whoa, there. Take it easy, fella. You guys need any

help?" The guy gestured at his pocket, and with a nod from me, he inched out his ID and held it up. "Agent Cooper Colins, FBI."

"Recon John Black." I lowered my knife and offered my hand. He gave me a firm handshake, and I relaxed a little. I was damn glad he was here. I noticed a ring on his right hand that looked a little flashy for an FBI agent but figured I couldn't judge, considering I was helping a repeat offender in the one percent club.

"This is a friend." I indicated Brick, whose face showed a distinct lack of friendliness.

"Well, looks like you both have seen better days. Need a phone?"

"Please." I took the phone he held out and quickly dialed a secure number. The agent shook his head at some lowlifes who were slowly moving toward us. Who the hell *was* this guy?

I focused back on what I was doing, and as the phone rang, I finally activated my personal GPS.

"Go," someone answered.

"This is Recon John Black, ID 135241493," I paused and gave my code word, "clear."

"Code word verified. Give your location."

There was a moment of silence while someone typed in the number to see who it was assigned to on this mission.

"Did you activate yourself?" He cleared his throat like he wanted to say more, but we both knew he couldn't.

"Affirmative." I glanced down at my watch to see the tiny green light that showed it was working.

"You need medical?"

"Negative for me, and I also activated a second tracker," I glanced at Brick and saw he was now glaring at the agent, "but yes, I will need medical for one I need to get out. I'd like to make a request to stay put."

There was a pause. "Give me a moment."

I moved to the window and scanned the place to see if our company had arrived. All looked clear, not that that meant anything. They were slimy suckers and knew the land better than I did.

"In twenty-four hours, meet at checkpoint two. Clock starts now. Leave your company where you are someone is on the way."

Second tracker confirmed."

"Ten-four."

"Ten-four." The line went dead.

"Wait." Brick propped himself up against the wall after I told him I was out. "You're leaving me here with a fucking FBI agent and some John Gotti-looking assholes?" Sweat dripped from his forehead, and he looked pissed. "I'd rather be back with the fucker on the cliff." He tried to stand, but I pushed him back down.

"Irons is on his way. He'll get you back to Cali," I whispered.

"Look, I don't want to sound like a pussy, but—"

"Then don't," I interrupted.

"Shit, at least Mike is friendly."

I ignored him and stood to check my wounds. The gauze was holding fine on my side and arm. It wasn't anything I couldn't handle. I dabbed at the blood on my cheek and figured I was ready.

"You can't go out emptyhanded." Agent Colins passed me a handgun with three clips. It bothered me that he'd overheard my conversation with Brick, but I was thankful for the weapon.

"Thank you." I gave a curt nod and glanced at Brick. He still looked pissed, and it was obvious he didn't like being so close to the FBI agent. "Will you be here for long?"

"No," Colins checked the time, "we're following a subject who's now on the move again." He signaled for his men to stand. "Good luck, Black."

"Same to you." I watched them leave the diner and turned back to Brick. "Happy?"

"I'd be happier if you got me a drink and a lighter."

I tucked the gun away and stored the extra mags in my pocket. I leaned down and took one last look at Brick's leg.

"Why were you in Mexico?"

"I told you—"

"I don't want your bullshit answer."

His gaze shifted, and his expression was pissed again.

I wanted to beat it out of him, but I was losing time. "Logan and Irons have been good to you," I held up a hand to stop him from interrupting, "and you've been good to us. I just want to make sure you aren't involved in something that will hurt this operation."

"It wasn't me who screwed up your operation. Mine was completely unrelated." His gaze returned to mine, and I saw he was being honest.

"Okay." I stood and checked the time.

Shit, I'd wasted eighteen minutes.

"Irons should be here soon, but keep watch in case those sons-of-bitches show up. You good? I don't like it you don't have a weapon. Keep your head down."

"Yeah, no shit. Me either, but," he smacked his leg, "I'll be just dandy." Then his expression changed, and his smile turned genuine. "Thanks for the help out there."

"Same to you. Stay alive." With that, I left and scoped out the area before I slipped into the tall weeds that would be my protection as I raced back toward the last location I'd known my team had been.

Nightfall came just as I reached the top of the cliff Brick and I had been on earlier. The man I had slipped the tracking device on was gone. I knew wherever they were, they still could be close by. My fingers inched across the rock to get a strong hold before I lifted myself up and twisted to sit on a high peak.

I had a solid nine hours before my team came to retrieve me. Now I would sit and listen to who came and went. My gut told me there was much more to this story than we knew.

Once the sun peeked above the horizon and the stars faded away, I started my descent from the cliff to the next checkpoint. Sadly, nothing was spotted, and I needed to move on. It wasn't long before my watch vibrated to get my attention. It was time to haul ass.

A single loud bang echoed through the air, and the sound waves traveled through my chest. Every instinct in my body screamed at me to follow that sound.

Moving as quietly as I could, I struggled not to let my mind think it was one of my brothers. I saw the body lying face down. He was stripped of all his clothes except his boxers. A signature move of the cartel, along with a single bullet to the back of the head.

I dropped to my knees and rolled over his badly beaten body. I recognized the poor rookie. He was only twenty-two, fresh out of school, and was our target to find. Someone had helped him get a hookup to join North Rock, and against all of Frank's protests, he was overruled from somewhere higher up. I remembered his anger over it when he had to let the boy in when we all knew he wasn't ready.

The *no brother left behind* mantra kept racing through my mind.

I wrapped his arm around my shoulder and slipped him over my back to carry him to the checkpoint.

The chopper blades beat the trees, and as it lowered into a secured area, I stepped out and caught Chamness's horrified face. I raced across to the chopper and handed the kid to him.

"Who is it?" Mark asked as he grabbed for my arm.

"Nick Stewart."

"The rookie operator?" I nodded before he asked, "Are you hurt?"

I shook my head in spite of his raised eyebrow at the blood seeping from the hole in my side and settled into the seat next to him. I watched as the men carefully covered the kid and started the protocol by calling it in. Chamness cursed and closed his eyes. The loss of any man was hard, but it hurt even more when we all knew this had been the wrong place and team for the rookie.

Frank was going to flip his shit over that one, because he knew he wasn't ready to be on the team.

Chamness finished loading up his sack with more ammo and rations before he disappeared back into the Mexican forest to find the rest of his team.

I settled in for the long flight home, and my head hung with fatigue. I draped my arms around my propped-up knees and felt the heaviness in my heart. I needed to sort through what the hell just happened.

My head still spun by the time I arrived back at Shadows and made my way up to my room. I barely remembered my shower or how I even got changed before sleep called my name.

The moment my head hit my pillow at Shadows, I was out cold. I faintly remembered Mia saying something, but I couldn't focus enough to listen. I needed sleep badly, and then I needed time to process.

———

"Is he dead?" I heard Shit One's little squeak from the doorway.

"Nah, he isn't gray yet," Shit Two hissed.

"You mean blue?"

"Gray means dead for good."

I cracked open an eye and glared at Mark's twins as I licked the inside of my dry mouth. Screw the troubled twos, when you were a Lopez, six was the dangerous age.

"Should we poke him just in case?"

"No! Remember what happened last time?" Liam warned. "He hung us from Abby's clothesline and left us there until Mom heard us screaming."

I smirked at that delightful memory and tried to muffle my laugh.

"Oh, shoot!" Liam yelped. "He's awake. Run!"

"Boys!" I heard Mia shout from the hallway. "You better be ready for school, and you better not be not bothering Uncle John."

"We're not!" they both lied together.

"Move it," she warned with a sigh. Poor Mia was exhausted a lot lately. Tabby was two and a handful in her own right.

I rolled out of bed, and the reality of the past two days hit me like a ton of bricks. I slipped on my pants and headed to get my day moving. I was good with heavy shit. I'd dealt with enough of it to know I was, but last night's mission went wrong very fast, and I knew something was definitely off.

TWO

"Sorry. I know this isn't what you wanted to have happen, Sloane." Frank offered me a hand as the tips of my heels found their footing in the loose gravel. "Where is Logan?" He shaded his eyes and scanned the property. "It's like herding cats with these men." He chuckled with a grin. I could tell he preferred to be here rather than in Washington, and I could understand why. I mimicked him and shaded the tops of my glasses against the glare and took in the breathtaking view of the famous Shadows safe house. I'd always known this place existed, but I never thought I would be brought here, especially under these circumstances.

"Trust me, Frank," I grinned when I saw the lake and heard a loon call off in the distance, "I am not complaining." This was the better option. A cool breeze brushed over my exposed skin and swirled the ties on my jacket.

I missed the wide-open spaces of the country and the fresh clean smell that came with the mountains. I really needed to get out of the city more often. Well, I guessed I was now; I just wished—

"Ready for some madness?" He broke into my thoughts.

"Bring it on." I forced a smile and followed him up a staircase and into a delicious-smelling entryway. Was that nutmeg? My mouth started to water.

"May I take your jacket?"

I shrugged out of the heavy wool pea coat and handed it to him, and a chubby white cat flopped on his back and spread his legs, awaiting attention.

"Take my advice and don't touch it." He wrinkled his nose at the cat. "He's a shameless flirt who only has eyes for Savannah."

"Good to know." I avoided eye contract as I stepped over the meowing fur ball.

"Follow me." He led me through the entryway and into a massive living room. An older lady dressed in a pair of slacks and a green sweater greeted us with warm smile.

"Welcome back, Frank."

"Abigail." He gave a polite nod before he turned to me. "I want to introduce you to Sloane Harlow. She'll be staying with you for a little bit."

I held out my hand, but she wrapped her arms around me instead. At first, I was taken aback, but her warmth was so infectious I hugged her back just as tightly.

"Lovely to meet you, Abigail."

"Any friend of Frank's is a friend of ours." Her love for people poured from her, and I instantly missed my mother.

Frank whirled around when a nice-looking man came in. "Logan, where's Black?"

"Peak," he said through a bite of an apple and tapped on a tank that held a lively fish with weird eyes.

"Shit, seriously?" Frank muttered.

"Pardon me?" Abby turned to Cole, and to my surprise, spoke to him bluntly. "You let him go to the peak? He just got home, and he was shot, for goodness sake."

"He must need it."

"Still, Cole." She rubbed her cheek, obviously worried.

Cole shrugged, unfazed by her comment. I hadn't had much time to brush up on the Blackstone men. I had just finished up my last case and was told to stop everything and meet Frank at the airport in only two days and to bring enough clothes to last me awhile. Once I was in the air, I was told where I was going and why, and even though I was beyond upset with the decision being made for me, I knew I didn't have a choice. I knew he was right, but I still didn't like being told to pack up and move without a say in the matter.

Normally, I'd make sure I knew all the ins and outs of

everyone, but there hadn't been any time. Frank did, however, gave me a file on Cole and Savannah, so I wasn't completely out of touch on the family dynamic, but the rest of them I'd have to learn about. He mentioned that some boxes would be waiting for me when I got settled. At least I wouldn't be wasting time and would be useful. I was good at my job, and I was determined to help in any way possible. I would do anything for Frank.

"He's a grown-ass man, Abs." Cole took another bite. "What am I going to do?"

"You could have stopped him."

That made Cole chuckle in amusement.

"Telling John not to go to the peak is like telling Mark there's no dinner. It doesn't happen."

A chair hit the floor in the other room, and someone shouted. "There's no dinner?"

Cole's eyebrow lifted. "Case in point."

"Cole," Abby put her hands on her hips with a sigh, "he's injured, and he should be resting, not to mention he found—"

"No, really," a boyish-looking man was in the entryway of kitchen, "what's going on? Savi promised to cook."

"Don't worry, Marcus, I'm about to start dinner." Abby shook her head at me, but I could tell she loved every moment of it by the way she looked at the guys. Love and patience were written all over her face.

"That's not funny." He pointed at Cole before he grabbed two cookies off the counter and spotted me.

"Company? Why didn't anyone tell me?" He shoved a cookie in his mouth before he held out his free hand. "Mark Lopez." Crumbs fell from his lips, and I couldn't help but laugh.

"Sloane Harlow."

He tilted his head to study me. "I see a little Latina in you and…" He waited for me to finish.

"Hungarian, Latina, but born in America."

"Oh, that explains your intense blue eyes."

I smiled at his mannerisms. He was like a sweet boy trapped in a man's body.

"*Köszönöm*," I replied, *thanks* in Hungarian.

His hand landed on his chest. "That was so sexy."

"Right." Frank rolled his eyes. "How much longer until Black returns? I'd like to have a meeting sooner rather than later."

Cole grabbed the binoculars off the counter and headed for the living room. Frank motioned for me to follow. He adjusted the center knob and raised them to look somewhere up on one of the mountains.

"Can't see him, so he must be on his way back."

"Or dead on a ledge somewhere." Abby scowled.

"He's been climbing since he could walk, Abby. Today is no different."

Mark strolled in with more cookies and sprawled out on the couch, perfectly at ease with someone new in the house. It was oddly comforting. I'd spent a lot of time around awkward, uncomfortable people, so this was new and welcome.

The back patio door opened, and the sound of someone hitting their boots together had Abby sighing with relief.

Cole responded with a "told ya" smile.

"Don't start, young man," she warned as she turned and placed her hands on her hips.

"Johnathan Davin Black, march your butt in here."

A light chuckle could be heard as he moved about. My cell rang, and I quickly fished it from my purse. Checking the ID, I groaned.

Cole's face questioned, and Frank shook his head. "The line is secure."

"Excuse me," I lowered the phone, "I have to take this."

"Please, take my office," Cole said softly as I answered the phone and told Henry to hold on.

"Ah…" Frank took a step toward me, but I shook my head for him to stop.

"Just act normal, right?" I reminded him I knew my part.

"Just be careful."

"That's why I'm here, right?"

He backed off, and I followed Cole down a hallway.

Henry was just like the rest of them. Well, I could tell myself that, even though deep down I knew he was different, but most of the time clients just needed to let the anger settle before they could move on. I hoped that eventually Henry would too.

Cole's office was gorgeous, just like the rest of the

house. The fireplace was on, so I moved to stand in front of it.

"Take your time." He nodded before he left me.

With a heavy sigh, I felt the weight pull at my chest as I lifted the phone to my ear.

"Randy, you know you're not supposed to use this number."

"When I call the other one, you don't answer."

I closed my eyes to calm my nerves. "That's because I'm working on a new case now. I don't have time to chat about ones that are over."

"Says the lawyer who didn't win the case."

Ouch.

"I'm sorry for what happened, I truly am. But, Henry, facts are facts, and the truth can't be bent to fit what you want."

"You know he didn't do it."

"Do I?"

"Really, Sloane?"

"The judge made up his mind, the decision was made, and there's nothing I can do. My hands are tied on this."

"You didn't bring in the third witness, Sloane. You got sloppy, and now—"

"Randy." I cut him off because the anger inside me bubbled to the surface at his words. I took pride in my work, and I was a damn good lawyer. "Five months, three weeks, and two days I spent on your son's case. It's not my fault the defense found a mistake that *you* made, and one you failed to mention to *me*. You and the others need to let it go. His days are numbered, so use them wisely."

"Maybe I should have hired Grant instead," he snapped before the line went dead.

My head dropped, and my hand reached out to the mantel to stabilize myself. I'd had difficult cases before, but Randy's had been the hardest by far.

The phone rang again. I didn't have to look at it; I knew it was him. He always snapped, flipped out, then called me back. He was so draining and heavy, and he always knew just what to say to hit all my weak spots.

Like a battered wife, I answered the call and heard the same song and dance that had weighted me down for the past six months.

"Sorry." He paused. "I just get frustrated."

"I know. But, Henry, you need to let this go and move on. Please stop calling. Nothing is going to change. The only person who can put this behind you is you. So, do it."

"I know." His voice softened a little.

"Please, I have a meeting with a client," I lied, "and I need to be able to focus. No more calls, okay?"

"You moved on fast."

And there it was again. *Oh, my God. I can't win with this guy.*

"It's my job."

"It was also your job to get him off."

The ache between my eyes increased, and I pressed to try to relieve some of the pressure.

The loud noise of a chopper filled the house, and I moved to the window to see a black helicopter landing up on the side of the hill.

"Where are you? Because you're not home."

That grabbed my attention. "How do you know I'm not home?"

"Because I'm outside your place, and there isn't a light on."

"That's creepy, Randy. You need to go home."

What the hell?

"I have a file I wanted to you to look at, something new I found."

The office door opened, and Frank was standing there with my coat draped over his arm. He motioned to me that I should hang up.

"Look, go home. There is nothing I can do for you or him. You need to leave me alone. I'm not your lawyer anymore." I hung up and closed my eyes to gather myself.

"Sloane, you really need to distance yourself from them." Frank took a step inside the office.

"Yeah," I tried to clear my head, "I'm trying."

"Who was it this time?"

"Randy."

"I really don't like you talking to him."

"I'm a big girl, Frank. I'm aware of the dangers, and I'm doing what you and *he* asked, but you have to let me be me too. I changed my number to the secure line like you both insisted a few weeks ago, and somehow, Henry figured it out, and he's just hanging on to a hope. He'll go away soon, and everything will go back to normal." I sighed. "Do you want me to have a look through your stuff now?"

"Yes, but you will have some minor restrictions."

"Of course." I motioned for him to lead the way.

To my surprise, I was led back outside and down a stone path toward a small cabin.

"Things have changed around here a little now that some of the guys have families. There was a time when all our business was conducted in the conference rooms downstairs in the main house. Savannah," he paused to look at me, "that's Cole's wife," he reminded me, "insisted that since you'll be here for a while, you should have your own space. Somewhere you can have privacy if you need to hide away at times."

"That's really nice." I so appreciated that. "Are you here a lot now, Frank?"

He laughed a little before he tucked his hands into his pockets. "Now that Mia and Mark have three kids, I am."

"I bet she loves that."

"We've become a lot closer." He smiled warmly.

I didn't know Mia very well. My own parents had traveled a lot, but Frank had always been in my life in some way. I knew he had a reputation for being a hard-ass, but he'd always been kind to me.

"Mark sure seems like a character."

"It was hard at first. We bumped heads for sure, but he's a really good guy, and Mia adores him. The ladies do seem to flock to him. I didn't really get it before, but I think I do now."

I actually laughed out loud at that comment. "I'm not going to lie, Frank. I wasn't expecting that to come from you."

"Yeah, well, he's a charmer." He eyed me. "You all are."

"What, me?" I smirked.

"Sloane, you're a smart girl, just the type of person who would fit in at Blackstone. Not to mention you're already vetted, so you're a perfect candidate."

"I might be a perfect match, but all it would take is *his* name to get dropped, and I'd be like poison to the touch."

"Yeah, about that." His tone changed. "I haven't shared anything, but Grant was asking about you."

Ah, yes, the wonderful ex was asking about me again. I hid my annoyance. "And I would appreciate if you don't share anything. I will when I'm ready. Grant can know I'm away on work."

"And that's what I told him."

"Thanks," I huffed.

"Here we are." Frank pointed to the small cabin with its tin roof.

He opened the door, and I gasped. It was so pretty. One side of the house had a huge, long, rustic wooden table that looked to be made of a single piece of solid wood. White boards covered two walls, and a long window looked out over part of the lake which could be seen through the tall, thick trees. A cast iron maze of light above the table flickered in all directions, and oversized, dark brown leather chairs sat eight. On the other side was a stone fireplace, flat screen, and a matching couch and two chairs.

"There's a small bedroom up in the loft." He pointed to the high ceiling where a bedroom was apparently nuzzled somewhere above in the cathedral ceiling. "Wait until it rains. The tin roof was Savannah's idea."

"Wow," was all I could say.

"Kitchen and bathroom are right through there, and one more bathroom is upstairs. Also, Abigail has arranged for you to have a driver if you need to go to town."

"Wait," I was confused, "I thought this was just for my workspace. I thought I was staying in town?"

"Cole and Daniel thought it was best that you stay here."

I immediately felt uneasy. I liked my alone time and space, not to mention my freedom to come and go as I pleased. This felt smothering.

"I'm not sure, Frank…"

"If you're not comfortable with this setup, you can talk to either John or Cole about it." He seemed to make an effort to keep his face expressionless, but a small smile showed. "Now, I'll let you look around while I go grab your bags and boxes from the car. I know you, Sloane, and I know you'll want to jump right into work. I'll send Black down so you can start."

Before I could protest further, he was out the door and up the path.

This wasn't exactly our agreement.

I was about to close the door when a familiar sound caught my attention and drew me back outside. I found myself crossing the yard and, still following the sound, up a set of stairs. I chuckled at a little sign that read "If you lived here, you'd be home now" that was posted outside an open door. I peeked inside and watched.

"If you hold down your thumb and shake the controller, you can kill him and jump to the next building," I said.

Two sets of identical brown eyes swung to stare at me, not with concern but with intrigue.

THREE

JOHN

"**R**eally?" Mia felt around my stitches. "You could have done more damage, John."

"Did I?"

"That's not the point." Livi stepped out from behind her with a stethoscope wrapped around her cute little neck. "You were supposed to rest, and you didn't."

"Does Daddy rest when he gets hurt?" I challenged the littlest Logan whose dark eyes and smile made my heart melt daily.

"Daddy doesn't get hurt." Her pigtails bounced around.

Mia stepped back. "Stand and put your hands over your head." I did. "Does that hurt?"

"Nope."

"And if it did?"

"It doesn't."

"Fine." She rolled her eyes and looked down at Livi. "He's good to go."

"You get a sticker." She reached up and stuck a Doc McStuffins sticker over my heart.

"I feel so much better. Thanks, doc." I rubbed her cheek.

God, I love that little girl.

"Come on, Aunt Mia," she ordered. "I heard Auntie June sneezing earlier. We should see if she's sick."

"Lead the way, little lady." Mia turned back to me. "Seriously, John, take it easy." She paused. "Mentally too."

"Will do," I lied. If I stopped, I'd go crazy. It was just how I operated.

I pulled on my heavy green knit sweater and caught a glimpse of myself in the mirror. I looked worn out, and my eyes probably gave away a lot, but I'd promised Frank I would do my best to answer a few questions from some mystery lawyer. How a lawyer got this type of top clearance and was here at all was beyond me. Apparently, that was a trend lately. I brushed the cliff dust off my black Army pants and ran a hand through my long crew cut. Scruff was visible, I knew, but I had zero desire to shave. I headed for the stairs.

"Hey," I stopped Mark who snatched up Liam by his beltloops as he raced by us, "you met the lawyer? What's she like?"

He looked over his shoulder to where Frank was in the living room and lowered his voice. "Redhead, raging

B, dressed like a crazy cat lady, kind of smells like one too. Good luck, buddy."

"Good luck, buddy," Liam repeated.

My stomach sank. "Great," I muttered sarcastically.

"Yeah, and whatever you do, don't mention the giant-ass mole on her face."

"Why would I—" I stopped myself. "Never mind. I need to just get this over with."

"Good luck, man." He quivered, and when Liam repeated him like a parrot, I tugged on his pants to increase his wedgie. I stuck my tongue out at him and left with a laugh. Mark's boys were a handful, but Christ, they were fun.

"Frank?" I called.

He motioned for Daniel to follow us as he pulled me aside.

"First, your target's tracker hasn't moved in hours. Looks like he may have been killed or the shoes have been ditched."

"Damn."

"Okay, here's a quick rundown. Logan can fill you in on the rest later. She's vetted, she has a secure line for her cell phone and laptop. She signed the NDA. She's incredibly smart, and it's said she can find a pebble in a snowstorm. I've never seen someone who can research the way she does. She'll be working on some things for me and some of her own stuff as well."

"Wait." I was confused. "She has that kind of clearance. Who the hell is this woman?"

"Let's just say she's a friend of the family."

"Frank, does anyone else know you have her working on this? There's a lot of lines being crossed here—"

"John," his hand landed on my shoulder, "I trust her like I do my own daughter, so I need you to trust me on this."

I glanced at Daniel, who nodded for me to go with it.

"Okay, so you want me to share a little of what happened on the last mission? How much do I tell her?"

"Just what she should know."

"Which is?"

"For now, the timeline. If she starts asking helpful questions and you see she's on to something, you can decide to go into more if you'd like. Just use your judgement."

"All right, and why is she here, again? Something about a bad case?"

I knew I wasn't getting the entire story.

"Ex-clients weren't happy about the ruling they got and are giving her some trouble. I thought it would be best for her to be here."

"Must have been a big client for Blackstone to take her on." The skin around his eyes creased, and I saw deep concern. "Who is she to you?"

"She asked me to keep some things under wraps for now, and I respect her decision."

I hated secrets.

"And Cole knows everything."

"He does."

Great, so the *vault* of the house knew the story, which meant I wouldn't know anything until I had to. Even with his last breath, Cole wouldn't whisper a word to anyone, not even Savannah.

"John," Daniel spoke up, "she's only here for a bit, and for now she's confined to here and town. We'll get Davie or Dell to drive her around when she needs to come and go. Frank just wants her out of Washington for a while until the dust settles on the trial."

"Why do I have the feeling there is more to this story than I'm being told?"

Frank smirked and hit my arm playfully. "Because there's always more, son."

I rolled my eyes, and Daniel chuckled.

"Be nice, John." Savannah poked her head around the corner.

"I'm always nice."

"You can be, but you also can be a bit cold too."

I pointed at her, and Daniel shrugged like he agreed.

I wasn't cold, I was quiet. People misunderstood that about me.

"Would you mind meeting with her tonight?" Frank jumped in. "She's down at Tin House getting settled."

"Yeah, okay. But I would be kinder," I glared at Savi, "if you gave me something on her." Frank closed his eyes before he spent the next three minutes giving a tiny rundown of who she was to him.

I headed outside and started to jog down the pathway. The cold wind made me hunch my shoulders. Winter was quickly taking over the crisp nights of autumn. We were warned this winter was going to be harsh, and nights like this proved it.

Once I got to the steps, I swallowed back the urge to turn and head back up to my peak and ignore the rest of the world. It was my little oasis and one no one could touch or take away from me.

The last twenty-four hours had been shit, and the idea of discussing it with some citified- privileged lawyer didn't sound like a good time.

With a deep breath that felt cold in the lungs, I knocked on the door.

"Come in," a muffled voice called.

I stepped inside to see a woman bent over a box. I closed the door, and when I turned back around, she was balancing a stack of files.

Wait?

I looked around, confused at who I was seeing.

"I'm here to see Sloane Harlow." I jolted forward to grab the papers just as they began to slip off the top stack. Slipping my arms under hers, I took the stack and put them on the table.

"Thank you." She pushed her hair off her face, and I couldn't help but stare. Her indigo blue eyes latched on to mine. She was shorter than I was, and if she removed her heels, she'd probably only come up to my shoulder.

"Agent Black?"

"Yes, and you are?

"Sloane Harlow."

"Son of a bitch," flew from my lips. *Fucking Mark.*

"Are you calling my mother a bitch?"

"No." My eyes popped out of my head at the realization that it sounded like I had insulted her.

She smirked playfully. "Good."

"It's just, Mark said you were…" I stopped myself again. Why was I talking out loud about this?

"I was what?"

"Just, ah," I stumbled and felt like an ass. "Nothing. Sorry. He's just a—"

"A son of a bitch," she finished for me with a chuckle.

"Yeah," I chuckled.

"Now that we have that cleared up, why don't you take a seat?"

"Sounds good."

Oh, yeah, that was a great first impression. Savi will have a field day with this.

I couldn't believe that in all the time I'd known Mia, she never once mentioned Sloane. A friend of the family, Frank had said. I wished I'd been prepared for how friggin' gorgeous she was. What was the catch here? Maybe she was married? I moved my attention to her hand, but there was no a ring.

Divorced? Maybe that was it.

She pulled out a notepad and recorder and started to look around for a pen. Her long, dark, glossy hair brushed across her silky gray blouse, one that was unbuttoned seriously low on her chest. I wondered if it was intentionally that low or if it had come undone. Given her lack of order and the way she was tossing through things, I guessed the latter. I'd bet Frank had thrown this at her pretty quickly. When she bent back over the box, I couldn't help but notice how tight her skirt was and how it hugged her slim hips.

"Sorry." She held up the pen. "I promise once I get settled, I'll be a lot more prepared."

"No doubt."

Stop staring at her eyes. Look away. Damn, she was pretty. She was so hot, not just classic gorgeous lawyer hot, but foreign hot. She was a mix of something I wanted to ask, but she beat me to it.

"Hungarian and Latino."

"Really?" I smiled happily, entertained she had guessed my thoughts. "I'm sorry. I didn't mean to stare."

"It's fine. I get it a lot." She shrugged like it was normal and settled into her chair. "Do you mind?" She pointed to the recorder, and I nodded for her to go ahead. She leaned forward, and my eyes moved to her slender neck with its thin gold necklace that sparkled in the light. Such a simple piece of jewelry that was incredibly sexy.

"October twelfth, North Dakota, with Recon Johnathan Black." I noticed she didn't say our actual location, which was a sign she was good at her job, and Frank clearly gave her a crash course on what location we often use as a cover. Info like that would be the end of Shadows if anyone ever got their hands on those tapes. "May I call you John?" I nodded. "Why don't you tell me a little bit about yourself?"

I shifted uncomfortably, but when her eyes moved to meet mine again, I eased up slightly.

"Ah, I joined the Army when I was seventeen, three tours in Afghanistan, joined the Green Berets, and then was recruited to Blackstone."

"Seventeen?"

"Yes. I graduated early and joined as soon as I could."

She scribbled on her notepad and brushed her long bangs out of her eyes. "How long have you been here at Shadows?"

"Um," I thought for a moment, "seven years."

Her pen stopped moving. "You moved up in the ranks pretty quickly."

"A lot of us have," I said.

She pulled out a file and started to flip through some papers. "So, you were here when Savannah Miller first came to the house?"

"Yes." I wasn't aware she would know something like that.

"Interesting."

"Why?"

"Nothing." She shook her head. "Umm, tell me about what happened on your last trip to Mexico."

"It was a trip." I slipped into my habit of not sharing anything.

"Okay," she pressed her lips together, "I see here Blackstone got a distress call to leave at zero five hundred hours, and you touched down at zero nine hundred. Were you in contact with First Class Chamness the entire time?"

"No."

She kept her head down but moved her eyes from the paper to mine.

"When did you hear from him, from the time you left to the time you arrived at your location?"

"Right before we rappelled down."

"How did he seem?"

"Stressed."

She flipped through some papers before she leaned back with a heavy sigh.

"I'm not going to pretend I understand anything that goes on when you leave for a mission. But I'm here to help, and from what Frank has shared with me, something isn't right, and I have a feeling you feel it too or you wouldn't have gone back after calling in your location at the diner. I know Blackstone has a reputation for keeping things close, and I fully respect that," she leaned forward, "so if you don't want to share anything, you don't have to. I was just hoping for a little more understanding so I know what I'm supposed to be looking for."

I cleared my throat and tried to push away the uneasy feeling of breaking my brotherhood oath.

"We're trained to turn that side of us off. It's not easy for me to sit here and speak to a stranger who isn't even our JAG and share the details of a mission."

"I understand that. I'm just trying to help."

"What makes you think you can help? You're not part

of the military. You just said you have no idea what it's like on our missions, so how can you have any hope of finding something at all, especially when you have no clue what you're looking for?" I challenged.

She pushed her pen through her slender fingers as she watched me.

"I've never shot anyone, I've never wrapped someone in a carpet and pushed him into the Hudson River, nor have I ever sold anyone on the black market, but my job is to find out every single detail that took place when those things happened, and I do. I see things that most don't. That's what makes me a damn good lawyer. I understand right from wrong, and what is happening to Blackstone and North Rock is wrong. And this interview with you, Agent Black, is where I am starting, per Frank's request." She raised a hand to show peace. "But I can turn the recorder off and start with Lopez or Logan if you'd prefer."

I rather liked her approach with me. She could've just backed off, but instead she played diplomat and showed her intentions.

"How much of this has Frank shared with you?"

"Enough."

"Does he know something that we don't?"

"I don't know." Her eyes softened. "You haven't shared anything with me."

True. I took a deep breath and cleared my head. It went against everything inside me, but I opened the door a little.

"We got the call to move out at zero five hundred. We were told North Rock had been monitoring a house at the last known coordinates of their lost team member. He had been separated from the team during their last raid, six days ago." I paused to clear my throat. "They were in their second position when they were ambushed from the south. Which is odd, considering North Rock, like us, changes their location constantly. They are extremely unpredictable, they barely use radios, and when they do, it's nearly untraceable. We have our own codes so if anyone *is* listening, it wouldn't mean anything to them."

She didn't move, she didn't write anything down, she just listened.

"When we touched down and followed the last coordinates, we either walked into a trap or we were followed. I don't think I want to know which is the truth. And in case you were thinking it, no, Agent Chamness is one of the best God damn soldiers I've ever known, next to my family up there." I pointed to Shadows.

"I wasn't," she whispered.

"There was a lot of chaos and times where I lost sight of my team. But when you're over there, it's do or die, so we do. It was pouring for most of it, which doesn't work in our favor because you have to account for slippery gear and ground. I was hit by a bullet, and my gun was cut from me, and then after some hand to hand, I lost my footing and fell backward down a cliff."

She winced before she jotted down a note.

I shifted in my seat and spent the next hour and

fifteen reliving the story. Once I was finished, she stayed in a trance like she was letting the movie I painted finish out in front of her.

"Um…" She suddenly moved and pulled on a pair of blue-rimmed glasses and studied a paper.

"You mentioned earlier, there was a tattoo on the man's arm you fought with. Can you describe it?"

I stood to grab a marker off the whiteboard ledge and began to draw a spider web with a seven drawn through it.

"Seven spider web," she whispered to herself.

"Have you heard of it before?" I sat down and watched as she pulled out her phone to Google something.

"Huh." Her eyes squinted as she read something. "I don't know yet."

"But it does sound familiar?"

"Maybe." She forced a smile. "It's a possible starting point."

I wanted to push further, but I also didn't want to be overwhelming either. Savi's words echoed in my head.

Her phone went off, and she cursed under her breath then lowered the phone and ignored the call.

"Everything okay?"

"Yeah." Her tone changed a little, almost nervous, or maybe she was just beat from her trip. "Um, I think that's all for now. Let me do a little more digging, and I'll see what I can come up with." I went to stand when she said, "Who was the man you were with? Brick or Bret?"

"Brick?"

"Yeah, is he here? Can I talk to him?"

"He's not here." I smirked, knowing this was going to be entertaining. "He's with the Devil's Reach."

"The what?"

"Devil's Reach Motorcycle Club in Santa Monica."

She leaned back in her chair and looked up at me. She nibbled on the top of the pen cap. "Let me guess. He was there on business?" Her eyebrow arched, and I couldn't help but smile at how sexy her brow looked behind her glasses.

"Something like that."

"I'd like to meet with him."

"I highly doubt Frank will let that happen." I smiled then stood and checked the time.

"Mm, we'll see," she muttered.

I liked that she wasn't scared of Frank or the fact that Brick was with a motorcycle club.

"Oh, John?" She stopped me when I got to the door.

"Yeah?"

"Can you get me clearance to get a hotel room in town?"

Huh?

"Frank said I should talk to you about getting the all-clear to leave."

Interesting.

"You don't like it here?"

She crossed her legs, which drew my eyes to her long, slender calves that led my gaze to her black matte heels.

"It's just that I don't want to impose, and I like to be able to come and go as I please."

My hand dropped away from the door handle, and I leaned my hip against the windowsill. It would be better she learned now than later.

"Frank tossed this at you last minute, right?"

"Something like that, yes." She pushed off her chair and started to gather her paperwork.

"*If* this case is something, which my gut is telling me it is, you're best off here and not in town."

"I appreciate the concern, John," she clicked off the recorder, "but I've been living in Washington for a very long time and have dealt with some pretty scary people, and I've been okay."

Then why are you here?

I rubbed my chin and thought about another angle to take with the conversation.

"The people up in that house," I nodded toward the main house, "have seen all kinds of ugly, and though you might think you'll be okay, I'd appreciate it if you'd humor them by staying."

She stopped what she was doing and seemed to hear me. "Okay," she nodded, "I respect that."

Good.

I glanced at my watch. "Dinner is at six."

"I'm not really that hungry. I think I'll just stay here and get myself organized." Her hands twisted together. Poor thing was very uncomfortable. I actually felt bad for her, but I also knew Savannah wouldn't have it.

I smiled. "One thing you should know about this place, Sloane, Savannah is relentless. Unless you want her bringing the whole cavalry down here, you'd best be there at six."

"Okay," she held her hands up in defeat, "I'll see you at dinner. Oh, John?" I looked over my shoulder. "I'm sorry for your friend."

The painful knot returned when I pictured the rookie's lifeless face. Though I didn't know the kid, it didn't mean it didn't hurt.

"Me too." I headed outside and up the path.

The house smelled of peppercorns and baked potatoes when I entered the living room. I could hear Savannah in the kitchen singing her heart out to a country song. Cole and Mark were in deep conversation by the fireplace, and Mia was rocking Tabby to sleep.

I sometimes felt like the odd man out without a family of my own, but I just had to look around me, and I knew I had the best of both worlds. I was free as a bird to climb my mountains and do what I wanted. I knew warmth and love were all around me, and that was all I needed. Besides, I also got to play wild games with their little squirts.

"Have you washed up for dinner yet, Uncle John?" Livi popped out of nowhere like she often did.

Damn her father. Their games of hide and seek meant she knew all the *hidey spots* in the house.

"Not yet."

"Surely you're not wearing that to dinner. We have company."

I looked down at my dusty pants and fisherman sweater and then over to my little-lady niece, who was less than impressed.

"There's a lady guest in the house. You should brush your hair and at least change your shirt."

"She's right," Savi chimed in from the kitchen.

"Fine," I grunted and headed for the stairs.

"Oh, and Tripper ate Dell's radio again!" Savi called after me.

"Maybe he should put it away next time," I muttered back.

FOUR

I pushed open the huge wooden entry door of Shadows' main house. The sounds of voices had me curious. Who was all here? I recognized one voice I knew, Frank's laugh as it rang out. Good, he was still here.

I was used to being around people I didn't know. I was brought up in a constantly busy, constantly changing yet controlled household given who my father was, but I wished my mother was here to make small talk. I really should call her and let her know I was getting settled.

"Ms. Harlow," Daniel flashed me his famous smile and escorted me to the bar, "you look lovely."

"Thank you, Daniel." I caught my reflection in the window. My navy-blue sweater hung off one shoulder, paired nicely with my white jeans and thigh-high black boots. The one thing I did love was fashion. Since most of the time I worked in a courtroom, I was excited I didn't have to wear my usual business attire.

"What would you like to drink?"

Mark rubbed his hands together as he strolled up next to me, and another man joined him. "Would you like to try the famous Marcus Martini?"

"Or maybe a Tail of the Devil?" the smaller guy chimed in.

"Um…" I looked at Daniel, but he just shook his head like this was the norm.

"Both?" I joked.

"Ah," Daniel laughed, "smart answer."

Mark shoved the martini he held in my hand and made a show of waiting with bated breath for me to give it a try.

I took a small sip, then another larger one. "Okay, this is fantastic."

"My job here is done." He winked and snatched a baby from an older woman who hurried by. "Hello-rou wittle one." His voice rose about three octaves. "Yes, you love your daddy, don't you? Yeah, you do."

"Oh, she's yours?" My heart melted as the toddler giggled in his arms.

"Nope, he rents these kids and uses them to pick up chicks," the small one chimed in with a shit-eating grin. "Name's Davie."

"Nice to meet you, Davie."

"Trust me, the pleasure, I can assure you, is all mine."

"Come on, Sloane," Frank appeared out of thin air

and pulled me away, "you should meet the girls. You'll need some protection around here."

"Savi. June. This is Sloane." The lady who Mark stole the baby from had a lovely smile and looked a lot like Abby, then one of the prettiest women I had ever laid eyes on welcomed me with a warm smile. Then she looked down, and her mouth dropped open as she nearly cried over my boots.

"It is possible to have an orgasm over footwear? Because I think I just did."

June burst into laughter and ran a hand down the smooth material of my boots.

"All right, then," Frank covered his ears, "that's my cue to get the hell out."

"Hey, babe." Cole came in, and Frank turned him around.

"Trust me, just don't."

Cole didn't even look back. This place was pretty friggin' hilarious.

"So," Savi pulled me over to a stool where I could sit while she finished making a salad, "tell me about yourself."

June waited until I was done with my martini before she replaced it with a deep-red wine. I took a sip and appreciated the smooth, velvety liquid as I swirled it around my tongue. Their booze collection was something else.

"I have a little brother who has three amazing sons,

and they are my world. However, they're moving to North Dakota soon because of my sister-in-law's job."

"That sucks." Savi made a sad face.

"Yeah, it really does."

"What drew you to become a lawyer?" June asked as she washed her hands free of the rosemary.

I shrugged. "When I was only sixteen, I watched a family friend get destroyed in court when all the evidence proved he was innocent. The prosecutor just ate his lawyer for lunch. It took everything in me to not jump in and state the facts that I knew were true."

"When you were sixteen?" June asked through a laugh.

"I know it's young, but my older cousin is a lawyer and always took me to court with her when she was studying for the bar. I ate it up and begged her to take me whenever she could. We would watch together. It fascinated me, and the challenge of digging for the real facts thrilled me. I couldn't wait to be what I knew I was born for, to get at the truth of things. I don't know, I think something clicked in me that I wanted to help those who couldn't."

"That's very badass of you." Savi clicked her glass to mine, and I was happy that my story impressed them. Normally, the spotlight wasn't on me. "What about your parents?"

I skirted around the question. "Both my parents were in the military, but I didn't want to be a JAG. I wanted something that was mine."

"Were you up on the peak again?" I heard from behind me and turned to see who it was. It took me a moment, but then I saw a little of Frank in the woman and realized it was Mia. She was still just as pretty as I remembered.

"No," John said as he walked toward us from the direction of the kitchen, looking completely different then earlier. He was in a dark gray dress shirt, unbuttoned at the neck with rolled sleeves. His jeans were dark, which complemented his shirt nicely. "My niece gave me shit for looking too Army while we had a lady guest in the house." He smiled at me. "So, I showered and changed."

I couldn't help but laugh at that. He was wonderfully open and confident.

"Mia," Savi stepped in, "this is Sloane. She is working with our district attorney for Blackstone."

"Oh," she flushed with a squeal, "the last time I saw you, we were ripping the heads off your brother's GI Joes." She laughed as she came in for a hug. "It's really great to see you again, Sloane."

"You too." I smiled, happy that they didn't hide who they were in front of me. It was incredibly refreshing. John gave me a sexy, lopsided grin before he made his way to the fridge to fetch a beer. A tiny ping of something hit my stomach, and I tried to push back the feeling. I knew with my situation I shouldn't even go there, but if I was honest with myself, John was very attractive.

"You two know one another?" Savi asked.

I shot Mia a small plea to keep what she knew quiet.

"Sloane is an old family friend." She brushed off the question, but I could tell Savi caught it, and to my surprise, she let it go. She came around to my side of the island and leaned down to my level.

"Does John remind you of anyone?"

"Savi," he growled with his back to us.

I played along because she was right. He did. Since the moment I first laid eyes on him in the house, he'd reminded me of someone. I wasn't good with famous people, mainly because I always had my head in a book or a laptop digging up dirt on people, but John was painfully sexy, and I was surprised I didn't drop my entire stack of papers when he spoke to me earlier today. "Yeah, but I can't place him."

"I'll give you a hint." June joined in. "Like father, like son."

I chewed my lip while I raced through my mind. "Celebrity?"

"Mmhm…" Savi beamed.

"John?" I called over just to add to the shit they were giving him. "Would you mind turning back around?" To my surprise, he did, glaring at Savannah the whole time, but she seemed completely unfazed by his look of death.

Then it hit me like a hot need that worked its way through the center of my stomach. I willed my blush to leave, but it didn't listen. It shamelessly stayed right where it was.

"Oh…my…God." Each word fell slowly from my lips.

"Yeah," Savi stood, "she sees it too."

"Who does he look like?" Mark kissed Mia and looked around the room, thoroughly entertained.

"Crazy cat lady." John stuck his finger at Mark.

"I'm just sorry I missed the moment." Mark hooted in laugher at some inside joke they must have had. "Anyway, who does Black look like?" he repeated without missing a beat.

"Scott Eastwood," Savi and I said at the same time.

"Who?"

"Clint Eastwood's son," I explained.

"Mark, remember the movie right before my water broke? You and I both made the connection."

"What?" He pulled his phone free and started to search the name.

I glanced over at John. He was watching me. His light blond stubble intensified his jaw, and his straight eyebrows rose slightly when I held his stare. I was just happy I was sitting, because my knees went tingly.

"Oh, yeah," Mark snickered, "that was the guy from the movie you were all gushing about that day too. You watch that movie a lot."

"Yup," Mia grabbed the phone, "because of the way he rode that bull."

"Right!" Savi moaned, and Mark dipped low to whisper in Mia's ear.

"Pff," Mia scoffed, "the last time that happened," she pointed to the baby in the other room, "that happened."

We all laughed while Mark shook his head.

"So, I guess the question is," I waited for the noise to settle, "John, can you ride a horse?"

"I can." He nodded.

"A bull?"

"Perhaps."

"Interesting."

Savannah looked at the both of us with a sparkle in her eye that snapped us out of our moment. "And as much fun as this is, it's time for dinner."

"So, Sloane," Mark wrapped an arm around my shoulders as we walked over to the table, "I'm not one for being subtle, so I figured I should just dive in. I notice your left is naked."

"What?" I laughed as he pulled back a chair for me while John slid into the chair to my right.

"Married?   Engaged,   boyfriend,   ex-husband, widowed?"

"Mark!" Mia elbowed him in the arm. "Really?"

"What? That's a normal question," he shot back.

"I'm sorry, Sloane." Mia looked mortified. "He doesn't have a filter."

I shrugged. "It's refreshing, actually." Mark shot her a look, and she rolled her eyes. "No, no, it's complicated, no, and no."

"Complicated how?" This time Mark was ready for Mia's hit and grabbed her hand as it came at him. Damn ,he was a charmer.

"Sloane," Frank stepped in for the rescue, "I leave

tomorrow but will be back in a few days. Is there anything you need before I go?"

"Actually, there is." John handed me the mashed potatoes, and as I took the heavy plate, he was ready for me to struggle, so he kept his hands on it. "Heavy and hot." He chuckled and moved it to sit in front of me.

"Thanks." Having him so close made my mind foggy. I stumbled to remember what I was talking about. "Ah, I would like to interview Brick from the Devil's Reach."

The table went quiet, and I wondered what the deal was with this club.

"I can pack a bag and make day trip out of it. I just have some questions."

Frank glanced at Cole uneasily. "When does Irons return?"

"Not sure yet. He and Keith are finishing up the paperwork."

"I don't need an escort, Frank," I interrupted before Cole could say anything else. "You know what and who I've been up against before. A motorcycle club doesn't scare me."

Frank's lips pressed together like he wanted to say something, but the room was full, so I didn't push it further.

Suddenly, a stampede could be heard, and a door slamming brought a chorus of groans from around the room.

"Hey," Mark grabbed one of the little boys by the shirttail as he attempted to scoot by and wrangled him to his side, "Liam, meet Sloane. She's going to be here for a while."

"I know, Dad." He rolled his eyes. "We already met."

All eyes swung over to me, so I stuck up my pinky and pointer finger and screamed through a whisper, "*Call of Duty!*"

"Mark!" Mia hit his arm. "I told you they are too young to play that game."

"I can't help it if they find my games. Just be glad they don't find my porn or your toys."

"Oh, my God, I can't." She gave a pleading look to Savi, who was still staring at me with a smirk.

"*Call of Duty!*" Liam returned my hand gestures before he escaped his father's hold and raced away yelling, "See ya tonight, Sloane."

Cole was the first to laugh, breaking the moment.

"I think I'm a little turned on right now," John joked as he sent me an interesting look, one I couldn't quite interpret.

"You and me both." Mark let out a loud laugh before Mia shook her head. "So, you're kinda single?" Mark suddenly flipped topics again, and I started to laugh—so hard in, fact, that I teared up. He was relentless.

"At least she thinks I'm funny." He pointed a finger at Savi.

"Excuse me, Uncle John?" a young voice rang out, and a small version of Savi in a sweet black and white dress approached. A bright red ribbon was tied in her hair, and she wore shiny black shoes with a silver buckle on the side.

"Yes, little lady." He reached out and brushed the back of his finger down her cheek.

She leaned over and whispered something in his ear.

"I see." He nodded, and she continued to softly chat in his ear.

"That might be a Daddy question."

She gave a quick glance over to Cole before she spoke out loud. "Oh, Uncle John, you know what he'll say."

"What would I say?" Cole asked.

"Daddy, it's rude to come into a conversation that you're not a part of."

Cole turned to Savi. "Whoa, who does that sound like?" Savi covered her mouth to stop her smile while she pointed at herself.

"If you're talking about me, shouldn't I be in it?"

"No," they both answered without looking at him.

"Ah ha," Cole huffed and tried to hide his amusement.

"I think it's fine, Livi." John wrapped an arm around her shoulder.

"Will you join me later?"

"I'll try." She reached up and gave him a hug before she hurried off downstairs.

"Pssst," Savi whispered to John, who made a motion like he was playing the piano. "Oh, okay."

I stayed quiet through the rest of dinner in order to

observe the men and their families. A few things were for sure. They all loved and respected one another. Shit and insults were tossed out constantly, but there was always a line they never crossed, and when Livi returned a while later and sat on her father's lap, the tone at the table lowered and the topic was immediately changed to kid-friendly things.

I'd heard many stories over the years about the great team Blackstone, but I never thought I would be here at their massive dinner table surrounded by their stories and laughter.

"Thank you so much, Savi. Dinner was amazing." I threaded my arms through the sleeves of my jacket.

"I'm really glad you joined us. Breakfast is normally around eight, but if you sleep in, as I'm sure you must be tired after your travels today, you're welcome to anything in the kitchen. Our house is yours. Oh, and here." She handed me a basket. "Just a few things you might need and want down at Tin House."

I thought it was sweet they called it that. "That's very thoughtful." I leaned in and hugged the woman who felt more like a sister in one night than my best friend had ever been.

John appeared with his coat and took the basket from my arms.

"I'll walk you back down to the house."

"Oh," I wasn't excepting that, "okay."

"Have a good night." Savi closed the door behind us with a devilish grin.

Once again, my heels tried to find their way through the gravel, and my balance was slightly tested.

"I get women love heels, and so do I, but those are not Montana boots."

"Are you more of a four-inch heel guy, or do you go big and do six?" I teased.

"Six," he responded, deadpan.

"Now, that I'd like to see." I laughed. "Listen, I spend a lot of time either in a book or a courtroom, so any chance I have to wear my boots or high heels like these, I do."

"I'm not complaining, just pointing out the simple fact that you're," I stumbled, and he caught my arm, "going to break your ankle."

"Yeah, but what a way to go."

He smirked, and I couldn't help but stare.

"What?"

"You just really looked like an Eastwood."

"I hate Savi."

"Why?" I started to move again. "How is that not a compliment? I would love for someone to say I looked like a sexy celebrity."

"Are you calling me sexy?"

"I…" This time, I stumbled over my own words. "I'm just saying…" A loud panting noise caught my attention, and I froze. "Do," my words froze in my throat, "you hear that?"

Suddenly, John stood straighter and stepped next to me then shouted in a big, booming voice, "Stop!"

In a blur, a giant German shepherd came to a screaming halt in front of us, his tongue lolling out of his mouth while he waited for his next command.

"Oh!" I loved dogs. "Who is this big fella?" I bent down and held my hand out toward him.

"Okay," John ordered, and the dog wagged his huge tail and licked my hand. "This is Tripper."

"Hi, Tripper. Nice to meet you." I rubbed his ears as he pushed his head into my stomach. "Oh, my, you're a big baby, aren't you?"

"Not normally." John chuckled. "Normally, he will get in between me and whoever is with me."

"It's because you know I wouldn't hurt a fly." I addressed the dog and kissed the side of his face. His happy noise told me he liked it. "Oh, someone likes kisses, doesn't he? You're a big flirt." If a dog could look deliriously happy, his face was a picture of it.

"Seriously, Tripper?" John shook his head. "Compose yourself."

"Don't listen to him." I let him kiss my face. "I love a dog that loves to be loved."

"This dog has taken down more men than I can count. I'm not exactly sure what's happening right now." Tripper was now on his back, paws in the air, waiting for a belly scratch. John looked mortified. "He's like a big baby with you."

I stood, and John stared at me. "What?"

"Nothing." He gently took my arm and walked me

toward the little house with Tripper glued to my side, only stopping when we reached the door.

"So, the twins convinced you to play their game?" He gave me a sideways glance.

"Actually, I asked to play. Liam couldn't get past level one, so I offered some tips."

"Impressive." He nodded.

"Yes, my video game skills are widely talked about."

John opened the door with a chuckle, set the basket on the table, and went in to turn on the fireplace and a few lights.

"It will take a few moments, but the place will warm up."

"I don't mind the cold."

"Good, because winter is coming in fast this year."

We both stood by the door as Tripper pushed inside and crawled up on the couch.

"No, Tripper, you can't stay here."

"Can he?" I interrupted. "I mean, I don't know if he stays with you, but I'd love the company."

John eyed the fur ball on the couch and looked back at me. "Well, all right, I guess. But just so you know, the grounds are protected twenty-four-seven. No one can get in or out without someone knowing."

"Good to know." I removed my jacket.

"Well, goodnight, Sloane." He looked over at the dog and made a face. "Night, traitor." Tripper's tail beat the couch cushion, totally comfy already.

"Thanks, John."

I went to the window to watch him walk back up the path. When I turned back around, Tripper tilted his head to one side as he watched me.

"What?"

FIVE

"I have some questions myself, Trigger." I held my phone to my ear as I moved to the window and looked down at the lake. It had been one week since Sloane arrived at the house, and I might have seen her twice. Frank had sent some boxes down to her, and she'd been quiet ever since. I knew she was alive only because the girls had been bringing her food and checking in, and whenever I asked how she was doing, they'd simply say she was busy. I knew I was being cold and edgy when she was around, but that was because I couldn't figure out why she drew all these new feelings out of me. Feelings I didn't deserve to feel. I knew I shouldn't be interested, but...I rubbed my head, frustrated. I hated that a woman got inside my head. Not to mention my dog seemed to have totally fallen for her. But along with the excitement of an interesting woman came the acid in my stomach. Happiness just didn't sit very well inside me anymore.

"Because you helped get my VP out of that shit hole," Trigger broke the storm in my head, "I'll agree to chat. But, ah, some shit has been brewing, so you gotta come here or we can call again."

"All right, but I need to know why Brick was there. Can you tell me that much?"

There was a long measure of silence before he cleared his throat like he was annoyed.

"He was following up on a personal lead but also trailing the president of the Stripe Backs. Guess he's stepping down, and the rumor is his nephew Caleb may take over. We're trying to learn what they're up to since that surfaced, and our new guest in Hawaii has made his mark. Think it's best to watch all that want to take us down. Since Brick was already heading that way, I got him to tail the president, but shit went down, and that's when he ran into you."

"What was the personal lead?" I knew I was digging too far, but I needed answers to rule out Brick.

"Nothing that concerns Blackstone."

"Fair enough. I appreciate the time."

"Yeah." The phone went dead.

"All right, bye," I said to no one. He always was a guy of few words.

I changed into my camo pants and t-shirt and headed down to where the guys were training. I raced to catch up. I hated to show up late, but Cole knew I needed to make some calls. We were all a little extra forgiving lately with the present situation.

Three of North Rock's members were still in the hospital, one in critical condition. We all waited, desperate for intel to come back on who had messed with the team and killed our guy. We were waiting for the call to ship out to even the score. It was painful not to just go, but we had our orders, and no matter what, we had to obey them.

I turned my ball hat around, so the peak covered my neck, and flipped the hundred and thirty-pound farm tire over and over again across the property. The effort felt good.

"Again," Daniel yelled, and we switched directions and repeated the same actions again. My muscles screamed, and I welcomed the burn that spread through my body.

"So," Mark grunted as he neared the finish line, "the lawyer is hot."

"Yeah." I lifted the chains over my shoulders, curled my fingers under the rubber lip, and stood with the tire around my waist then started the Farmer's Walk move.

"You should take her to dinner at Zack's."

"I don't think she's totally single." I reminded him of the dinner when the words *it's complicated* were used.

"'It's complicated' is very different than 'I'm seeing someone.'"

"City and country don't mix."

"That was my excuse," Cole chimed in while a vein popped out on his neck. "Now look."

I dropped the tire, wiggled my arms to get the blood moving again, and dumped my water over my head. It instantly cooled in the chilly air.

"Savannah was an exception to the rule," I pointed out. "She didn't have a city life to go back to."

"Stop hiding and date," Cole muttered.

"I'm not—" I stopped when Mark elbowed Cole, and they both grinned at me.

"What?"

"Afternoon, Sloane." Mark waved, and I glanced over my shoulder to see her jogging up the property in yoga pants and a zip-up sweater, and right by her side was the friggin' traitor. I guessed I couldn't blame him. She looked damned gorgeous.

She removed her earphones and slowed her pace. "Hey, guys." Her cheeks were pink from her workout. "Beautiful day."

"It is." Cole shaded his eyes to see his father coming in our direction.

Tripper bolted for me, and like the crazy pup he was, he leapt into my arms. "Oh, you do remember me?" His long tongue started to lick my face all over.

"Sorry." Sloane tried to hide her amusement. "I

brought him up to the house three nights ago, but he wouldn't stay there."

"Smarter dog than some I know," Mark whispered at me with a grin. "Hey, Tripper, wasn't that you who took down that big guy on a drug bust last year?" Mark shook his head at Cole. "Now look at you, buddy." Tripper wagged his tail furiously when he heard his name, then suddenly tuned in to Daniel and wiggled to get free.

"Hey, boy." Daniel gave him a pat on the head. "Sloane, I wanted to ask, has Henry made contact with you at all this past week?"

Her face fell, and she wrapped her arms around her midsection. "Once, yes."

"Did you let Frank know?"

"I meant to. I just fell down a rabbit hole and guess I forgot."

Daniel glanced at Cole before he spoke again. "Did he seem any different?"

"Different how?"

"Agitated?"

She thought for a moment. "A little, but I didn't think anything of it. They're always intense and know no boundaries."

"Boundaries?" Daniel questioned.

"It's nothing. Henry was just outside my place the other day. He's watching for when I come home. Claimed he had more evidence for me to look over."

Daniel pulled out his phone and excused himself.

"Cole, it's really nothing." She turned to him. "This whole thing has been blown way out of proportion."

"Maybe," he shrugged, "but if Frank brought you here, my guess is it isn't."

Her hands rubbed her shoulders like she was cold, but I knew it was nerves. I really wished I knew what was going on.

"You mentioned you fell down a rabbit hole." I jumped in. "Did you find something?"

"Um, maybe?" Her face scrunched up. "I came out for a jog to clear my head before I dove in any further."

"John is off for the rest of the afternoon if you need any help." Mark grinned.

So subtle.

"Thanks," she smiled back, "but I think I could use one more run before my mind will let me work again."

"Have you been up the mountain yet?" Mark asked.

"No, not yet."

"Well, that's John's second home. Maybe he can show you?"

"Yeah?" Her eyebrows rose in interest.

"Sure." I started to walk with her but glared back at Mark, who was in a fit of laughter, and Cole was about to join in.

Dicks.

We headed up the path. I began to jog, and she seemed to easily keep up with my pace. I decided to take a harder trail just to test her endurance.

"So," she hopped off a ledge where I figured she might ease down, "does your family live in Montana too?"

"Yeah." I jumped over large split in the rock and turned to offer her a hand, but she dove straight across.

"Brother or a sister?"

"Yeah." I barely heard her and moved onto a small ledge and inched across it. If I fell, it was only twenty feet down, but I wanted to see if she'd follow or just go around.

"Both parents still alive?" She slid her right foot onto the rock to test her balance.

"Yeah." I watched once I got to the other side and couldn't help but let my eyes roam over her tight pants. I was always respectful with women. My parents raised me well, but they hadn't prepared me for Sloane's tight little body all smothered in spandex.

She crossed, hopped off, and brushed her hands clean of rock dust.

"Are you always this forthcoming, or do I just bring out the one-word answers in you?"

I smirked and stared down at her, loving her in my element. Some of her hair had worked loose from her ponytail, and the dark color framed her intense blue eyes.

"Most women." I stopped myself, curious as to why I even felt I should say anything. I closed my mouth and continued to climb.

"Have we graduated to two words now?" She chuckled behind me. "All right, then."

I hated how much I enjoyed her banter, and the fact

that she didn't pry to know what I had been about to say made me almost want to elaborate. We slipped into quiet mode as we moved around the mountain. On the steep part, I turned around to help her, but she'd found her footing and jumped up next to me.

"You don't have to look so surprised." She tucked a piece of hair behind her ear.

I lifted a hand. "Sorry. I guess your heels threw me off."

"Is that why you took me the hard way around the mountain?"

"Huh?"

"Abigail told me about the different routes." Her hands went to her hips, and she lifted an eyebrow at me. "I know there are two other ways to get here."

I pressed my lips together to hide my smile. She'd known and had never once mentioned it the hour we'd climbed. She was good.

"Are you testing me, Black?"

"Possibly."

She nodded and looked down before she laughed. "Well, you're going to have to try harder than that."

"Seems that way."

I turned and fell into a fast pace, and she followed in silence until we reached the top of the lowest peak.

"Wow," she scanned the panoramic view, "miles and miles of wide-open space." She closed her eyes and let the afternoon sun warm her face. "I can see why you like it here."

"I don't stop here," I corrected her, really just wanting the opportunity to stare at her a little longer with her eyes closed.

"What do you mean?" She turned to look up at the wall of rock that rose another sixty or so feet and jutted outward. It was an intense climb and one I did at least once a week. "You climb that?"

"Yeah." I nodded and pushed off where I was standing.

"That's insane," she huffed.

"Hence the reason I do it." I grinned as I stepped toward her. I pushed down my usual wall. I deserved at least one moment of freedom from the hell I carried inside. "What do you like to do for fun?"

She let out a long sigh before she shrugged. "I don't know. I don't normally have a lot of free time anymore."

"But when you do?" I was pretty close now and enjoyed how much I towered over her. She was slim and tall, but I was taller. She tilted her head back to look into my eyes.

"I love to be outdoors, no phones, no computers, no TV, just unplugged."

I nodded, extremely happy with her answer. I'd misjudged Sloane, thinking she was all city. Not that she would be happy in the country, but it was good to know she wasn't an uptight-citified woman who couldn't handle outdoor life.

"Why do you get to ask questions and I can't?"

I shrugged. She was right, but I wasn't good at opening up like she was.

"You owe me an answer."

"One."

"Okay." She tapped her fingers against her pink lips. "Do you mind me being at Shadows?"

That threw me for a loop.

"Why would you ask me that?"

"Because you seem to get annoyed when I'm around. You're one way with the family and another with me."

I swallowed down the knot in my throat. "Reasons." I shrugged.

"You promised me an answer, John." She filled what little gap there was between us.

"Ask me another."

"No, I want this one."

"Pass."

She suddenly smirked. "I never pegged you for a quitter."

"I'm not a quitter."

"Okay." She went to turn, but I snagged her arm and whirled her back to me. Her chest rose, which drew my gaze to her cleavage. I shook my head clear and tried to think straight.

"There are things about you that make it hard for me to be around you. It's not something I can discuss very easily."

"Okay," she whispered as her gaze dropped to my lips.

My pocket vibrated, and I pulled it free and slowly let go of Sloane. "Hello."

"Son, you need to come home. We can't get..." Screaming in the background made my stomach coil into a familiar hard knot.

"I'm on my way."

And just like that, my reality came screaming back to me, and I felt myself pull in again.

"I need to leave," I muttered to her and raced back toward the path.

"Is everything okay?"

"No."

We made it down the mountain within thirty-five minutes. I jumped into my truck without saying a word to Sloane. I wasn't trying to be a jerk; I just had bigger things on my mind. My world wasn't meant to be shared with two.

I arrived at my parents' house in just under an hour. Even from my truck, I could hear her screams. I rushed inside and found my sister with her hands over her ears, her mouth wide open, with tears streaming down her face.

"Oh, thank God!" my mother shouted.

"What happened?" I dropped to my knees and held my twin sister's head between my hands.

"We were trying to get her in the car, and she just panicked." My mother pleaded, "She has a doctor's appointment, and now we're going to be late. I-I just don't know what to do anymore."

I glanced at my father, who was in the hallway, his face expressionless. He looked checked-out, as he often did these days.

"Ellie," I whispered. "Ellie, look at me."

Her bloodshot eyes opened, and she finally registered me. "John?"

"In the flesh," I joked, knowing she often reacted positively to humor.

"I can't go in the car." Her speech was slow, but I was patient. "The last time I went in the car, I got hurt."

My mother sank onto the couch and started to cry.

"El, that was years ago. You've been in the car a lot since then."

She looked at me, confused, and I knew she was trying to search for those memories inside her head.

"Come on," I helped her to her feet and handed her a tissue, "I'll take you to the appointment. I think Mom needs to stay home right now. Let's just go, you and me."

"Thank you, John." My mother was beyond emotionally and physically spent. I wished so much I could do more, but I didn't know where to start.

By the time I dropped my sister off back at home, it was late. Mom had finished making dinner, and Dad was out in the barn.

"Doctor said she was okay, just to watch her salt intake." I dropped my sister's pills on the table and kissed my mom's cheek. "I'm going to check on Dad."

I walked across the yard and into the red barn that sat a few yards from the house. It had been our favorite place growing up. Our parents had let us decorate the loft and turn it into a clubhouse. Over the years, it became our place to escape from the world of grownups, and now it was where my father came to escape what was happening in the house. I took the twenty-foot ladder three steps at a time and found him sitting on the edge looking out from the massive barn doors, feet dangling, head back, and beer in his hand.

The white twinkle lights lined the opening, giving a warm glow on chilly nights. Three hens cuddled together in the hay and clucked when I came closer.

"Hey, son," he greeted me with as much warmth as he had inside of him. Lately, there wasn't much left.

"Ellie's appointment went well."

"Good." He looked away, but I saw the stress that deepened the crow's feet around his eyes. His dusty jacket hung open, and bits of hay clung to his sweater.

"I can come by tomorrow if you want and help move the hay."

"It's all done. We finished up today."

"Okay." I tucked my hands in my pockets. "How's Mom?"

"Hanging in there, I guess." He tipped his beer back and finished off the rest of it.

My heart squeezed tight; we were not that kind of family anymore. There was a time we were happy and light and full of life. My father would drop anything he was doing for any of us at any time. Now we were zombies going through the motions of life with no end in sight. Mom carried her emotions on the surface, and Dad carried them deep in his gut. Both as checked-out, just in different ways. Which left me to be the floater. I helped out in any way I could, but I had a job—a very high-stress job. The fact that I loved it helped, but I just didn't have time for anything else in life anymore. My job and my homelife were all I could handle.

"You want a beer?" Dad pointed to the box of beer. I knew I should get back, but I could tell he needed company.

"Sure."

SIX

I checked the mirror one last time. My black sweater hugged me tightly, a soft V-neck, with a dark gray heavier knit that lined the cuffs. My dark slim jeans looked good with the gray suede booties. I admired the chunky high heel and thought John would approve.

My smile fell when I thought of how we had parted ways after our hike. The past two days, it wasn't lost on me that he was avoiding me. Once again, I wondered what the phone call was that had so quickly changed his mood.

Threading a gold-leaf earring through my earlobe, I shrugged off the uncomfortable feeling that came with John. I had really hoped that we were connecting, but now he was once again incredibly guarded around me.

I grabbed my purse, headed downstairs, and checked

my watch. Dell had mentioned he was heading into town today, and I was hoping I could hitch a ride with him.

"Morning, Sloane," Daniel greeted me as he came in from outside. "Where are you off to?"

"Town, actually. I need to get out and thought I'd like to see what Redstone is all about."

"Dell has just loaded some packages into the trunk if you'd like to go with him."

"Yes, I would. Thanks."

As I turned to leave, he spoke again. "I don't need to remind you of the—"

"House rules?" Mia piped up from behind me. "You have my word, Daniel, that she knows the consequences."

"Of course." He smiled warmly. "It's just a habit."

"It's a good one," I agreed. "I promise."

Mia pulled her hair into a ponytail as she joined me.

"Thanks, Mia. I appreciate the trust."

"No problem. Enjoy yourself today." She gave me a hug.

I found Dell closing the trunk and asked to go along, and he assured me he would be glad to have some company.

"Three checkpoints," Dell explained as he held up an ID to a guard who scanned it before he waved us through. "In and out, we document everyone. The only time they don't is when the chopper comes in to pick up Blackstone for a mission. That's the one exception." I nodded as he continued to explain a few more things.

Once we got to the open road then into the town, I

felt better. I was excited to see what they had for stores and food.

"If you need anything mailed, there's a UPS." Dell pulled into a free spot. "I'm warning you, the chick who works there is insane, and I highly recommend that you don't share you know Cole, Mike, or John."

"Why?"

"Just ask Savi."

"Ah, she's jealous?"

"Understatement."

"Okay, so, avoid the UPS. Got it." I pulled my purse onto my lap.

"I'll be a few hours, but if you need more time, Daniel will be coming back in town tonight, so he can drive you back if you want. You have my number, so just stay in touch."

"Will do."

Redstone was beautiful, and as I walked along the street, the most amazing smell of coffee drifted to my nose. I headed that way on autopilot. After a quick trip inside, coffee in hand, I window shopped for hours. I found the softest white sweater and matching Ugg boots. From there, I played around in a few Christmas stores and found my mother a sweet little ornament. It wasn't until my stomach begged me to stop that I realized I was hungry. Hmm. I whirled around and backtracked to a restaurant I'd spotted earlier.

"Good evening, and welcome to Zack's," a young man

greeted me as I stepped inside. "Table for…?" He waited for me to finish for him.

"One, please."

I swore I saw his excitement.

"This is one of the best seats in the house. Zack, the owner, will be over to explain the menu to you. Can I get you something to drink?"

"A glass of Cab, please. Thank you."

"Adam." He pointed to himself.

"Sloane."

After he left, I pulled off my coat and removed an iPad mini from my purse. I fired it up and waited for my email to open. Thirty-two new emails waited to be answered. I scrolled through the ones that weren't important.

"You must be Sloane. I'm Zack." A nice-looking man in a black apron smiled down at me. "I was wondering when you were going to stop by."

"You were?" I was confused.

"Are Savannah or Abigail with you?"

Oh, he must be friend of theirs.

"No, they're at home."

"I see. Will there be anyone joining you?"

"No, just me."

He looked puzzled before he pulled out the seat across from me and sat.

"Well, in that case, welcome. Do you mind if I explain the menu to you?"

"That would be nice." I smiled at his ease and listened

as he warmed up to explaining all his restaurant had to offer. In the end, I couldn't choose, and he was delighted to make the choices for me.

He rose and called out my order to someone in the back then turned back to me. "Will your father be joining you at some point during your stay?"

My stomach twisted. How did he know my father?

"Ah…" I stumbled. "Not that I'm aware of."

"If he does, please let me know. I have a bottle of Oban with his name on it."

"Will do," I whispered as he hurried away to speak to someone else. *How strange was that conversation?*

My phone pulled me from my confusion, and without looking at the caller ID, I answered.

"Sloane Harlow."

"Are you avoiding me on purpose?"

My eyes shut as my annoyance took over. My ex…

"No, Grant, something just came up."

"So I heard." His tone dripped in sarcasm. "Well, I need you back in the city by Friday."

"That won't be happening."

"You promised you'd be free."

I shook my head. He never listened to me; he only barked out orders. Sometimes I wondered what he really saw in me. He often treated me like more of a client than someone he recently dated.

"I'm not even in Washington, Grant." I tried to even out my breathing.

"So, your father was telling the truth. You are working

on a case in North Dakota." *Seriously?* I was going to kill my father. "Or is it that you're still mad at me?"

"I am still mad at you."

"Come on, baby, you know it was a misunderstanding."

"That's not how I remember it."

"She is a colleague—"

"Colleagues don't spend the night."

"We were working late, and we fell asleep."

I felt my anger rise to the surface. "Grant, there is so much more than just what happened with her."

"Like what? It's no secret I'm an ass, but I love you, and I know you love me too."

I mouthed a "thank you" to Adam as he set my dinner down.

"I'm your arm candy when you need someone to puff up your ego."

"Is that such a bad thing for you to do for me?"

"No, if you returned the favor once in a while, maybe, but you don't. You know that deal was mine. I worked hard on that client, and you took it from me."

"That's what you're pissed about?" He laughed like I was crazy for thinking that was a big deal. "Sloane, look what you just landed, one of the biggest mob cases of the decade. Mind you, I know you lost, but still, you got the job."

Holy Christ! Jab number three hundred.

"Grant, we are too different. You really need to find someone who is more what you need."

"We're perfect for each other. You know it, I know it, and your parents know it."

"Just because my parents like you doesn't mean we're a good fit."

"I want to see you."

"No." I went to hang up when something plowed through my memory. "By the way, did someone call you looking for my new number?"

"One of your field runners called about two weeks ago. Why?"

Oh, my God, Grant!

"Because that wasn't one of my runners, that was a client who I'd very much like to not hear from ever again."

"Sorry," he muttered sarcastically. He hated to be proven wrong. "But, Sloane, seriously, I need you—"

I hung up the phone and rubbed my forehead. I wished I known how vain Grant was before he burrowed his way into my life and my father's. He reminded me of an alley cat I'd fed and now he wouldn't leave no matter how many times I sprayed him with the hose.

"Everything okay?" I heard Zack ask.

"Not even a little," I muttered with my head in my hands.

"Well, my mother always said a hot meal and a sweet dessert helps the heart heal faster."

"How did you…"

He stepped closer. "Call it intuition." He smiled knowingly.

After he left, I dove into the amazing fig and prosciutto pizzettes, and if I had been totally alone, I would have licked the plate. My glass was never empty, and once my dinner was finished and I'd settled back in my chair, a lovely glass plate of tiramisu was placed in front of me. I took the first taste, and before I knew it, I had eaten the whole thing. It was to die for.

Zack refused my money, and in spite of my protests, he sent me on my way. He said family was everything and that I was family. How could a complete stranger be so kind?

I sent a quick text off to Dell and headed for the door. Just as I was about to step outside, I saw an older woman with her shoulders hunched over sitting on the side of the room. She looked beyond finished. When she sniffed, I pulled out my package of tissues and handed them to her.

"Oh," her bloodshot eyes found mine, "thank you, dear."

"Of course." She went to hand the package back to me, but I shook my head. "I have more."

She dried her eyes, took a deep breath, and brushed her sandy blonde hair off her shoulders. "I never knew a person could cry this much."

I could tell she needed someone to talk to, but I knew Dell would arrive any minute, and I needed to go.

"I hope your evening gets better." I sent her the best warm smile I had in me, and that seemed to help her a little, because she matched it with an attempt at a smile and a nod.

I hurried up the street to where I had agreed to meet Dell. The wind whipped my hair and blocked my view as I placed my bags in the giant trunk then tugged the handle and hopped onto the warm leather seat.

"Thanks, Dell, for getting here so—" Oh! My hand went to my chest as John waited for me to buckle up. "Sorry. I thought Dell was coming for me."

Tripper's big wet tongue licked the side of my head. "Hey, boy!"

"Back," John ordered, and he obeyed. "He called and said he needed to get back to the house, and as I was on my way into town, I offered to swing by and grab you."

"I hope I didn't put anyone out by staying so late."

"Nope, you're good." He pulled away from the curb. "Did you have fun?"

"I did." I tried to warm my frozen hands in the air vents. "I met Zack and Adam—who, by the way, is quite the little charmer."

"So I hear." He smirked behind his hand.

"I don't think I have ever had such a great meal before."

"Zack's our town gem. Best food and the best bar for miles."

"I believe it." I started to say more, but his phone rang through the car, and his mood suddenly shifted to serious.

He switched off the speaker phone and pushed it through to his earpiece. "Hey."

When I felt I could, I looked over at him and noticed his jaw was clenched. I could just barely hear a man's voice on the other end. His hands tightened on the wheel, and he mouthed a curse word.

"I'll come," he said quickly and ended the call. Before I could ask what was going on, he pulled a U-turn, and we headed in the opposite direction.

"I need to deal with something before we can head back to the house. I'm sorry, but you'll have to come along for the ride. It shouldn't take that long."

"That's okay." I wasn't really sure I wanted to know what made him this stressed, so I remained quiet. When we pulled onto a side road, I noticed his grip on the steering wheel was literally turning his knuckles white. A big red house sat on top of a hill with a matching red barn a few yards away. It was a huge piece of property and looked to be some type of farm, although I couldn't tell what they grew because of how dark it was. Lights shone on the lower half of the house, and it looked as though a man was pacing behind a curtain.

John parked and turned to look at me. "You could stay here, but I don't like to leave you alone out here, so I think you should come in."

"It's okay. I'm fine here." I really didn't mind, but the look on his face had me quickly open the door to follow him toward the house. Tripper trotted along on my heels. We walked up the stairs to the house, and he hesitated at the door.

"I'm sorry you have to see this."

He opened the door and let me walk in first, and I

spotted the woman on the couch in tears and a man in the corner looking like he was about to break down.

John hurried over to the woman and sat next to her, while Tripper followed cautiously. She started to panic when she saw the big fur ball, but John reminded her that she'd met Tripper before and that he'd been around for a while now.

"Ellie," he said calmly, "what's wrong?"

"I don't want to leave. I don't want to get into the car."

"Hey, it's okay." He rubbed her back. "You don't even have to go until tomorrow."

Her breathing picked up, and her panic rose to the surface. Her words were slightly delayed, and I could see it took an effort for her to get them out. "I don't want to die."

"You won't," he assured her. "Just like last time, you didn't die then, right?" John glanced over his shoulder at me, and I looked away when I saw the rawness inside him. I took it he didn't share this side of himself with many people.

"Pops," he called to the man in the corner, "I want you to meet Sloane. She's a friend of mine. Could you maybe get her something warm to drink?"

The older man's lifeless eyes found mine, and a small flicker of something flashed across his face. He stepped in front of me and put a hand on my shoulder.

"Hi, Sloane," he said quietly. "Can I make you some coffee?"

I didn't want any, but I could tell John needed me to be anywhere but here where he was.

"That sounds good, thank you."

"Oliver." He smiled warmly.

The kitchen was modern but had a lovely farmhouse feel to it. A chicken with jacked-up eyes stared at me from a shelf. It was creepy but funny as hell. I tried to hide my smile, but he must have caught it in the reflection of the window.

"That's Hennie." He filled the pot with water as he stood with his back to me. "John gave us that when he was thirteen. We were horrified at first, thinking the kid just bought us a thoughtful gift and we'd have to pretend we liked it, but after a few days, we caught him moving the ugly thing around the house just to tease the heck out of us." He let out a small chuckle, but it was soon weighed down by the sounds from the other room. "John was always good at making us laugh."

It didn't go unnoticed that he spoke in past tense.

"It's pretty comical looking," I added just to fill the silence.

"Mm," he grunted in agreement. Oliver moved about the kitchen until the coffee was finished. He handed me a large mug and motioned for me to follow him out onto the wrap-around patio. It was cold, but I knew he wanted me out of earshot.

"How do you know my son?" He handed me a warm wool blanket from a box that sat next to the porch swing, and I happily snuggled into it.

"I know his boss in Washington." I sipped the warm coffee and let its heat spread through my insides.

"What brought you to Montana?"

I sighed and decided the man deserved the truth.

"I'm a prosecutor, and my last clients were pretty shady and forgot to provide me some rather important information that was later brought to light, and we lost the case. They were pretty unhappy with me for losing and started to give me some trouble. Frank—you know Frank, right?" He nodded. "Well, he's a family friend, and he thought it would be best if I got out of town for a while."

"It is pretty serious?"

"I suppose so." I shrugged. I was used to having clients upset when the evidence didn't work in their favor. "Honestly, I'm not really afraid of them. I didn't really care that I lost because I think a part of me wished something would come to light and sink them."

"That bad of guys, huh?"

I pressed my lips together and nodded. Henry's son always had a way of speaking about what happened like he was telling the weather, emotionless. He wasn't sorry for anything he did; he was just sorry he was sloppy and got caught. "They're ruthless."

He leaned over the railing and let out a deep sigh. "It's a good thing you're here, then."

"Yeah, my father certainly thinks so." I watched a dark cloud move in front of the moon and dull its shine.

"What do your parents do?"

I downed a little more coffee just to stay warm. Oliver seemed easy to talk to. He asked questions and seemed generally interested in me.

"They both work in the Army." I kept it vague.

He nodded and stood straight again when he heard a car coming up the driveway. A lady stepped out with three plastic bags, and I strained to see who it was.

"That's John's mother, Kelly." Oliver filled in my unasked question. "She went out for dinner."

I suddenly felt like I was in the way. I really wished Dell had picked me up. Kelly walked up the stairs, and when she spotted me with her husband, she stopped short.

Oh, shit. She was the lady who had been crying at Zack's.

"Kelly, this is John's friend Sloane."

I reached out and pretended like we hadn't met earlier. "Lovely to meet you, Mrs. Black."

She shook her head free of the trance she seemed to be stuck in. "Please call me Kelly." Her worried face swung over to Oliver's. "Everything okay?"

"Just a little misunderstanding, but John's inside."

"Okay." Stress outlined every wrinkle on her face. "Are you hungry, Sloane?"

"No, thank you. I'm fine."

I felt my phone go off in my purse. I fished it free and saw it was an unknown number.

"I'm sorry, but would you mind if I took this?"

"Not at all." Oliver steered Kelly inside. "Come on in

once you're done. It's much too cold to be out here for long."

I smiled at his warmth before I answered the call.

"Sloane Harlow."

"Why aren't you home?"

Just like that, a frost layered my insides.

"I told you I was working on another case—"

"And I told you we weren't finished yet."

"Henry," I pinched the bridge of my nose to stop the headache that wanted to come on, "let's look at this another way. I lost your case, so why would you want me to re-open something if I did a bad job in the beginning?"

"I know you have connections, Sloane." His voice changed to a more serious tone. "I know your father can make things happen with one phone call."

"How do you know my father?" We went by different last names on purpose. It just made things easier.

"I know a lot about you, Sloane."

"Well," I lifted my hands, finished with this, "if you're so good at finding out information, why don't you call him yourself?"

"You will do it."

"Not going to happen."

"Sloane," again his voice was laced with a sharp undertone, "remember what Ken Wind did to that girl at the bar?"

I froze on the spot and let the notes from Henry's case flip through my head like the pages of a book. It stopped when it came to the photo of the girl flung into a field like she was nothing more than a burger wrapper. She had been beaten and raped for witnessing a meeting between two of the head mob bosses. Though he went to prison for it, he got out on bail and was never seen again.

"I take it from your silence you remember." He seemed amused. "We are not your normal gang-banger clients, sweetheart. We are organized, methodical, so why don't you get your sexy little ass back to Washington so we can finish what you started?"

"The judge signed off on the case, Henry." I repeated the usual response Frank coached me to use. "Neither my father nor I can get you your guys back. I didn't do those crimes, I didn't kill those people, I didn't lose your son's case. You did. Until you can see that, I can't speak to you. Don't call me again." I hung up and sucked in a huge, deep breath of cold air.

"Everything all right?" John asked from behind me. I jumped and nearly had a heart attack.

"Yeah…yes, just work."

He studied me for a moment before he looked up at the sky. "Can I ask you for a favor?"

"Sure."

"I need to help out my parents tomorrow early in the morning for Ellie's appointment—"

"I can drive back." I cut him off, trying to give him an out before it got even more awkward.

He studied me for a moment. "I'd lose my job, so that's not an option." He stepped closer. "Do you mind if we spent the night? I can drive you back right after we drop them off."

"Oh." I glanced around at the huge property, wondering if I was even welcome. I knew I was now an inconvenience. His shoulders were tense with discomfort. "Of course. Let me know if I can do anything to help."

"Thanks." He shrugged and motioned for me to follow him inside.

SEVEN

I felt bad for Sloane. I could tell she felt our discomfort with the situation, and that wasn't on her, that was on us. My life wasn't easy anymore. A lot rode on my shoulders, and the guilt ran bone deep.

Despite her protest of not to want anything to eat, she did join us at the table while Dad and I ate. She helped us through the uncomfortable silence that usually settled on the room as we ate by asking questions about the farm.

"Mostly cattle, organic wheat, and some of the best eggs Redstone has ever seen." My pops spoke proudly, and my mother eyed me as we both thought the same thing. He was finally chatting.

"Sounds like a lot of work," Sloane sipped her water, "but a lot of reward."

"It is." Pops nodded in agreement. "A dream does not

become reality through magic. It takes sweat, determination, and—"

"Hard work," she finished for him, and he eyed her curiously. "Colin Powell," she added.

"That's right." He glanced in my direction like he was trying to figure her out. "Do you get out of the courtroom much, Sloane?"

"Only when I've made someone mad." She chuckled darkly, but I could tell something was bothering her.

"Do you horseback ride?"

"When I was a child, I did take lessons, yes."

"Maybe sometime you and John could take a ride and see the property."

"You should take her to the lake." Ellie appeared at the doorway, and the mood shifted back to reality. My hand went out to ease Tripper, who wanted to greet her but knew better. She just couldn't retain who he was. "We were there last week, and we found these pretty dark pebbles that shine when they're wet."

I glanced at Mom for help. "Oh, Ellie, are you hungry? You said you didn't want any supper." She began to stand when Sloane spoke up.

"How many did you find?"

My sister held out her hand and thought. "Six, I think."

"Six? Wow, maybe you could show me sometime?"

Ellie's face broke into a smile that made my stomach twist with happiness, but it was quickly replaced with a jolt of pain. She didn't have the rocks anymore because that was almost fifteen years ago.

Mom got up and walked Ellie to the living room, and Sloane went back to the conversation like my thirty-two-year-old twin sister didn't just come into the room after the world's worst meltdown.

"Oliver, you'll have to share your secret about your creamer. I've never tasted coffee so creamy before."

And just like that, my father slipped back into talking, and when my mom returned, her face showing her usual strain, she was pleased to join in the conversation. It had been years since I'd brought anyone over. We weren't like the Irons, Keith, or Logan families. We had "hidden" stress that I didn't want to project on anyone else.

Later that night when Mom went to bed and Sloane and Pops were hanging out in the living room, I escaped outside, just needing a minute to clear my head. I found myself gravitating to the barn. I climbed the steps, flipping on the twinkle lights and special heat lamp that was safe to have near the hay, and I scooped up Doug, my favorite rooster. We both sat on the edge, and I let my legs dangle over the side. Using my phone, I played Brothers Osborne over the speakers in each corner of the room.

"How are the ladies?" I rubbed Doug's head, and he prattled some chicken noise. "That so? Maybe you should tell her how you feel?" He pecked my hand. "Calling the kettle black, hey?" I joked at my own expense. "It's complicated." I defended myself and leaned my head back to rest on the frame. "There's so many complications in my life that I'm not even sure where to begin." Doug clucked a few times before he settled on my lap and nestled into his feathers. It was freezing tonight, and the dark clouds tried to hide the moon. Weather was coming.

"Man, that's a long way up." Sloane came into view and brushed her hands free of dirt. "Your pops ratted you out." She grinned when she spotted Doug. "You really are a country boy."

"Well, seeing that you stole my dog…" I smirked.

"Not my fault. He's a giant flirt."

Can't blame him.

"This place is pretty amazing." She looked around with her arms wrapped around her midsection.

"Look, Sloane, I'm—" I wanted to address the elephant in the room, but she cut me off.

"I really like Oliver." Her face changed with a softness that made the rest of the words fade away. "He's very proud of all that he's done, and the two of you. He told me about the wagon rides he used to do for the town. That must have been fun."

"He told you about that?" Who *was* that man down in the house?

"He told me a lot." She sat down opposite me and stretched out like I was, so her feet were near mine. I loved how at ease she was. "You just have to ask."

"You asked about my childhood?"

"I did."

"Why?"

"Why not?" She seemed genuinely surprised that I'd

question her interest. "I shared that I have a brother moving to North Dakota and how much I'm going to miss him and my three nephews."

"But don't you have my entire life sitting on your conference table back at Shadows?" I muttered darkly and felt my walls twitch to shoot up. She rubbed the side of her leg before she moved her gaze out to the night sky. "You dig up dirt for a living, so you tell me what my life looks like."

Annoyance flickered on her face. "The file they have on you and Blackstone doesn't share the little moments you've had as kids, those moments that have molded you to who you are today. To me, those are the moments that count, not that you are some Green Beret who most likely was a Delta at some point." My face dropped at the word Delta. It was a no-go line she had just crossed. She pulled at her sleeve. "Please don't toss darts at my career, John."

I felt the unfairness of what I said and reminded myself she'd been vetted already. I was confused where this conversation was going and why she hadn't brought up Ellie. I found myself wanting to get angry at her. I didn't deserve her interest.

"I'm not stupid and know a lot more about the Army and what's going on in your life than you think."

"I highly doubt that." I hated that I was being a dick. I truly didn't want to be, but she brought up feelings I didn't want to have surface.

She moved to her feet and shook her head. "Sorry I bothered you."

Everything inside me told me to call her back, but the words wouldn't come. I turned away and closed my eyes and tuned in to the sound of her feet as they descended the ladder.

I woke to Doug burrowing into my sweater, and pieces of hay were stuck to the side of my face. I had fallen asleep in the barn again, something that used to happen all the time when Ellie and I were younger. I rolled my wrist and caught sight of the time.

Shit!

I jumped to my feet and slid down the ladder and landed with a heavy thud. I raced across the property and into the kitchen, where I came to a stop.

"Where's the fire, little bro?" Ellie called out with a plate full of pancakes. She was dressed and had her shoes on.

"We're the same age," I reminded her and spotted Sloane and my mother over the stove.

"Then why did I slip out first?" she joked, and my mouth dropped open. Ellie hadn't cracked a joke in years.

"Nice." I playfully scowled but still was beyond confused on what was happening. Normally at this point, Ellie would be in a fit of rage, ready to hurt anyone who came close. "Pops?" I questioned him when he opened the door from the living room.

"Sloane wanted to help." He was just as shocked as I was at what was happening. He sniffed the OJ like it might be laced with something.

"Here you go." Sloane sat a pile of blueberry pancakes in front of him. "Kelly said they're your favorite."

"They are." He glanced at me, still concerned. "Thank you."

"Okay, Ellie, we made a deal." She addressed my sister. "I'm finished. Are you?"

"Almost." She took three more bites before she pushed the plate away.

"Can you bring your plate over here?" Sloane patted the counter, and to my utter surprise, Ellie hopped up and did what she asked. "Thanks!" She grinned like she was talking to anyone else. "You good?"

"Yes."

"Great. Let's go."

My mother slowly turned to peek over her shoulder at me as the girls left the kitchen.

"What the hell is happening?"

"Don't question a good thing." Dad shoved a forkful into his mouth.

After a quick shower, I heard voices outside and pulled the curtain back to find Sloane and Ellie out by the car. Sloane was explaining the car to her and where they were going.

I slid my watch back over my wrist as I headed downstairs and outside, but not before I noticed both my parents were in the same room. They weren't talking, but they were both in the same room. The fact that Pops didn't immediately run outside and my mother wasn't already in tears was...*strange*.

Once Sloane spotted me, she helped Ellie in the back and slipped into the front seat. During the drive into town Ellie told stories, and the few times she got nervous, Sloane steered the conversation in a different direction. I zoned out, wondering what the hell was happening with the North Rock situation. It has been entirely too quiet, and we should have been sent back to Mexico days ago. It was hard having your head split in two different halves, home and work.

The waiting room had a fish tank, which entertained Ellie while I checked my email. Three calls came in on Sloane's phone, and I noticed each time she would decline the call.

"Ellie Black," the nurse called, and Ellie looked at me in sudden panic.

"Just like we spoke about." Sloane pulled Ellie's attention to her and used a calm voice as she reached out and helped Ellie walk toward the nurse.

"I'm scared, John."

"Don't be." I forced myself to allow Sloane to take the lead as we moved into a secondary room.

"What-what are we doing here?" She started to panic, and Sloane asked to speak to the nurse outside the room. "I don't like this room, John." Tears broke her dam, and she ran to me. I was ready for another epic battle.

Shit, sometimes I was just too tired for the fight. Again, guilt and pain smacked me across the face like a heartless bitch.

"I know it's scary, but I'm here, and I'm not going anywhere."

She curled into a ball on the chair, and I wanted to hug her and make all the panic go away, but I knew that wouldn't help. Nothing seemed to help.

"Hey, Ellie, check this out!" Sloane came in with energy, and I sagged into the chair. I had nothing left.

"Okay," she sat next to Ellie with her phone and showed her some pictures, "this is where they're going to take you. See this room right here?" She swiped the phone and pointed to something. "You'll lie down, and then they'll take pictures of your head. Just to see what's going on in there."

"Because of the accident." She sniffed like she was following.

"Right, to make sure everything is still okay."

"If I'm not?" she challenged.

"Do you feel okay?"

"Yeah."

"Then you're okay."

The nurse came in, and Sloane handed Ellie the phone. "Follow the pictures, and you'll know what's going on."

"'Kay." She nodded once before she looked at me and left. No screaming, no fights, just left.

I wanted to talk to Sloane to ask her how the hell she knew to do all this stuff, but my phone rang.

"Black," I answered sharply.

"You planning on coming to California, or did you

get what you needed from our last phone call?" Trigger's voice boomed through the speaker.

"Been a rough couple of weeks, man, but if that's all Brick was doing in Mexico, I think we're good."

"Well, I got something for ya. I tried calling Irons, but he's busy with shit, so I'm bringing it to you."

"All right."

"Cray heard that a cartel had one of your radios. Said it had orange buttons."

I felt my stomach twist.

"They must have poached it from the kid."

"Any way they can find your channel?"

"There's no way, and we talk in code."

There was a long stretch of silence.

"What?" I asked.

"Don't know, man. Something feels off."

"It has from the very start," I agreed, but I also knew Trigger was extra sensitive since he'd found a mole within his club.

"Any chance you have a—"

"No." I cut him off.

"How do you know?"

"Call it gut intuition." We learned our lesson with York.

"I'll keep my ears open, then."

"I appreciate you doing that."

"Yeah." The line went dead, and I turned to find the room empty.

Ellie returned ten minutes later, and she seemed okay.

We found Sloane out in the waiting room. She stood when she spotted Ellie.

"Here." My sister handed her the phone. "Grant called three times."

Sloane's face fell as she tucked her phone away. Who was Grant?

After we dropped my sister off at home and said our goodbyes, we picked up Tripper and headed back to Shadows.

Sloane was quiet and stared out the window while Tripper rested his head on her shoulder from behind. He must have sensed her mood was off. Just as we passed the last checkpoint, I slowed the car to park.

"Thank you," I whispered, "for your help."

"Sure." She kept her eyes away from mine as she unbuckled her seatbelt.

"Look, I don't discuss my personal life with the guys, so I'd—"

"So why would I?" She grabbed her things from the trunk and headed down toward her cabin with the fucking traitor right on her heels.

I closed my eyes and sighed. I really wasn't good with anyone anymore.

I needed some sleep.

Three hours later, the click of the radios and squeaky voices woke me from a restless sleep. Liam was in my closet shouting codes to his brother in the middle of an epic battle.

I groaned and covered my head with my pillow, but

the sound of my phone pulled me from my desperate need for sleep.

Cole: Conference room, now.

John: Be there in 5.

With a quick shower and a swipe at my teeth, I hurried down the stairs to find the men at the conference room table. Coffee and pastries lured me to the plate on the side. As I sipped the brew, I tuned in to their vibe and realized something was up.

Cole cleared his throat and tapped a button on the computer, which sent a photo to the big screen behind him.

"As of this morning, Frank got word that North Rock was ambushed and three of the guys are now separated from the team." Cole paused while Daniel joined us. "We got the order we ship out at eleven hundred."

So, four of North Rock were now in the hospital, the rookie was dead, and now another three were missing. *Christ, almost half the damn team has been picked off!*

Daniel stood next to Cole with his phone in hand. "Mike and Keith are on the way and should be here in an hour. I want all comms double checked, extra ammo, and watches charged."

"Cole," I drew the attention my way, "I don't know if you got my text, but Trigger did confirm that the cartel has the rookie's radio."

"I did. I'm not concerned. It's not the first or last time

that will happen." I gave a quick nod in agreement. "All right, men, eleven hundred."

As I raced up the stairs, I spotted Tripper playing with Butters in the living room, outing Liam's position. I glanced around to see if I could spot Sloane, but instead, I found June working in the kitchen.

"Hey, handsome, what are you up to?"

"Getting ready to ship out."

Typical, June skirted around the subject of us leaving and went directly to the elephant in the room.

"I don't know what happened last night, but Sloane sure is quiet this morning." She gave me the eye.

I picked up an apple and began to polish it on my shirt as I considered what to say. Her warm hand covered mine from across the island.

"The boys might be oblivious as to what's going on, but this wise old lady sees all. It's not lost on me that you keep your family's pain from us. I know there's a lot more going on with you than you want to share, but it's okay to be happy, John. It's okay to let someone in."

I hated that she saw the truth, but her words hit home.

She rounded the island. "The last time I saw her, she was heading down to her cabin." She kissed my cheek, handed me the last piece of my apple, and turned back to the sink.

On my way out the door, I whistled for Tripper to join me, but it took me half a second to realize he was already on his way down there. *I get it.*

EIGHT

SLOANE

I pushed some papers aside and found my phone that alerted me a text came through.

> Dell: Hey, Sloane, I wanted to apologize for not picking you up last night.

> Sloane: It was no problem, Dell. No need to apologize.

> Dell: I just heard you had to spend the night at Black's, and I know you may have preferred to come home instead.

I smiled at his comment. It was true. I did love my own space, but what happened last night was completely fine, and I was really happy I could help out.

> Sloane: I was fine. Thanks for checking in.

> Dell: Oh, good. When John told me to go home and that he was on his way into town to find you, I thought about texting you, but he assured me you'd be fine with it.

Oh, really, now, I couldn't help but grin like a teenager. Maybe Mr. Black was a bit of a softy after all. I sent another thanks his way and went back to my work.

> Daniel: After a lengthy conversation with Frank, we both decided you could have a video conference with Brick. We'd still rather you not go to California. Here's his contact number –He is waiting for your call.

My mind flipped through a hundred questions, but I calmed my head and angled the camera at the blank gray wall, propped my phone up, and tapped in the number. I didn't want to waste any time. It took the camera a second to clear, but the sounds of people yelling and music filled my cabin. When the photo focused, I swallowed hard. Brick was a good-looking man, but I could see by the way he squinted at the camera he was high as a kite.

"You guys don't waste any time, do ya?" He laughed and held up a finger while he walked outside. He slipped on a pair of sunglasses and leaned on a lounge chair. In the refection of the glasses, I could see a pool in front of him and someone moving around on a truck under a tree.

"Hi, Brick." I was warned by Frank to be respectful and use his nickname. "I'm Sloane Harlow, and Daniel gave me permission to use this number."

"Save the formalities with me. Just shoot the shit and ask your questions."

"Okay." I leaned back in my chair and studied him for a moment. "Why were you in Mexico?"

"Like I told Black, why I was there had nothing to do with his operation."

"So, why were you there?"

He scratched his beard and cursed. "Personal."

"Can you elaborate?"

"I can, but I choose not to."

"Fine." I tried a different direction. "It's no secret you've been around the cartel before. I read up on Trigger and his rather colorful past." I couldn't help but smile. Trigger's rap sheet was longer than the test for the bar exam. "Before you ran into Black that day, did you see anything strange or out of order?"

"Nah, not really." He tilted his head as if something might have jogged his memory. "One of the younger rats was running his mouth about watching after that rookie kid who got killed."

I sat a little straighter and pulled my notebook beside me. "What did he say?"

"Something about his belongings."

"His belongings," I repeated as I scribbled it down. "Anything else?"

"I didn't stick around. I was outnumbered and was

trying to wait out the rain. The last person I ever thought I would turn my gun on was Black. Guess I'm fuckin' thankful he was there."

"Did you physically see the rookie kid with any of them?"

"No." He lit a cigarette but nodded like he had more to say. "They have these deep square cut-outs in the ground, like four-by-eight," he motioned with his hands, "with a makeshift covering that acts as a roof. Once they catch someone, they'd strip 'em down and toss 'em in there until their leader arrived. You could run right over it and never know anyone was down there."

"Really?" I cringed.

"Yeah, so most likely, that's what they did to him for the six days he was taken. It's like their own version of a snatch and grab, but they don't have roads, they have the jungle."

"How did you know he was taken for six days before he was killed?"

He chuckled like it was a stupid question. "We might be an outlaw biker gang, sweetheart, but we know just as much as you do."

"Fair enough." I didn't have much to go on, but I still could dig with what he gave me. "Thanks. I appreciate your time."

"Sorry I couldn't be more helpful, but like I said, I walked into their shitstorm, not the other way around."

"Got it." I gave him a wave and ended the call. Still, something nagged at me. The truth was always there; you just needed to remove the fog to find it. With my notebook in hand, I moved closer to the fire to sit on the couch. I studied the satellite photos of the last mission Frank had sent over. With a red marker, I traced North Rock's position and then traced Blackstone's in black. Something just didn't add up. In the past, the cartel had typically crossed their paths, but this time they were coming in directly behind them as if they knew and followed their route.

"How could that be?" I whispered to myself.

"How could what be?" I looked up to find John in the doorway. "May I come in?"

"That depends. Are you going to play nice?"

As he closed the door, he shot a look at Tripper, who was now snuggled down by my feet. He wagged his tail in delight. John stood in place and looked like he wanted to say something.

"Do you want something?"

He tucked his hands in his pockets then quickly removed them to finger comb his hair.

I leaned back in the couch and sipped my wine, waiting for him to speak. When he didn't, I turned back to my work.

"Years back, my sister was in a car accident. Well, actually, she was hit by a semi. The driver was eighteen hours over his logbook. Her head bounced off the window, severely damaging her frontal lobe. Though she doesn't remember much of the accident, she remembers everything before it. She just has trouble with everything after it. Damn, I really wanted to hate that driver, I really did, but after I learned who he was and that he had a five-year-old daughter with cystic fibrosis, how could I? After all, he's really not the one to blame."

His haunted eyes found mine, and I knew there was a lot more to the story, so I remained quiet, allowing him to find his words.

"My dad's equipment was getting old. For his birthday that year, I wanted to buy him a weather station to help him predict the barometric pressure. It would help him decide when to harvest the grain. I told Ellie about it. She knew I ordered it, but I got called out on a mission and didn't have time to pick it up. When the cops were finished with the investigation, they found it among the wreckage. She had gone to pick it up for me." His shoulders sagged. "It should have been me. I should be the one stuck in time."

"John—"

"I've never told anyone that before."

"Does it feel better?"

"What?"

"Telling me. Does it make you feel better?"

"I don't know. I've felt this way for so long, it's hard to recognize any other feeling."

"Why now? Why tell me this?"

"I don't know. There's something about you that makes me want to tell you."

"That's a really nice thing to say."

"I'm leaving."

I shook my head to keep up with his spinning thoughts. He must have caught my confusion. He glanced at the satellite photos on the table.

"North Rock's team got separated, and we're going to make an attempt to locate them. We leave in an hour."

I felt my chest tighten at the idea of him leaving. I didn't want him to go, but I knew he had to.

"I think they know ahead of time where you are landing."

"Impossible."

"Is it?"

"Yes. I know where you're going with this. You heard they have one of our radios, but like I've said before, we use codes and speak in different languages. It would be impossible for them to decode our messages."

"Then explain to me why every other time they've found you, they've come in from the sides, but this time," I pointed at the photos, "they came in directly behind both your teams' locations."

He pulled out the photo I had traced on with the marker and studied it.

"Coincidence."

"Well, in my line of work, there are no coincidences."

He turned back to study the photo again, this time a little longer, then he let it drop to the table. He looked at his watch, and I knew his head was already in the mission.

"Tripper," he addressed his dog, "watch over her for me." I felt my face blush, so I removed my glasses and stood, not sure where to go with that. He headed for the door, hesitated, but stepped out and closed it. I stood there not moving, mulling over his words. He'd opened up to me and shared a secret no one else knew and was about to leave on a dangerous mission. I felt my legs move before my head caught up. I swung open the door and ran down the stairs when I heard him speak behind me.

"For the first time in five years, I had a moment where things felt normal, and that happened because of you." He stepped down a stair, and his broad shoulders blocked some of the sunlight. "For the first time in fifteen years, I had a moment where I didn't want to leave on a mission, because of you." He joined me on the ground. "For the first time in my entire life, I don't know what I'm doing."

"Because of me?"

He reached out and tugged me to him then leaned down and stared intently into my eyes. I could barely think, he was so close. My hands landed on the sides of his shoulders, and they flexed under my hold. His was strong—country strong. Lean and cut in all the right places.

"Yes, because of you." His fingers wove into my hair, then he dipped lower and caught my lips. He was warm, and his mouth tasted like he had just eaten something sweet. I allowed my body to relax against him, and I fell into step with his rhythm. I mirrored his movements with my tongue. Never had I ever felt such sweet warmth burst through my entire body during a kiss. It was as if fate was saying, "See! He's the right one to take a chance on."

His free hand slid down my back and under my

jacket to my bare skin. I jumped at the sudden rush of cold. I giggled at my reaction and felt his smile against my lips.

He broke the kiss and closed his eyes like he was drinking me in. So many things at once.

"I have to go."

"Now?" I felt the excitement plummet.

A wicked grin made the lines of stress around his eyes fade away.

"Welcome to Blackstone, baby."

My hands went to my hips, and I lifted an eyebrow at him.

"That's a little unfair."

"Trust me," he brushed a finger down my cheek as I'd once seen him do to Olivia, "nothing about this is fair."

"John…" My words caught in my throat.

"Be here when I get back, okay." He wasn't asking, and I oddly liked it.

"Okay."

He squeezed my hand, took one last look into my soul, and left.

My fingers brushed my bottom lip, wanting to savor his kiss.

"Be careful," I whispered into the chilly air.

I watched the team head up the mountain to catch the chopper. I decided to go for a walk to clear my head and ran into Savannah in one of the cabins next to Mark's. I saw her through the window as she draped a blanket over the coach.

"Knock, knock." I stepped into the cabin that mirrored mine.

"Oh, hey, Sloane," Savi greeted me with a smile. Her eyes narrowed in on my face, and I could swear she knew what just happened with John and me.

"What are you doing?" I noticed some boxes marked "living room" in the corner.

"I'm just getting ready for some company."

I picked up a glass ornament that sat in the window and rolled it around my palm, not sure what to do.

"I spoke to Brick," I blurted for something to say.

"Oh, yeah?" She laughed. "Was Rail there? Because the two of them are incredibly entertaining."

"No, but I was able to talk to him a little. He didn't have much to say, but he did give me a small lead."

"Well, that's something." She smiled, and I could tell she was waiting for me to go on. *Dammit.* I wasn't even sure where to begin. My head was swimming.

"It's strange at first, but the feeling becomes normal."

My gaze moved to hers. "Is it really that obvious?"

"No," she chuckled lightly, "I just recognize that look, and I know how you feel."

I sank into the chair, oddly relieved that I had someone to talk to about it. "Honestly, Savi, I don't know where to go from here."

"What do you mean?"

"John seems to be a troubled soul. One moment he's great, but the next his walls shoot up, and he shuts me out."

Savannah pulled some green pillows from the box and set them neatly on the couch, then took a seat and faced me.

"Ah, yes, our Blackstone boys. They're complex men with complex jobs who got into it thinking they would always just be married to their career. Each one carries their own personal demons, some big, some small. John has always kept us at arm's length, and according to Cole, he was especially closed off after his sister's accident. I know she must have been hurt more than he lets on and that he carries a lot of what happened on his shoulders, although none of us knows why. If John wanted to share, he would, so we respect his privacy."

"Any advice on how to open him up?"

"Do you know how to climb?" She chuckled.

"No, but I'd be willing to learn."

"Look, Sloane, it's baby steps with John. Enjoy the moments when he opens up, and at those times really show who you are, so you break through that barrier. It will take time, but he will see who you are and will let his guard down with you more. All the men married very strong women, so there is something to be said for that. Sometimes they may need a little push to see what's right in front of them."

I stood, feeling a little better inside, and asked Savi if she needed any help.

By mid-afternoon, the cabin looked inviting and ready for company. We made our way back up to the main house and wandered into the kitchen to help make dinner. Savi suggested that I pitch in, as it would be a good way to keep my mind busy.

An entire "cow" and a bushel of potatoes later, we started to fill the table with tonight's dinner. I noticed Dell, who was also one of the Green Berets, was extra quiet this evening. Savannah said they often hung around while dinner was made, but tonight it was more than that. Something seemed off. I wished Frank was there so I could ask him. As I was setting the last platter of meat on the table, a strange noise blew over the roof of the house. Savannah froze, and her glance flew to Abigail, who had the same expression.

"What is that?" I asked, curious to know why the mood had suddenly changed in the room.

"It's the chopper." Abigail moved to the window and pulled back the curtain. "It's back early."

Savannah dropped the forks on the table and rushed toward the front door where Dell was already waiting.

"What's going on, Dell?" Savannah opened the door, only to have Dell close it on her.

"Let's just give them a minute."

"So, they *are* back." Savi looked over at me and hesitated. "Dell, we have an agreement when they are back on US soil, you can tell me if they're okay or not."

"They are okay."

Savannah's shoulders sagged inward with relief, and she didn't press further. Instead, she came over and stood next to me as if to offer me comfort in unknown territory.

One by one, the men entered the house. Their clean

gear didn't go unnoticed, but their stressed expressions sent a chill up my spine.

Cole immediately made a beeline for Savannah, and a fully tattooed man granted me a halfhearted smile.

"You must be Sloane. I'm Mike," he pointed to himself, "and that's Keith. It's a pleasure to meet you."

"You too." Before I said anything else, he disappeared upstairs.

"Hey," John appeared, "change in plans."

"Are you okay?"

"Yeah." He glanced over my shoulder to someone before he brought his eyes back to mine. "I'm going to change out of my gear, then I'll meet you at the table."

Cole slapped Dell on the shoulder, giving him a thanks and let him know they'd be down to dinner in a few minutes.

Fifteen minutes later, the team joined us at the hastily reset table. Before the men had even settled, Mark had two steaks on his plate and was reaching for the potatoes. He looked over, catching my amusement.

"I'm eating for two. Mia isn't here tonight."

I grinned at him, but it slipped when Cole sat at the head of the table. The tension was as thick as the steaks in front of us. John was the last one to join us and sat next to me. His warm hand reached over and squeezed my leg as a silent hello. I covered his fingers and returned the gesture.

"All right, boys," Abigail spoke first, "there's no strangers at this table. Out with it."

Keith cleared his throat and pointed his fork in John's direction. "Shouldn't the hero speak first?"

"Luck," John corrected.

"You can call it luck," Mike's voice boomed across the table, "but that luck saved your brothers."

Keith waited for John to speak, but when he didn't seem to want to elaborate, Keith picked up the story.

"We were getting into position to rappel down when John suddenly shouted at us to stop. With North Rock screaming in our ears, we waited for an explanation."

"I had a bad feeling." John finally spoke up. "Our gut is everything in this job."

"Well, then what happened?" June leaned forward on the edge of her seat.

"At least fifty cartel were waiting for us like rats in the grass," Keith snarled. "If we hadn't stopped when we did, we wouldn't be sitting here right now."

"To brothers 'til dust, in instinct we trust." Mark raised his glass in lieu of a toast.

"Hear, hear," Cole chimed in, and we all joined him.

After dinner, the team left to debrief with Frank via video chat, while we spent the next hour cleaning up and preparing for tomorrow's breakfast. I found myself alone with everything done. At a loss as to what else to do, I shrugged my coat on and headed out into the cold. A layer of frost blanketed the ground and muted my footsteps as I walked to my cabin.

"I don't want to scare you." His voice came from somewhere above. He stood with his back against the door, his face in a shadow. I loved how attractive he was. No man would ever compare from here on out.

"I thought you were still with Frank."

"Wasn't a lot to debrief about. I just had a bad feeling."

I took two steps and admired the view in front of me.

"So, you're a hero?"

"Only because of you," he whispered.

Huh?

"I've had a pretty strange last seven hours." He stepped into the light and held out a hand for me to take. "I'd really like to spend the next seven with you."

As soon as I closed the door, he hovered above me again. He brushed my hair back and cupped my face.

"They call me a hero, but really, it was you, Sloane." He leaned in and kissed the corner of my mouth. "You had my instincts on high alert, and when I felt that kick in my gut just before we descended, everything inside of me screamed it wasn't safe." He paused. "I have to question myself. Would I have stopped my team if you hadn't honed my senses with your questions?"

"But you did." I returned the kiss and craved more of him. "Focus on that, John."

"All I could focus on was you, Sloane, getting back to you. I saved my team, my brothers, the people I would die for, and all my mind wanted to think about was you."

"Lust is a bitch." I tried to give him a sloppy out, but I didn't really want him to take it.

"No." He pulled his lips from the slope of my neck

and gently held my chin in his hand, so I was forced to look at him. "Not lust, need. There's a difference."

I couldn't recall the last time someone had spoken to me the way John had. Maybe never.

"I'll ask you this once. Are you dating anyone?"

"No."

"Good answer." He grinned.

An ache settled in the center of my chest then plunged straight down between my legs. I shifted my weight to the other foot to find some kind of relief. A storm brewed inside my veins, and I wasn't sure how much more I could take. Heat and hunger bubbled to the surface, and my clothes suddenly felt too hot.

Both his hands pressed above my breasts and slowly slid upward to remove my jacket. It fell to the ground as his fingers inched to trace my collarbone.

"Now I know how Cole felt," he whispered more to himself. "Sometimes it only takes one look to be captivated by someone."

I wished I had something to say, but I was lost in the moment, so I reached for his sweater and held on to the bottom of it. He stepped back and reached over his head to tug it off.

The low light cast shadows in the grooves of his stomach, and when he took a breath, his chest puffed up, and I wanted to cry. No man should be this good looking.

"This…" I ran my fingertips over his tattoo that spread across his shoulder and half his chest. A lion was nestled between some swirls, and a scroll had been inked over his pec. It was John 14:6. "It's my favorite verse." I smiled warmly. "Yours too?"

His eyes moved away for a moment, and when they returned, I saw it was raw topic. "I lost my way once, and now I won't."

I nodded and let the topic go.

Slowly, I worked the buttons of my blouse through the tiny holes while his hands flexed at his sides. A small grin traveled across my lips as I saw him fight for control.

Flexing my shoulder blades, I let the sheer fabric slip away from my skin and float down to land on top of my coat.

"Wow," he whispered as he took a step toward me and backed me up to the cold wooden door. I was soon trapped by his hips. "I didn't want to like you, Sloane. I don't deserve your smile, but when I saw you and this," his hand slipped over my bottom, "I lost my fight to stay miserable." His eyes squeezed shut like he was struggling. "This isn't going to be easy. I carry a lot—"

I shook my head and ran my hands up his chest to place a finger over his warm lips. His eyes opened.

"When is life ever easy, John?" I whispered and saw so much pain there it seemed to settle into the sexy lines in his face. "But having someone to share it with makes it a lot easier." Before I could go on, he leaned back and sucked my finger into his mouth. A jolt of lust spread through my stomach, and just like that, I was ready to go.

It had been such a long time since a man made me feel this way.

I moaned.

Wait, did I just moan? Oh, my God. I was thankful for the low light because he chuckled as he sucked a little harder. My free hand went to his belt and tugged it open while he did the same to mine.

Removing my finger, he dove down and caught my lips, and his hand pressed flat to my stomach and moved inside my panties. A fever heat flashed across my face when his finger found my slick opening and pushed in.

I tried to gasp for air, but he kissed me harder, so I shamelessly ground myself into his hand and took everything he offered me. Two then three more fingers pushed my walls, and I whimpered, wanting more. His lips broke the kiss and traveled to my neck, and I sucked in a much-needed gulp of air.

"John," I half moaned, and my head flopped backward, just needing some support—anything to let me fully enjoy what he was doing.

"I need to see you." He pulled his fingers free of me, lifted, and carried me to the conference table. With one arm, he pushed my paperwork aside and laid me back, so I was sprawled out lengthwise on the mahogany table.

"Jesus," he huffed.

NINE

Using all my willpower, I slowly peeled her out of her shoes and jeans. As much as I ached to ravish her in the alpha way, I took my time. Sloane deserved to be treated like a lady. She was everything I wanted in a woman, and I had waited way too long to ignore that.

Her slim, naked body waited for mine, and all I could do was stare and savor the moment, almost afraid this couldn't be real. Guilty thoughts tried hard to break through this happiness, so I knew I'd have to do something fast before they consumed me and ruined the moment.

Removing the rest of my clothes, I eased between her legs and gawked at the feast that was before me. I reached forward and dragged the tips of my fingers from the tops of her plump breasts, down over her nipples, through the lines of her toned stomach and between the crease of her thighs. She bit down on her lip and closed her eyes as though she could barely handle the feelings I was bringing to her.

"John," her words had my erection flexing toward the warm slit that begged me to enter, "so help me God."

I loved that she was on the brink of losing it, because so was I.

With the pad of my thumb, I circled her nub twice, then I lined up and slipped in all the way to the root. Her back bowed, and a marvelous sound fell from her lips. Her long dark hair spread wildly around her and bounced about when I started to thrust. I couldn't get enough of this woman. I didn't know where to look. My eyes left her hair and her face as I now found myself fascinated by her stomach that flexed as I dove deeper and deeper. My God, she was beautiful.

A thin layer of sweat broke along the back of my neck, and my vision blurred as I lost control. Her nails dug into my arms as she desperately clung on, but I needed more. So much more. I crawled above her, hauled her up, and balanced on my knees as she rode me. Every time she came down, I would thrust harder. Her screams only fueled my need to go on. As her walls fisted me, I buried my face between her breasts and let go. We both came. She shuddered and bucked, and I held tight to her shoulders to keep her against me.

"John," she mumbled.

"Yeah." I kissed her neck.

"Before, when I was at Zack's, were you already in town or did you come to find me?"

I smirked at the realization Dell might have told her what I did.

"Truth," she added.

"Yes," I admitted, "I came to see you." She was putty in my arms as I walked her to the shower to clean up.

"I'm glad you did."

"Why?" I figured I knew why, but I wanted to hear what she had to say.

"Because I got to see a side of you that you don't share with anyone else. It makes me feel special."

"Good." I carried her up the stairs cradled in my arms. It felt good to be naked with her, like our bodies were meant to coexist. I kicked the door open and turned on the water.

"How are you?" I grinned as the warm spray soaked her long hair.

"Mm," she moaned, "so good."

"Me too." I kissed the drops of water from her temple, loving the way my body reacted whenever I kissed her. Soap lathered between my hands, and I turned her around to massage her scalp, and her body leaned back against mine. Her silky skin awoke my erection, so I pressed it into her back, and she started to move to create friction.

Damn, she felt amazing.

Removing my hands from her hair, I traveled down to her neck and chest and spread the soap as I moved about.

Her nipples grew firm and erect while I played with them, and she let me know she liked it by the way she reached back and started to pump me. My fingers inched farther south, and to my surprise, with her free hand, she directed me back to her opening. We both built one another up. Our moans and grunts filled the steamy bathroom, and I was glad we were in her cabin and not inside the walls of Shadows.

When I found my release, I bit down on her shoulder, and she bucked and shook in my hold. It was the sexiest thing I'd ever seen, Sloane losing herself in my arms. The way her body jolted and vibrated drew my animal instinct to the surface. I whirled her around and spoke slowly through my locked jaw.

"I want more." I craved to be inside of her, but I could see she was spent. "But I'll savor what we just had until later."

Her big blue eyes looked just as hungry as I felt, but she gave me a nod, and I turned off the water.

I tucked her into bed. I wrapped my body around her and nuzzled my head into her hair and drank in her sweet scent. I wasn't tired. Truth be told, I could have done that all night, but she was spent, so I let her sleep. Once again, I took the time to admire this gorgeous, sexy woman. I knew she had just given me two of the greatest moments I would ever have. In the last how many years, I realized I had been dead inside, and I wanted to savor the memory as long as I could.

Just after three, I felt her stir and I knew she was awake. With her head on my shoulder and her hand on my chest, she started to trace my muscles.

"You should be asleep," she whispered. I smiled and kissed the top of her head. "Thinking about your last mission?"

"A bit, yes."

"Want to talk about it?"

"There's not much to discuss."

"We either talk about it here or across the table we just christened."

We both laughed.

"I don't know," I rubbed my head, "I rather like you in that silk blouse, tight skirt, and glasses."

"Mm." She laughed a little more. "Well, what else are you thinking about?"

A nagging question did linger in the back of my mind. It had for some time now, and I was sorry she had brought it to the forefront. I wasn't sure I wanted to bring this topic up yet. I so enjoyed the lightness we had just now.

"Tell me something about you." I decided to start there.

"Like?"

"I don't know, just something." She went back to her delicious tracing as she thought.

"I have been around hospitals since I was nine," she

started, and that immediately caught my attention. "My mother is a neurosurgeon." I flinched, and I felt her fingers stop. It took all my effort not to change the subject. If she noticed, she didn't react, which I was learning was an amazing quality in Sloane.

"I thought you told the girls she was in the Army?"

"She was but later stepped away. She helped me understand how the brain worked and why things happened the way they did. Understanding how the brain works is key to understanding how to help when things go wrong. You can begin to understand how to navigate through new brain pathways, how to help people find a new way, a new path. It can make life a lot easier, in an otherwise frightening situation," she paused, "for everyone." She shifted to her belly and looked up at me.

I was sure every negative emotion I'd kept hidden from the world was now written in bold big letters across my face. Panic and anger fought to bubble up inside me, but her eyes flickered with something completely different, so I forced it back down and went for a puzzled smile instead.

"Something tells me the great Agent Black, hero of his team, was holding back on me earlier." She moved to her knees and straddled my legs, and the heat from her arousal had my hands twitching.

"You have no idea." I flipped her over and spent the next two hours showing her what a Special Forces officer's endurance was really capable of.

Just after dawn, my alarm went off, and I carefully

unfolded myself from Sloane to get dressed. She looked beautiful in the early morning light. The tip of a breast was highlighted in a beam of sunshine. I couldn't help myself as I leaned down and softly sucked her nipple into my mouth. I forced my hands to stay put, and along with it the desire to dive down between her legs for a taste.

*Oh…*but it tested all my willpower.

She stirred, and I waited a beat before I broke contact with her. With one last look, I slipped out of the cabin and into the cool, brisk air.

I should get a fucking medal for leaving her alone this morning.

"Morning." Savannah winked as she whisked by with a handful of toys from the living room.

"Morning." I beamed back, but the silly grin quickly fell from my face as Davie appeared with a radio and clicked the button a few times.

"Another one bites the dust."

"Fuck!" I snatched the shitty device and headed to the morning meeting I was about to be late for.

I tossed my broken radio in the middle of the conference table with a growl.

"We have drones that hover and drop bombs, we have navigation systems that can get us out of the darkest corners of the world, but yet the military cannot make a damn radio that works."

"Jacob," Cole jumped in, just as pissed as I was, "our CIA informant tried multiple times to reach us through our comms on the last mission to warn us of this." He tapped a key on the board, and video footage from a drone showed the cartel moving in on us, something we should have known in real time.

"General Csaba," Frank's voice crackled through the speaker phone, "has not taken this lightly and will report it to the appropriate party." Mark glanced at me with the fear of God on his face. General Csaba had a reputation for being a fierce son of a bitch. Cole had to deal with him after he returned home from his captivity in Mexico a few years back. I knew it was hard on him mentally to relive what he went through with Csaba, who questioned his every move on his disappearance. The fact that he was still reeling from the loss of his and Savi's baby didn't help. Even Keith and Mike had a taste of the general when they were starting up Dusk. I had my own view on the man but kept it to myself.

Dell appeared at the door and held up his phone. "Logan?"

"Not now." Cole dismissed him with a short wave.

"Logan," he repeated in a voice that caused us all to look at him. Cole gave him a curt nod to continue. "Another video has been leaked."

"Toss it up," Cole instructed as he looked at the screen.

To say the tension was already thick was an understatement for what we were about to witness. Once again, my team, my brothers, were the stars of a YouTube sensation called *Cartel Versus US Special Forces*. I recognized Chamness, BT, and Rick as they moved through the thick terrain in Southern Mexico. The cameraman looked to be several yards away, up high. Mike cleared his throat as the next clip showed him running through the trees.

"Holy shit," Mike spat angrily, "I hate being on some fucking reality show."

I stood and moved closer to the screen. I squinted as something caught my eye, and I asked Dell to rewind it three seconds.

"We are shadows that move in the night. North Rock is our mirror image across the border. We are ghosts as far as they are concerned, so how the hell do they know our route?" I reiterated, "How the hell are we not catching their cameras?" I pointed to the screen where a camera was mounted on a tree trunk. "How can they know our movements before our boots even touch down on their territory?"

A heavy silence filled the room. For the first time in Blackstone's history, we were unsure of our next move.

After three more hours of digging under every rock and going through every possible scenario, Cole dismissed us. We were all exhausted and frustrated, and it didn't help that I'd gotten very little sleep last night…not that I was complaining.

"Savi, have you seen Sloane this morning?"

A knowing eyebrow lifted at me, and a playful smile ran across her lips as she went back to cutting up grapes for Mark's little one, who was buckled into a chair at the table.

"All I know is she showed up in the kitchen earlier

with Dell. She had an overnight bag and a stack of files. She said she had to go to North Dakota for something. Don't worry, though," she added looking up at me. "She said Daniel approved it." I sank down on the counter and pulled out my phone.

John: I feel used.

I started to put my phone away when I saw the dots to show she was texting back.

Sloane: I left two hundred on the bedside table.

I laughed, and Savi glanced over at me with a question.

John: You good?

Sloane: I found something that couldn't wait. I saw you were still in the meeting, so I couldn't say goodbye. See you tomorrow, at the latest.

John: Call tonight?

Sloane: Sure thing.

"So," Savi started, "I couldn't help but notice your room was empty this morning, and Tripper was missing again."

Just as I went to feed her some bullshit line, I spotted

Olivia outside about to attack Liam and Ethan with her Nerf gun.

"Look at her go." I nodded in her direction proudly. "That's my girl. Take out the little shits." As Savannah watched, I slipped out of the kitchen and headed for my beloved peak. I needed to clear my head.

"You play dirty, Black." She chuckled as I headed for the door.

I jogged down the path and gave a wave to the guys who were at their posts scattered throughout the woods. This really was the one place I could relax and not be hyperaware of my surroundings. The base of the mountain welcomed me as I prepared myself for another climb.

The toe of my shoe wedged into a tiny crack while my hand swung out and gripped a barely protruding bit of rock. My mind calculated my next move. With no ropes, no cleats, no helmet, just the clothes on my back and my brain hyper-focused, I slowly made my way up the familiar cliff face. I glanced down at the forest seventy-five feet below me and felt energized. As a member of Blackstone, we faced death on every mission. We were all responsible for each other. If one slipped up, we all slipped up. Here on my mountain, I faced death on my own terms. I challenged myself constantly to be the best I could be. I'd let down one person in my life, and I refused to repeat that with my brothers.

Once at the top, I plucked one of the yellow flags from a baggie I kept up there. I would add it to the others back in my room. This would be my seventy-third successful climb to cheat death.

I brushed the dirt off my hands and made my way down the path toward Shadows, but before I hit the driveway, my phone rang. I didn't have to look at it to know who it was. "Hey, Dad, what's up?"

"I was wondering if you and Sloane were going to come by today. Your sister seems a little off."

"Sloane is away with work. Is Ellie okay?"

There was a pause before he spoke again. "She's all right, but your mom would like you two to come by again soon, maybe for dinner this week."

"Dad, I don't see that happening. Things are really stressful here at work."

"Okay, just if you have the time, it would be nice to see you."

"I'll try."

The heaviness the mountain had relieved settled right back down on my shoulders and ate away at my gut. A rustle in the trees told me Keith wasn't far. I spotted him next to the trunk of a tree.

"Everything all right, Black?"

"All things considered, yup." I didn't know how much he'd heard, so I turned the conversation. "When do Lexi and Baby B arrive?"

"Tomorrow afternoon. Catalina comes in the next day."

"Have you told Abby yet about Lexi?"

He shrugged with a small grin. "I thought it might be more fun for them to see it for themselves."

"That'll be fun. It's about time things got back to normal around here." I paused. "Well, almost."

"Agreed. Long overdue." He gave a short wave as he sank back into the trees.

> Sloane: Just got back to the hotel.
> Going to have a quick shower. I'll call in
> twenty.

With a grin on my face, I jogged back down to the house.

TEN

SLOANE

My laptop was balanced on my knees as I tried to type up my notes. The weaving roads of Montana made it difficult, but I wanted to get the information out while it was still fresh in my mind. I had the opportunity to speak to a couple of friends of BT and Danny, who were members of North Rock. Frank had mentioned a possibility of a leak somewhere and asked me to dig a little deeper into their lives. Though the military knew almost everything, only friends really knew the little hidden secrets of your life, things that could make someone flip. I didn't want to believe it, but it wasn't my job to pick sides. My job was to dig.

"I'm sorry you weren't able to find anything to help Blackstone, Sloane." Dell glanced at me in the rearview mirror. I had chosen to ride in the back so I could spread my papers out around me.

"Sometimes what we can't see right away can lead to something later."

"Can I ask you something? Off the record."

"Sure," I answered without looking up.

"North Rock has collaborated with Blackstone for the past twenty years. I heard your last case you worked with members of the mob, so you know evil when you see it. In your gut, do you believe one of North Rock could have flipped?"

I removed my glasses and thought about my answer. "Humans are capable of pretty much anything. Given the right amount of money and the right incentive, anyone can flip. However, in this particular case and in my gut, no, I don't believe a member has flipped."

His shoulders loosened, and his grip on the wheel relaxed. Dell was younger and wore his heart on his sleeve. I really admired him for wanting to see the good in his friends.

I unpacked and got dressed and saw a missed text from Savannah explaining we were having company tonight and to dress accordingly. With the mystery guest on my mind, I chose a simple, black blouse and a pair of dark jeans, and then chose a pop of color in my heels, silver to match my earrings and bracelet.

I should have caught the mood in the house. The lightness that usually hung in the air was replaced with stiff postures and stiff drinks. Mark immediately handed me a martini and nodded across the room. I thought my stomach was going to bottom out when his blue eyes latched on to mine.

"There she is," he boomed across the room with a proud smile.

"You know the *devir-al?*" Mark whispered in shock. "You know who that is, right? That's General Csaba."

"You could say that." I took a step forward. "Hello, Father." I greeted him with a kiss on the cheek. I could swear the air was sucked out of the room in one fell swoop.

"Damn," Mark hissed behind me, "now we know how Mike felt when he figured out who Catalina was."

"Marcus!" Abigail scolded. "Mind your manners."

"What are you doing here, Dad?"

"Frank invited me to visit, and I felt it was about time I came to see how you were doing out here in the wilderness." He eyed my shoes.

"Ah, let's all go to the table. Dinner is ready." Abigail hastily waved her arms toward the dining room.

I took a gulp of my martini on the way to the table and graciously accepted a glass of red wine from Frank.

He leaned into me and whispered, "It's all good, kid. You got this."

John arrived late and took the seat next to me. He didn't miss a beat with his hand on my leg to greet me with a private hello. He eyed the table, picking up the vibe, and glanced at me with a questioning look.

"Hey, John," Mark smirked, "I would like you to meet Sloane's father, General Csaba."

To my surprise, John spoke confidently. "Welcome to Shadows, General." He didn't seem to be fazed like the others.

"Agent Black, I've heard of your recent mission. Well done, son."

"Actually, it was Sloane who planted the seed of doubt in the mission for me, so really the praise should go to her."

My hand froze as I reached for my wine. I was so used to Grant taking all the glory, even when it wasn't deserved, I wasn't used to someone putting the limelight on me.

"Well, that's very nice to hear." He raised his glass to me.

The conversation slowly picked up, and I glanced at John and mouthed "thank you." He returned a smile and put his hand over mine. Mark stopped talking and homed in on what he just did. John was normally very private, so this was new.

"Sloane." My father's tone changed and caught my attention, and I noticed his eyes on John's hand too. "Grant has called a few times and is worried about you. I think we can both agree he deserves a phone call."

"I have spoken to Grant, and we both know where we stand. Thank you, Father." My tone was not lost on him or the table.

"Very well."

Abigail and Savannah started to discuss decorating the house for Thanksgiving and what supplies they would need. Mark chimed in a few times with menu suggestions, and Keith made sure cookies were on the list. I appreciated their diversion and swallowed down a few more gulps of my dry red, thanks to June, who just topped up my glass. John removed his hand after a few beats while I glanced out the window and saw Liam and Ethan playing laser tag and wished it was me out there.

"Today's pain is tomorrow's strength." John's words broke into my thoughts and brought me back mid-conversation. "Those were the words, sir," he addressed my father, "that you said to me at a time I really needed to hear it."

I looked from John to my father, who had placed his fork on the table and leaned back in his chair. He studied John's face intently. I was unsure what this was all about.

"I remember that, son."

"I always wanted to thank you, but I wasn't sure how."

"No need for thanks. That's what the Army is for, family, one blood."

Mark, through a mouthful of food, shook his head. "I'm so lost right now." Laughter followed as dessert was served.

Abigail's earth-shattering squeal from the kitchen made Mark jump up and slap a hand over his mouth. He looked guilty as hell.

"You didn't." John pointed his fork at him.

"It wasn't meant for her!"

"Marcus!" she shouted.

My father glanced around the table, just as confused as I was.

"It was for Savannah," Mark appealed. He was red in the face from holding back his laughter.

"You promised that thing would never enter this house," Savannah hissed.

"It was Mike!" Mark was already in tears of laughter when Savannah turned to face my father.

"Forgive my family, General." She swatted Mark with her napkin. "We sometimes forget our manners."

"It's quite all right, dear, but I must say I'm curious as to just what is going on."

"It's a Dusk tradition." Dell spoke up. "Cole's daughter got a Furby for a gift one year, and it was supposedly left at Dusk. It speaks whenever its motion sensor is tripped."

"You can imagine the fun we have." Mark was still trying to get hold of himself.

My father laughed, and I cringed at the fury little monster in Abby's hand.

"I'm tossing it out!"

"Over my dead body." Mark jumped up and chased her into the kitchen while the table all burst into laughter.

"This is what I get for living with a bunch of boys." Savannah sighed playfully.

Once again, the house managed to make me smile even when I was completely out of my comfort zone.

I stood in the living room by the fire, feeling a little

lost, when my father came up to me and put a warm arm around my shoulders.

"I missed you, sweetheart."

"I missed you too, Dad." I really did. My father and I had always been close, just as my brother and mother were close. As a family, we were all very tight growing up. I knew my brother's move was weighing on all of us.

"You seem happy here."

"I am." I glanced at John across the room.

"He's a good man." He nodded to where I was looking. "Great soldier and well respected within his team. That says a lot to me. I know you had your problems with Grant, but I thought he was a good fit for you. I just want you to be happy."

"I think I am, now. I know this lifestyle may not be easy, but it's not like I'm not used to it, Dad. I did grow up in it."

"God, I raised you well, didn't I?" He beamed proudly. "I had a little help from your mother, of course." He chuckled as he glanced at his watch. "All right, I can report back to your mother you are well, so my job here is done. I will let Grant know to back off and that you've moved on."

"I would appreciate that, thanks. Maybe he'll finally back off if you say something."

"Of course." He nodded. "I fly out in a few hours, and I have a few things to wrap up, so this is my goodbye." He kissed me on top of the head. "I love you, sweetheart."

I noticed the team seemed to be in deep conversation at the table, and the girls were still planning events, so I slipped out and headed toward my cabin with Tripper on my heels. I peeled off my clothes and stepped into the warm spray of the shower, trying to let my mind accept that the General *devir-al,* as Mark called him, was just here and apparently had a connection with John. Funny how one of my concerns was put to rest so easily. I knew my father had a reputation of being a very difficult man to work with and had very little patience for those who annoyed him. As I towel-dried my hair, I skipped my clothes and went straight for a plushy bathrobe, then picked up my favorite book went downstairs and snuggled down by the fire to read. It wasn't long before my eyes grew heavy.

Something warm pulled me from the dream I was having. It faded away and then returned with a vengeance; the force of it made me gasp. I struggled to pull myself from sleep.

"Ohhh," escaped from my throat as the heat became more intense. My insides clenched, and my stomach coiled like a snake.

John reached inside my mind, his blond hair messy, his eyes hungry, and his muscles taut as he thrust inside of me.

I reached for my nipple, and I gently rolled it between the pads of my thumb and finger. A wild storm brewed inside my chest and stomach and created a feverish heat that warmed my blood as I sucked air into my starved lungs.

"Open your eyes, Sloane." John's cool breath brushed over my neck, but I was too far gone to care if this was real or just one hell of a fantasy.

My legs were spread open, and velvet nudged at my opening.

Yes! Oh, my God, yes!

"Open your eyes," he whispered again, and I cried out, needing release. I wouldn't risk the dream. I wouldn't risk waking up to find myself alone. I was too pent-up. *No, I'm so close.*

A deep growl vibrated against my chest from his, and just as my eyes fluttered open, he plunged inward. His neck muscles ticked as he waited for my walls to adjust to him.

"Are you always so hard to wake up?" He strained to speak.

"I didn't want to risk it." I tried to think as he moved from side to side to get a little deeper. "It was so good, too good to wake up and find out it might be just a dream."

He hauled me up so he could sit, and I straddled his lap. My breast brushed by his lips, so he stuck his tongue out and flicked my nipple.

"Do women often have dirty dreams?" He gently used his teeth to nibble the sensitive skin.

"Only when given a reason to." I tipped my head back and bowed my spine when his hands came around me and a finger dragged down the center of my back slowly.

"Did I not give you enough the last time?" he whispered in amusement.

"That's the problem." I nearly wilted at his touch. His erection was warm and wet against my leg. "It's all I can think about."

His hand landed on my hip, and the other moved around my front between my breasts.

"Well, I guess that makes two of us." He looked up at me with such a hungry, content look on his face it nearly made me come right on his lap. "I think," his eyes dragged down my front, "this is my most favorite spot." His hand swiped down to my stomach, and his thumb circled my sensitive nub.

"That's not fair." I squeezed my eyes shut and begged myself to find some control.

"No, Sloane," he leaned forward and kissed my collarbone, "what's not fair is finding you half naked on the couch and having to fight all my inner instincts not to toss you over my shoulder and haul you away, to take you the way I want to."

"Mm…" I pulled back slightly and cocked an eyebrow. "So, you like control?"

"I don't like it, Sloane," he lifted me up and lined his erection up with my opening, "I need it."

As much as I wanted to drop down and let him have his way with me, I felt a little playful. Both hands landed on his shoulders, and I lifted myself to my feet in one quick motion.

"What are you doing?"

"Maybe I like control too." I couldn't help but break into a smile when he folded his arms, unamused with my game.

"What kind of control would you like, then, Ms. Harlow?"

"Hmm," I pretended to think, "where to start?" I eyed the staircase but jumped when he reached out to grab my hand. "Oh, no, no, Mr. Black." I scowled him. "No touching…yet."

"Is that so?" He stood and pressed his chest into my aching nipples. "You see, we have this code among our team, *Code 45*, and when used in situations like this, it can be very effective."

"Oh, yeah?" I tried to think if I'd ever heard the guys use that code around me.

"Oh, yes." He suddenly bent down and scooped me up and over his shoulder. The world spun and dipped as he climbed the stairs to the loft and carefully dropped me onto the bed.

"I've seen and done many things that would make most cower and head home. I don't judge them for that. Our line of work isn't for everyone." He spread my legs and stood back to admire my naked body. "Control is the only thing we have, Sloane." He dragged a finger along my inner thigh, and I felt a delightful shiver. "If you want control, I'll try my hardest to step back, but," he leaned over me with a dangerous grin, "when we're naked and you're looking at me like that," he pointed to my face, "I need to be in control."

"I can agree with that." I shamelessly spread my legs farther, and he wasted no time diving straight in. I jolted upward and lifted my back off the mattress.

"Jesus, Sloane," his jaw tensed, and sweat broke out along his forehead, "you can't do that."

"What?" I lifted higher, which tightened my muscles again, and watched his face fight for control. *Ohh, so I do have a little power.*

"Sloane," he warned as his face flushed and his neck contracted. When I reached for his neck, he grabbed my hands and held them above my head and devoured my mouth while thrusting at a deliciously rapid rate. Colors, sounds, and the smell of the cool night seemed to vanish as he made love to me in his way. I couldn't care less who had control, as long as this man kept doing what he was doing. I wished I had a mirror, just so I could watch every inch of the man who was doing what he apparently did best.

My stomach coiled to the point of pain when he changed the angle, and I was catapulted off the ledge.

The last thing I remembered was him burying his face in my neck and his moan as he found his own release.

I woke to the feeling of my pillow vibrating. Inching my fingers along the mattress, I pulled my phone to my ear, while visions of John roaming my body danced inside my memory. I squinted at the unknown number on the screen and hesitated to answer it, but when I recognized the area code was the same as John's, I accepted the call.

"Hi, Sloane, this is Kelly Black, John's mother." *Poof*, and there went my dirty thoughts. "I hope it was okay that I got your number from Daniel. I feel that John wants to keep you all to himself." She chuckled self-consciously. "I was wondering if you would like to meet up for lunch sometime today. It was really nice having you at the house the other day. Oliver and I appreciated the change in pace," she rambled.

"I would love that, Mrs. Black. When and where?"

"Oh, dear, please call me Kelly. How about Zach's at noon?"

"That sounds great. I'll see you there."

I sent a quick text to Dell asking him if he could drive me into town and tossed my phone aside. A crinkle of paper interrupted my effort to get comfortable. It was a note from John to say he would be out for most of the day and that if I needed anything to call him. I laughed out loud when I saw he had added, "And give me back my dog." After a few moments, I convinced myself to get up and get going.

I sat in the front window of Zach's a few minutes early while Adam busied himself around the table to make everything perfect. A red Ford pulled up, and I saw Kelly dab at her eyes as she stepped out onto the curb. She took an obvious deep breath before she entered the restaurant. As soon as she spotted me, a genuine smile raced across her lips and lit up her dull eyes. I stood and was wrapped in a bear hug, which instantly warmed me.

"Sorry," she sniffed, "I'm a hugger."

"Me too." I laughed and pointed to the chair for her to sit.

"I can't thank you enough for meeting me today. I just needed a moment of normalcy. You seemed so kind and at ease with us, and by that, I mean our family situation. I wish I could get through to my daughter the way you do."

"That's only because I've been around cases like Ellie's my whole life. My mother is a neurosurgeon and brought me into that world, so I can really understand what you must be going through."

We paused to order, made small talk over lunch, but to my surprise, she brought back up the difficulty she had been having with Ellie.

"Oliver and I hate to rely so much on John, as we want him to have his life, but we just can't seem to move forward without him. Ellie is so difficult." She pulled out a tissue to blot her eyes. I reached out and covered her hand with mine.

"Kelly, at the risk of overstepping, may I offer you some help?"

"I'd love some," she whispered, teary-eyed.

"At Ellie's hospital, there is a brain-injury support group that is there for families like yours to show you that you're not alone." I raised my hand to stop her when I felt her need to protest. "Honestly, Kelly, you would get a lot from it, make friends who understand what you're going through and can be a shoulder to lean on."

"I don't know, Sloane. That's really out of my comfort zone. We're just not good at letting people in."

"You don't have to go alone. I could go with you." I could see the idea was rolling around in her head, and to my shock, she asked when the next meeting was.

"I already checked, and there is one this afternoon at three."

"Okay, if you'll go with me. Thank you, Sloane."

We killed time by checking out some of Kelly's favorite stores. I found an amazing shoe place that carried my favorite boots and a Papillon outlet that just happened to be five minutes from Zack's. There were a lot of hidden gems in the town that I missed the first time around. I was in love and could have spent all day there, but we needed to head in a different direction.

I threaded my arm through hers, and we walked into the support group where there was a horseshoe-shaped arrangement of chairs with a small podium in front. Eleven women and three men all sat, some talking together in small groups, and some who looked totally zoned out. Kelly took a long, shaky breath and patted my hand as we took the chairs closest to the podium. We listened to the speaker as she encouraged us to introduce ourselves and explain why we were there today. I was proud of Kelly as she told her story and expressed the stress her family carried day to day due to Ellie's injury. Every so often, Kelly would reach over and squeeze my hand when I knew other people's stories touched home. At the end of the meeting when they were wrapping up, Leslie, a woman whose son was in a motorcycle accident, offered to exchange numbers with Kelly, as she was also new to the group.

"Kelly," the instructor reached out and shook hands with her, "I'm always so pleased when new members come into the group. The first step is realizing your life is forever changed, and not for the bad, and not for the worst, just changed. The second step is to remember that no brain injury is alike. Everyone is different. What might work for one person may not work for you, but that's why you're here to learn all of this and gain some tools." She stepped a little closer. "Remember you are not alone, and we really hope to see you again soon."

Kelly quickly turned to look at me and in a panicked voice said, "Oliver and I would really like it if you came to dinner tonight. Please, won't you join us?"

How could I say no when she had just taken such a giant leap in the right direction? I knew my mother would be very proud of me, and I couldn't wait to share this experience with her. So much information was at people's fingertips. It was whether they choose to use it or not that could make the difference in their future.

"I'd love to." I followed her out to the car. I sent a quick text to Dell explaining I needed more time and asked if that would be all right. He was visiting a friend and was happy to stay longer. When we arrived at the Blacks' house, I spotted Oliver on the porch swing staring out over his crop. I wondered what was going through his head and how much of it was stuck in the past.

"I'm crashing dinner." I grinned and climbed the steps. He pushed off the chair and wrapped me in a hug.

"Never crashing, dear. You're always welcome here."

"Thanks." I followed him inside and spotted Ellie in front of the TV watching *Saved By The Bell*.

"Hi, Ellie." I sat across from her in the big La-Z-Boy chair. "I'm John's friend. I was here the other day."

Her eyes moved back and forth as she tried desperately to recall that memory. She couldn't locate it, so I just moved on. "Hi," she smiled politely, "are you here for dinner?"

"I am."

"Where's John?"

"He's at work, but he might be by later."

"Oh." She looked at her mother before she went back to watching the show.

Oliver waved me into the kitchen and put the kettle on for some tea.

"You're good with her," he muttered like it was hard for him to speak about her.

"I just understand, that's all." I wanted to say more, but his face looked a lot like John's when he didn't want to talk about something, so I knew better than to push. "How have the chickens been this week? Lots of eggs?" His face instantly relaxed, and I knew he had now had something he wanted to share.

It was like a light switch with the Black family. As

long as you kept the conversation on the things they felt safe talking about, they could pull themselves out of their stress bubble and focus elsewhere. So, that was what I did all during dinner, and it was really fun to watch them relax and enjoy themselves for a while.

"So, wait." I laughed so hard tears leaked out. "He lost his shorts swimming and had to walk all the way home stark naked?"

"Yeah." Oliver reached over to Kelly, who was in a fit of laughter, and held her hand. Kelly's face lit up and dropped to his hand on hers like it was something he hadn't done in years. I saw how hard their love had been tested. "Now," he continued, "John mostly worked in his jeans, so just image how white his legs and bare butt were!"

I could barely breathe, my insides hurt, but the picture in my head was so worth the pain.

"What's so funny?" Ellie came into the kitchen confused. "Who are you?"

And just like, that the cloak of stress was draped back over their lives.

"Ellie," I addressed her, "I'm John's friend, Sloane."

"Where's John?" She glanced around the room as the phone rang on the counter. Kelly slowly excused herself from the table.

"He's not here right now, Ellie." Oliver's face slipped back into his normal *checked out* stare. I didn't judge him for that. It was a coping mechanism that happened a lot, especially with men. Asking for help just didn't seem to be in his DNA, nor was showing any kind of real emotion when the stress took over.

"Nothing, dear." Kelly's worried tone made all of us tune in to her telephone conversation, and I suspected it was John. "I met Sloane for lunch, and then we…" She stopped when Ellie started to get upset over a commercial on TV.

"That's not true!" Ellie yelled, and I knew another meltdown was about to happen. "That never happened! Dad, the TV is lying again."

I hated that we went from one hundred to zero in a millisecond. I would have done anything to have heard them laugh again.

I texted Dell and asked him to come get me, and he said he was five minutes away. I grabbed my coat and watched from the porch for the headlights. I didn't want to be in the way or embarrass them as shit was about to hit the fan.

"I'm sorry, dear." Oliver joined me on the porch. "Our life isn't much fun to be around these days."

"I disagree, Oliver. I had a lot of fun tonight. I just hope I didn't," I fought my own emotions, "upset Ellie by coming over without John. I know it's confusing for her."

"You tried to help, and that's what counts. That's more than anyone else has done for a long time." He tucked his hands in his pockets and leaned on the railing. "We lost a lot of people when Ellie became like this. I think we're both holding on to some miracle that one morning everything will be right again."

Headlights lit us up, and I hugged Oliver a goodbye. "Please let Kelly know I'm sorry, and anytime she wants to meet for lunch, she's got a date."

"She'd love that, but don't forget about me," he whispered. "I need to laugh too."

"Anytime." I hurried down the stairs and gave him a wave before I disappeared into the black SUV.

I was pleased Dell was on the phone when I got inside. I really needed to check out and preserve the wonderful moments I witnessed this afternoon. Maybe, just maybe, I had helped Kelly and gained a new friend.

Back at the house, I decided after such an emotional day to hit the bed early. I dug through my purse and retrieved my phone. I walked up the stairs and went to reach for the door, only to have it whipped open, and there stood a fuming John. He took a heavy step toward me, and I took a step back.

Wow, what was going on?

"What the hell were you thinking?" His eyes were bright with anger, and it was directly at me.

"What?" I took another step back.

"Do you understand the damage you just caused?"

"John, I'm honestly totally lost. What are you talking about?"

"Weren't you just at my parents' place? Did you not just take my mother to some crazy brain AA meeting?"

"Not quite, but I did take your mother to a brain injury support group meeting. After we spoke about it at lunch—that she initiated, by the way—and we enjoyed—"

"She enjoyed it, did she?" he interrupted. "Because the phone call I just had sounded completely different."

"I was just trying to help. I—"

"And who gave you the right to step into my life and show my mother that life will never be the same again? You had no right."

I stood in shock, trying to recall the sequence of events that had happened. We cried, we laughed, we learned, but not once did I feel I had overstepped. After all, Kelly called me and seemed to appreciate my taking her there. Hell, even Oliver seemed to enjoy my company tonight.

His arms fell to his sides, and I saw his walls fly up tight.

"John?" I couldn't believe what I was hearing. We had made such progress. What the hell just happened? "Could we maybe just take a second and talk about this?"

"I can't." I could see this was much bigger than I had realized. "I let you into a part of my life that I hadn't even shared with my brothers, and you abused it and added even more pain to my family. I trusted you, I fell for you, and look where it got me."

"I never meant to hurt anyone. I thought I was helping."

He shook his head slowly. "This is fate's way of reminding me of what I did to my sister. Happiness is not in my future, so better I learn this now."

Panic swiped over me.

"I'm so sorry. Can we just go inside and talk about this? I'll make it right."

"No." His clipped tone made me flinch.

He walked past me toward the main house and called back over his shoulder, "Please stay away from my family."

I wanted to crawl into bed, pull the covers over my head, and cry. I wanted to shut the world away and not overanalyze where I went wrong, but instead I found myself digging my suitcase from the closet and dumping my belongings inside. I sent a quick text off to Dell, who agreed to take me into town. I was assuming from the delayed response he needed to check if it was okay or not. Twenty minutes later, we were on our way with no questions asked. Dell was wonderful for reading a situation and acted like it was a routine drop-off.

The airport was quiet, the lines were short, and the staff were happy to be getting off soon. I tried to match their smiles, but I found the pain in my chest tightened every time my smile did. Instead, I just gave up and kept my head down.

My flight left on time, and once in the air, I leaned my head against the window and pulled my sweater up over my face to block out the passengers.

Never had I let my emotions send me into this kind of state. I knew better than to run. I wasn't a runner. I talked things through and made sense of the situation at hand. But this was different; I'd never dated anyone like John. He just shut me out, turned off, and walked away. I wasn't allowed to defend myself. No, I was told to stay away. And just like that, we were finished.

Tears slipped down my cheeks and dampened my sweater. I closed my eyes and tried to calm myself using the sound of the engines to tame my hurt.

Hours later, I held my phone to my ear and waited for him to pick up.

"Hey, Frank, my flight was fine. Andy did a sweep of the apartment, and I just really need some sleep."

"I'm really uncomfortable with the way you returned. It's too soon, but I understand needing your own space. You've always been independent, Sloane. However, if anything seems slightly off in any way, call me."

"You have my word."

"Okay." His voice was kind. "Try to get some sleep."

"I will." I glanced in the mirror and saw the dark circles under my eyes. I officially felt as I looked on the outside. Drained.

After my shower, I changed into my sweats, grabbed a bottle of Francis Coppola and a glass, and curled up in front of the TV. I was way behind in my *Marvelous Mrs. Maisel* series, and we needed to catch up. I thought I made it to the opening credits before sleep got the best of me.

A noise startled me awake. I reached for the remote to mute the TV and tried to make sense of the sound. A small creak had goosebumps slowly inching up my spine. Without moving too much, I dug around the blanket for my phone when I heard it again. With two fingers, I pried the phone from between the cushions and called Frank, knowing he was closer than my father was.

"What's wrong?" He didn't miss a beat.

"Frank, someone's here."

"What do you hear? What do you see?"

"Nothing. I just heard something. I think someone is inside the apartment." I saw a shadow cross the kitchen door. "Frank," I nearly panicked, "someone's here in the kitchen."

"I'm on my way, getting in my car now. Can you get out?"

Just as I moved toward the front door, a dark figure stepped in my path. He was so close I could smell stale beer on his breath.

"I don't think I can do that." The man slowly shook his head and reached for my phone, ending the call.

"Sloane Harlow, we've been waiting for you. Henry will be very happy to see you."

I licked my dry lips and cleared my throat, hoping my voice would work.

"Like I explained to Henry, the judge has made his ruling. There is nothing I can do." His head tilted, still in shadow.

"Well, that's just a shame, isn't it? After all, you are the daughter of a general. You can find a way to fix it."

"That's not how it works."

"You can tell Henry that, then."

As his hand reached out to grab me, I blocked his arm, kneed him in the crotch, and as he fell forward, I grabbed the half-full bottle of wine and cracked him over the head with it. I leapt out of his reach and headed for the kitchen, only to be snatched up by another set of arms. He whirled me around to face beer breath, and his fist caught me in the cheek. A loud ringing noise blocked out any further sound, but not the pain that exploded in my head.

"Put the bitch in the trunk." His words seemed far away. Panic and adrenaline hit me at the same time, and I screamed for help as loudly as I could as they dragged me kicking and screaming down the stairs.

My legs broke free, and I kicked someone hard and heard a curse. "Grab her fuckin' legs, will ya?"

I clawed at the brick wall and used my fingers to grip the tiny grooves, which momentarily gave me a second of hope.

"Let me go, you piece of shit!" I wiggled hard and tried to use all my strength to break free. "Assholes!" Since I was already emotionally drained, all I had left was pure, hot anger.

"Feisty little bitch, aren't yet?" One laughed but stopped mid-hiss.

I was suddenly dropped onto the sidewalk on my back, beer breath landed beside me, and I struggled to make sense of what was happening. The lights from the parking lot burned my eyes as I tried to focus. Frank had a gun to the second guy, and I scrambled to my feet and grabbed a flowerpot and threw it as hard as I could into beer breath's face.

"Ahhh," I shuddered and put my hands to my aching face. "Fuck you, Henry!" I screamed into the night.

"Sloane," Frank reached out to steady me, "are you good?"

"Um…yeah. Yeah, I am."

"Go get into the car." I wasted no time and jumped into the front seat.

ELEVEN

JOHN

"Nothing like a twenty-mile run with ninety-five pounds on your back to make room for a second breakfast," Mark called as he trotted by me with a grin then slowed to a walk.

"Nice of Tripper to join us this morning," Keith said around his water canister. "I wondered when he was going to return to the team."

"Mm." I glanced over at Sloane's cabin, curious to know why he wasn't with her. "Maybe his guilt is getting to him." I snorted.

"You just need to feed him more cookies," Mark chimed in.

I laughed. "Not everyone is ruled by their stomach like you are, Mark."

"Women love men who eat. It makes them feel like

they're caring for me, and I need to be cared for." I shoved Mark's shoulder and rolled my eyes at Keith.

"Oh, my God, Abigail ruined him." Keith snickered as we heard footsteps from behind us.

"Uncle John!" Livi came racing across the yard and leapt into my arms. "We're still on for our practice, right?"

"Yes, ma'am."

"Good, because," she turned to look at Mark, who was listening, so she leaned in and whispered, "we're the fifth to go on."

"I promise, I'll be ready."

"Good!" She gave me her father's curt nod then immediately broke into her mother's smile. That little girl could commit murder, and I'd be right there digging the hole to hide the evidence. I dropped her to her feet, and she took off after Butters, who loved a good chase.

"Is someone keeping secrets?" Mark glared at me. "Just because you and Keith are her favorites doesn't mean I should get the Logan look from the little pipsqueak."

"She only loves me because of Baby B." Keith chuckled. "He's a charmer, just like his father."

My phone vibrated in my pocket and alerted me to a call.

"Hi, Mom." I stepped away from the others with a bad feeling in the pit of my stomach. Once again, I glanced at the cabin, concerned what this call might bring.

"Honey, I think we should talk. When you called yesterday, your sister was just starting another meltdown, and it really upset me. I was having a wonderful time with Sloane. We went to lunch at Zach's, and she welcomed me into a world I didn't think I needed."

"What? I thought—"

"John," she continued, "I realize I do need some help, not just with Ellie, but for myself and your father. Sloane opened my eyes that we can be okay again. Do you know what happened? Your father and I laughed together. We laughed for the first time in a very long time. Do you know how good that was for me, for us?"

I wanted to scream, my emotions were so raw on this subject. "Well, then, what was yesterday?"

"Yesterday was an eye opener for me, and it took until this morning for me to see that. We need to move forward, and if we allow ourselves to get help, we could. It's not fair for your father and me to rely on you all the time. I think I see things clearer now. Give it a little time, but I think things will change. I have to go, but I'll call you later. Sorry about yesterday."

"Okay, bye."

What the fuck.

"Who is up for some football?" Mike called, tossing the ball in the air. Just as we were about to start the game, I spotted Daniel, Frank, and Cole on the porch, deep in conversation.

"Irons." I nodded in Cole's direction. "Did Chamness call in this morning?"

"No." He dropped the ball, and we headed toward the

house. I noticed Daniel was spinning his watch around his wrist, a telltale sign that something was up.

"This can't be good," Mike muttered from behind us.

When Cole caught sight of us, he excused himself. "Black, can I have a word?"

"Well, shit, at least it's not me. See ya." Mark hurried off, avoiding Cole's glare.

Keith hovered nearby as the rest left. "Logan," he called, "are we all good here?" Cole motioned for him to join us. I leaned against the railing as Daniel and Frank approached.

"Black, I've always respected your privacy, and I know you've grown close to Sloane, but I have to ask. Did something happen last night?"

As much as I wanted to end this conversation, I knew Cole must have a reason to ask. Given the current company, I knew something was going on. "We had a few words last night that didn't go so well. Why, what's going on?"

"She left for Washington last night, and she seemed really off," Frank started. "It's not like Sloane to leave like that. She knows better. Now is the time, son. If she's not welcome here, please let me know. I can move her to Dusk. I need Blackstone to be one hundred percent focused right now, and if there's a negative distraction, I need to know."

Cole cleared his throat, and Daniel shuffled his feet as though there was more to come.

"No need to move her. We just had a disagreement, nothing that can't be fixed over a good night's sleep."

"Then you should know that when she arrived back at her apartment she was attacked and nearly kidnapped." I stood straight up and made a move toward her cabin when Cole put his hand on my shoulder to stop me. "So, maybe this would be a good time to mend fences."

"Is she all right? Is she here?" My voice betrayed the depth of my true feelings for Sloane, and I knew they recognized that.

"She just arrived. She's shaken up and a little bruised, but all things considered, she handled herself pretty well. She just might need some time."

"Go ahead, Black. I think she'd like to see you. She's with the girls." He nodded toward the main house.

I raced inside, feeling like shit, and realized I'd been wrong and once again had hurt someone. I was my own worst enemy, and I needed to make this right.

Sue stood as I entered the living room, cheeks flushed and concern all over her face. "Ladies," she whispered, "let's give Sloane a moment." Abigail and June hurried away to the kitchen, and Savannah and Sue wavered a moment. I heard Savanah whisper that I was here, then they left us alone.

Sloane didn't look up and sat hunched forward, her glass of brandy trembling in her hands. Her hair hid her face from my view. I moved farther into the room, but when she still didn't acknowledge my presence, I bent down in front of her.

I felt so many conflicting emotions bubble to the surface. I had no idea how to start or what to say to explain myself, so I just let my mouth go.

"I'm so sorry, Sloane. I was wrong to speak to you that way, so wrong," I repeated, feeling like a piece of shit. "I wish I could have listened to you. I wish I could have pulled back and realized you were only trying to help. And you did." I prattled on, knowing I sounded like my mother who I just had on the phone. "Mom called this morning and was happy. I'm not going to lie, I was confused. One phone call she was a mess, and the next she's seeing things totally differently. Do you know what that is like for me?" I shook my head and changed directions when she didn't respond. "I'm not like the other guys. I lash out when I shouldn't then shut down. I hide what I really feel. I push anything happy in my life away. I sometimes think I hide behind the pain of my sister's accident so I won't get more hurt myself."

I removed her glass from her frozen fingers and gently brushed her hair from her face. Then everything inside me went to stone when I saw her battered cheek and black eye.

"Oh, my God." I moved between her legs to get closer to her as tears started to leak from her eyes. "No, no, no." My chest caved inward, and I wanted to kill the sick son-of-a-bitch who did that to her. My thumb held her hair back as I examined her closer. "Are you hurt anywhere else?"

For the first time since I came into the room, she shook her head, once.

"John," Sue was in the doorway, "maybe she'd like to get some rest?"

I appreciated a little female guidance and went back to Sloane. "Would you like to get some sleep?"

She started to move, and I quickly jumped up to help her to her feet. I entwined my fingers through hers and led her out of the room, but instead of heading outside, I turned her toward the staircase.

"I'd feel a lot better if you were in my room today. Is that okay?"

She didn't protest as I led her up the grand staircase to the second level and down the hallway.

Inside my room, I pulled back the covers and watched as she sat like a shell of herself on the side of the bed. I stumbled inside my head. I'd been in Army mode for so long now I tended to forget how to be with another civilian, let alone a woman. Did I take charge, or did I leave her be? I went with the first idea, because I thought that was what she needed.

I bent down to remove her shoes, and that seemed to bring her back to me a little.

"Would you like something to sleep in? A shirt and shorts?"

"Pain pill?" She barely spoke.

"Sure." I reached into my bedside table and handed her a few while I raced to the bathroom to get her some water. After she took the medication, I helped her into bed and tucked the covers in around her.

I reached to turn the lights off, and her hand reached for mine.

"Don't tell Frank." Her voice was barely a whisper.

"Tell him what? That you're here?" I didn't care about rules anymore. Cole had paved that road for us, and right now I was just so friggin' thankful.

"No," her small body coiled tightly into a ball, "that I was so scared." She broke into sobs, and I pulled back the covers and molded my body to hers.

"Frank wouldn't care that you were scared." I kissed her head and wanted to take the hurt away. "He'd only cares that you're all right." I knew she knew this. They were quite close, but I also knew that when your life got railroaded that fast, you tended to think irrationally.

"You need sleep." I nuzzled my head into her neck. "Things will be easier after your brain gets some rest." I held her tightly and once again whispered an apology into her ear. "I'm so sorry, Sloane. Please forgive me for being such as ass."

Forty minutes later, my phone lit up the dark room, and I checked the screen.

Logan: Briefing in 5, ship out in 20.

Shit.

I grabbed my shirt, hauling it over my head, and rushed downstairs, nearly tripping over Scoot along the way. He just glared at me and continued to bathe himself on the bottom stair. I rolled my eyes and kept moving.

"Don't worry." Sue handed me a cup of coffee while I scarfed down my omelet. "I know you're worried about leaving, but you know we will watch over her."

"She needs to eat." I tried to push my discomfort aside, but it wasn't easy.

"Of course, dear."

"I'm sure she'll need some Advil when she wakes. She might not remember where mine are."

"I have some right here."

"And when will Dr. Rice be here to look her over?"

"Frank had her checked out before she arrived yesterday." I started to speak, but she held her hand up. "But of course I called the doctor to double check. I knew it would make you feel better."

"It would." I sighed and checked my watch. "Thanks, Sue."

"Don't worry, dear. I promise she'll be well taken care of."

"I know." I kissed her cheek, and as I raced toward the front door, I glanced up the stairs, wishing I could wake her to say goodbye.

"Black?" Mike called as we exited the living room. "Ready?"

"Yeah." As I shut the door, I whispered, "Goodbye."

The mood in the helicopter was abnormally tense because our new plan was one we'd never done before. We rarely broke our own protocol, but this was different. We needed answers. Mike was fiddling with his fingers, working out his side of the playbook, while I was mentally calculating the upcoming climb. When I glanced up, I saw each man was doing his own thing to prepare. Several glances came our way, which told me they were uncomfortable with the change in plan.

"T-minus five minutes, boys." Cole's voice came over our earpieces. All, including Mike and me, stood to check our gear one last time. We stepped back to let the others prepare for their jump.

"Join together, retire together." Cole recited our Blackstone motto, and we all chanted it back in unison.

Mark was the first to go, followed by Keith, but when Daniel stepped forward, he pushed Mike ahead of him and said, "You go. I'm going with Black."

Cole's face scrunched in confusion, and he started to protest, but then he gave Mike the nod and followed him out of the Blackhawk.

"What's going on, Daniel?" A last-minute change in plan was bad enough, but now this?

"No one knows the southern side of Mexico like I do. If you're going in, you get me. Besides, they've got some climbing of their own to do, and they could really use Irons." We both stood, arms above our heads, holding on to the handles while we got our heads back in the game.

We trained for years for the unexpected, and we understood the sacrifice and toll it took on us mentally and physically every time we faced a mission, but nothing could prepare us for this.

Bang!

A sudden jerk and a bright flash filled the belly of the chopper. We were thrown off our feet, and our grip tightened on the handles or we would have been ejected through the opening. Colors morphed together into horizontal line as we spun like a propeller.

"Mayday, mayday." I heard the pilot's call for help as he fought to regain control of the beast. "We've been hit."

Immediately, we went into survival mode. Somehow, I willed my brain to do an inventory check of the Blackhawk. Thankfully, we didn't carry much, only a few weapons. Nothing the cartel could use.

Bang! Again, we were thrown to the side, which stopped the spin but sent Daniel flying into the bench. He hit hard but managed to hang on. The pilot called in the second hit. The shriek of the alarms told me we were going down hard. I braced myself for impact and hoped the Blackhawk lived true to its design and landed on its belly.

Smoke and jet fuel made its way to my senses, and I searched for the source. If there were flames, we might explode before we even hit the ground, destroying any chance we had of surviving. But before I could even finish that thought, we hit the trees, sending debris everywhere. The sound was deafening. I squeezed my eyes shut until we finally stopped with a hard jerk on the forest floor.

I didn't remember letting go of the strap as I stood up on shaky legs and did a mental check of myself. Just a cut to the calf and some pain in my ribs, but all things considered, I was fine. I shook my head clear and immediately looked for Daniel. He lay crumpled against the wall of the cabin, not moving.

"Daniel," I hissed in pain noting a few broken ribs, "can you hear me?"

Nothing.

I knew the cartel would be hot on our trail, as they would have followed the smoke from our crash. I pushed aside some branches that had ended up inside and made my way to his side. Thank God Cole insisted we always wore our Spiritus Systems armor.

"This is going to hurt like a bitch, but we need to move."

I carefully laid Daniel flat on his back and pulled out the handle of the armor which had a makeshift stretcher inside. I glanced around and spotted the inflatable life vests, knowing the stretcher didn't float and the chance of being in water was high. It really was the quickest way to move without leaving a track. I hauled him to the edge. We need to get off the X. After I carefully splinted his broken leg, I jumped and eased him down as best as I could. My ribs burned like fire, so I figured they were broken, but that was the least of my problems right now. I got Daniel a safe distance away from the copter and hidden from view, then checked him over.

"Pilot?" Daniel's voice was weak but clear enough, and I knew it was an order.

"I'm on it." I raced back to the mangled Blackhawk and saw flames coming from the cockpit. Our pilot,

Chris, had a tree branch jammed into his neck. There was no doubt he was gone. I raced around the chopper and grabbed the door gun, and I was about to grab the last gun when the sound of cheering and hooting had me taking cover away from Daniel in some brush. As I bent down to take cover, my calf burned, and blood seeped out of a rip in my pantleg.

Fuck! I didn't have time to think before they came into view.

As the vultures came to pick the Blackhawk clean, I rubbed dirt over my face and arms and sat and waited to make my move. One had a GoPro Camera strapped to his head, and another had one on the grip of his gun. The sick fuckers recorded the crash, and I wanted to rip their eyes through their skull.

"*Fuego!*" a cartel yelled. Fire. "*Darse prisa.*" He ordered them to hurry.

I waited for most of them to step inside the chopper, and when two of them went for Chris, I pulled the pin and tossed the M15 light phosphorus grenade under the Hawk and hunkered down for the blast. A flash of heat hit the side of my body, but I was ready for it. When the dust cleared, I saw my plan had worked, and I took a half a second to mourn the loss of a friend.

"Sorry, buddy. See you on the other side." Better this than what they would have done to him.

Panic swept over the vultures as orders were yelled into the chaos to grab any weapons from the dead and to quickly move out to the east. I gritted my teeth, knowing they knew my team's location.

I watched a young boy, no more than twelve, scurry over to one of the dead cartel to take his weapon and clear his pockets. I had seen the dead man holding a phone earlier, reporting what was happening. After the blast, it had dropped not far from him, and I could see it on the ground. As the kid moved about, I prayed he wouldn't see the phone.

"Come on, kid, move away," I muttered under my breath. Luck was on my side for once, and with a sharp curse from their leader, he was told to get moving.

I stayed put until I was sure the coast was clear then Army crawled over to the dead cartel's phone and grabbed it. As I did, I noticed the seven inside a spider web tattooed on his arm. *Who the hell are you guys?* I took one last look before I headed for Daniel.

"Still faking it," I joked at Daniel's unconscious body, needing a bit of comic relief. "Look what I've got." I held the phone out toward him with a smile. "Let's get the hell out of here." Pushing the tiny buttons on the old flip phone, I dialed the secure line.

"Go," someone answered.

"This is Recon John Black, ID 135241493." I paused and gave my code word. "Clear."

"Code word verified. Give your locations."

I gave four locations, knowing only two would be used. I was told to sit tight and wait until dusk.

Once the line went dead, I lowered the phone and

took a moment to focus on the journey ahead of me. But all that came was bitter hot rage. How the hell did they know our every move? Where were the missing North Rock men? And who the hell was behind all of this?

Nothing made sense, and that was not something Blackstone was used to. We were the untouchables, but here we were stranded on enemy ground with one soldier barely hanging on to his life and three others missing. What a Goddamn shit show!

I shook my head back on straight and tuned in to the task at hand.

"All right, Daniel, time to move." I lifted him carefully, and the armor cradled his head while we started the hike toward our rendezvous spot.

It took me two hours, with four stops, to give Daniel a break from the pain that pulled him in and out of consciousness. It was true we were trained to block out someone else's pain along with our own in order to get the job done. But this was something else. Seeing your second father near the edge of death tested my limits as a soldier.

"I know, sir," I whispered, hearing him groan, hoping he could hear me to know he wasn't alone. "Did Cole ever tell you about the time we both got trapped in that basement hole in TJ?" I grimaced at the memory as I pulled him over a stump. "I had only been on the team about six months, and we'd just arrived in TJ for a mission. Remember when we found Senator Lee in that crate in that storage room? God, I hated that guy." I let my mouth run. "He always wanted something other than what Abby was making for dinner, and Mark always wanted to sit next to him to score extra food." I chuckled. The senator was an ungrateful ass. "Well, anyway, that night we had to clear several houses. Cole and I entered from the back, and once we hit the kitchen, the floorboards gave out and we dropped into the basement. The hole was clearly set up for us, and of course our radios were shit, so we had to wait for the team to find us."

I stopped to take a breather and to listen and scan my surroundings before I crossed a well-used path. I was happy when we were hidden by the undergrowth again. Quickly, I used my shoe to cover the marks from the stretcher.

"Where was I?" I thought for a moment. Sweat rolled down my face, and I swiped it away, refusing to acknowledge that my body burned hot in more than one place. I needed to concentrate on putting one foot in front of the other. "Oh, right, so, the way the basement hole was, we couldn't get a footing to get out. We used our weapons like pickaxes, but nothing worked. We had no choice but to hunker down and wait." I shuddered at the thought. "As much as we felt like we were stuck in a giant coffin, it gave me time to get to know Cole better."

I moved a branch out of my way and dodged the hole that could have broken my ankle in half.

"Given where we were, he told me about how when he was eleven, he and Mark were playing in the woods and they fell down that old well that was just off your property. They tried everything to get out, but it was no use. The walls were as slippery as butter. Mark started to get a little panicky with the small space and all, and Cole had to assure him that you would find them. That you could track and find anyone on this Earth. Night came, and then morning, and when daylight came, a shadow loomed over their heads, and there you were with Zack and his grandfather. He said he smiled at Mark as if to say, 'See? My dad always comes through.'"

I found myself getting a little emotional, so I waited a few beats to clear my tight throat. My neck felt like it was on fire, and the back of my shoulders was bothered by the fabric of my shirt. I would kill for a couple of Tylenols right now.

"He shared a few more childhood memories, some from the early years when he joined the Army, and some recent ones. And you want to know who they all included?" I glanced over my shoulder again. "You," I assured him. "And to be honest, sir, most of *our* stories include you. So," I lowered my voice a little, as we were approaching another clearing, "you need to hang on, because we can't have you gone. We can't have missing holes in our stories."

At the edge of the terrain, I lowered Daniel and did another quick evaluation on him. His hand moved to cover mine for just a beat before it fell back down.

"We got this, sir. Just stay with me."

Though it was clear his leg was broken, and he had a concussion, I suspected without removing his gear that he also had internal injuries. I worried about his condition, but I knew we had to keep moving. I had to push my own pain aside and keep my head clear because one wrong move could get both of us killed.

"Sorry, Daniel." I checked all around the murky landscape for another route, but the only way around would have added too much time—time we didn't have. "Sorry, sir, but you're going to get wet." I inflated the life jackets and did my best to place them under him, so he'd float, and to my surprise, it worked. I struggled to keep his head above water. Some places were deeper than others, but for the most part, it was mostly waist deep. I pushed what was possibly swimming around us out of my head and focused on the horizon. The mud under my feet was like quicksand, and the effort it took to cross was exhausting. Thigh-deep sludge had my muscles burning, and they begged for water as the rest of my body begged for some calories to keep me going. Every so often, I'd allow my mind to think of her. I'd remind myself of her smell, her touch, the way her intense blue eyes saw through my bullshit and made me live in the moment rather than the past. I stumbled during one of my memories, and the stretcher tipped.

"Shit, sorry." I regained my footing. *Mind over matter*, I thought to myself. Mind over matter was what was going to get us through this. That, and my training. So, I turned that side of my mind off and focused on nothing more than putting one foot in front of the other.

Once on the other side, I looked up the hillside ahead

of us and took a deep breath. The climb was going to be rough on both of us.

"Almost there," I reassured him through gritted teeth. Again, I let my mind wander where it wanted to and focused on the thought that I would be that much closer to seeing Sloane. She was the one person who had me moving forward. She made all the horrible moments seem obsolete.

Finally, we reached the top. I lowered Daniel on the ground and dropped down next to him, feeling exhausted, hot, and parched. There was still a lot to process, and my head just couldn't go there yet. I needed to focus on keeping us under cover and alive.

"Black." Daniel licked his dry lips and stared up at the night sky. We had been taking cover on the hillside, waiting the last thirty minutes until dusk. "Talk to me more about something," he barely whispered. "Make it up if you have to." He winched as he coughed.

"I bet Livi has Liam and Ethan tied to a tree somewhere."

"Ahh." He grinned through white lips. "That little girl has us all fooled."

"Yeah, she's just as bad as the rest, but it's her cuteness that saves her." I opened my shirt, desperate to cool off. "She is going to run that house someday. I guess she does already."

"I bet she's worried that you aren't there." He took a strained breath. "You two have been working hard on your project."

"I wouldn't do that for anyone else but her."

"I know that." He coughed and tried to keep the conversation going, but I could tell it was a struggle for him. "You're great with her, just like you will be with your own kid someday." His glazed eyes moved to find mine. "You know a father can't die without knowing all his boys will be okay." His eyes closed, and I knew he was too tired to keep them open.

"Don't even think of dying on me, Daniel. Cole will have my hide. Besides, you've been through a lot more shit than this. You really want the cartel to be the reason you go out?" I waved him off. "Nah, it would have to be something more epic than that. Like tripping over Tripper or stepping on one of Liam's Army trucks."

"God, I fucking hate those things. Worse than Legos."

We both laughed, but I pressed my hand against his arm as I heard chopper blades in the distance.

"I think our ride is here," I reassured him, but when he didn't reply, I looked down and saw his eyes were rolled back in his head as he was overtaken by a seizure.

"Shit." I quickly rolled him on his side as I snapped my smoke flare and signaled the chopper in our direction. I fought the dizziness that gnawed at me. I swore the place was trying one last attempt to keep us there. "Hang in there just a while longer, please, Daniel," I begged, knowing his condition was getting worse.

TWELVE

Thirteen Hours Earlier

SLOANE

I woke with a groggy brain and headed downstairs to look for coffee before I went to my cabin for a shower.

"Hey, Dell." I caught him on the steps, but his mood seemed off. He wasn't his normal chipper self. "Any chance we can go into town today?"

"Ah, I'll have to get back to you on that."

"Okay." I watched as he rushed off. I wondered if he was worried about how I'd feel today.

My face did hurt like hell. I glanced at myself in the hall mirror and felt nauseated as I took in my bruised and swollen face. I found Sue, Abigail, and June playing with

Mike's daughter, Gabriella, and Tabby, Mark's newest addition.

"Oh, Sloane, you're awake." Sue smiled warmly at me. "Is there anything we can get you? How do you feel?" She was kind enough not to mention the obvious.

"A little sore, but I'm okay." I noticed none of the boys were around. "Have you seen John?"

"They were shipped out with little notice around noon yesterday. They should be back sometime tonight," Sue explained, scooping up Gabriella.

Damn, how long did I pass out for? My stomach growled, and I felt the urge to visit the kitchen. Eggs and toast sounded perfect.

A black SUV pulled up and an engine turned off. Sue looked at Abigail. "Are we expecting anyone?"

Abigail shook her head.

"Dell just raced up stairs, so it can't be him," I offered.

The door opened, and Frank walked in.

I'd known Frank for a long time, and I could tell something major had happened by the way he avoided eye contact with me.

"Hi, Sloane. Have you seen Sue?" His tone was all business.

"I'm in here, Frank," Sue called from the living room.

He motioned for me to go first, and he followed. Savannah popped out of nowhere, and I joined her on the couch.

"I'm going to keep this as short as possible because

I've had multiple phone calls and finally have pieced things together."

He sat on the chair across from us as we all waited for the news, and we knew it couldn't be good.

"I hate this part," Savannah muttered under her breath, and Sue reached out to pat her shoulder.

"Sue," Frank turned his attention to her, "it's Daniel." Abigail immediately removed Gabriella from Sue's arms as her face drained of color.

"He's injured, but alive," Frank continued. "We are flying him to Redstone hospital for his safety. We had to change things up last minute to throw the cartel off our scent and didn't want to send him to the North Dakota hospital."

Sue had jumped to her feet, but Frank held up his hand, shaking his head.

"Not yet. The moment I get the call, we'll all go together."

Savannah leaned over and took Sue's hand as she sank back into her chair. She looked over at Frank.

"Is anyone else injured?"

"If they are, they haven't let me know." He rubbed his forehead and glanced at his phone then stood as though he needed to move. "Sue, I suggest you pack a bag so you don't have to worry about leaving the hospital and Daniel's side.

"Good idea," June chimed in, picking up Tabby. "Savannah, let's see if Davie is around to help watch the kids while Sue gets ready."

"Frank?" I moved closer to him. "What can I do?" He walked me toward the dining room and sat me at the table then sat next to me.

"North Rock called in. They were stuck in a ravine and, since half their team is either missing or in hospital, they couldn't hold back the cartel on their own. They called Blackstone for help." He pulled out his phone to show me some drone photos. "We purposely checked the area before the team got to their drop point, and we could see they were clear." He hesitated then added, "Mike and John were going to be dropped at a different point, but at the last minute, Daniel switched places with Mike." He looked directly into my eyes and went on. "Two RPG missiles hit the Blackhawk, sending them into the jungle."

"What?" It took me a minute to regain myself and pull out my inner lawyer. Frank had already said no one else had been seriously hurt that he knew of. I needed to hold on to that.

"John called in on a secure line. He got himself and Daniel to the pick-up point. The chopper radioed in that they both were safe and are on their way back."

"How bad is Daniel?"

Frank scrubbed his face with his hand and sighed heavily.

"Last I heard, he was unconscious. We just don't know yet. I had Waters, from Team Eagle Eye, assemble as much info as he could, and it's on here." He handed me a flash drive. "I need you to do what you do best, Sloane, and dig." He stood and leaned on the back of the chair. "I swear to God, if this ends up on another YouTube video, I will personally round up each member of the cartel and torture them one by one."

Could I help?

I hurried back to the cabin and gathered up my things, including my laptop. I knew I might be the only one clear-headed enough to help figure this out. I had to set my personal feelings aside and do my best for them.

Three SUVs pulled up to the front doors of the Redstone hospital. An outsider might have thought the president was visiting. We were a force to be reckoned with, whether it was the men or their women. When the doors opened on the third floor, it was utter chaos. Cole, Mike, and Keith looked exhausted, and they were covered in mud from head to toe. Savannah raced to Cole's side and flung herself into his arms. He broke when he saw her.

"The stubborn bastard never listens." His voice was muffled as he squeezed her tighter.

I handed Mark a water, and the normal humor that usually rested on the tip of his tongue was lost in his exhaustion and fear. I wished Mia was here. "Mia just left Dusk and should be here in a few hours. Can I get you anything?"

"No, thank you." He went back to staring at the wall.

Mike jumped up and looked over our heads, and we all turned around to see gowned people with a gurney rushing our way.

"All right, boys," Frank ordered, "I know he's one of us, but let's give them some room."

Sue ran to his side as Daniel was wheeled by. He had IVs and fluids attached to his arm.

"Sir, you must let me take a look at you. You're hurt," a nurse insisted behind us as she and John came down the hall. I wanted to run to him but forced myself to walk to his side. His lifeless eyes found mine.

"We didn't see it coming. We had drones watching, but it didn't help," he prattled on in shock. "One RPG hit, then another. We didn't have a chance. He lost a lot of blood. He was in and out of consciousness. I tried to keep him awake, but we had to keep moving." Sweat glistened on his face, and the collar of his shirt was soaked.

"John," I carefully held on to his shoulders to pull him from his memories, "you did great, but we've got him now. I need you to go get yourself checked out. Okay? I've got this. You did your job, now I'll do mine. You also have to let the nurse do her job and go with her."

The nurse mouthed a *thank you*, and Mike helped me steer John into an examination room. After a rather long argument, we finally got John into a hospital shirt, and the nurse wheeled him, still protesting, to x-ray.

"Whatever you need, Sloane," Mike said softly. "No matter what it is, you got it. But this needs to end today."

I nodded, understanding how bad this was. "I need a room with internet and updates on Daniel and John hourly, and as hard as this is going to be, I need to speak to each one of you while it's still fresh in your minds. If you remember anything at all, I need to know every detail."

Mike folded his massive arms and gave me a curt nod. "Done."

The team was surprisingly focused as each told me their own version of the story. Keith and Cole were the most matter-of-fact. Mike was oddly emotional but filled in a few empty gaps, and Mark, sadly without his usual sense of humor, was able to recall what some of the cartel leaders looked like. He noted how eerily confident they seemed. One detail in particular stuck with me.

"Um," Mark rubbed his head with his hand, and I watched as some dry mud crumbled to the floor, "one of them got close to where I was, and his radio went off. Someone was cheering about how Seven Webs was going to be happy."

"Seven Webs," I repeated and madly wrote it down on my notepad. So, it was a nickname for someone. Maybe it wasn't a gang symbol like I was researching. "Who do you think that is?"

"I asked myself that question whenever I let my mind idle."

"What was your conclusion?"

His dull eyes moved to mine, and I could see he was barely with me. "That someone out there named Seven Webs is going to die a very long, painful death."

"Let's hope." I nodded as he went to leave. "Thank you, Mark."

An hour slipped by while I was down a rabbit hole

digging for information on anything that could possibly help.

"Coffee?" Mark popped his head in the door holding up a cup. He seemed a little livelier since he'd cleaned the mud off—well, the best he could, anyway.

"God, yes, thank you." I stood to stretch my aching back and gladly took the brew and didn't question when he handed me a sandwich. I realized I was starving. "Any word on Daniel?"

"Still in surgery. That's all we know."

"What about John? Any word on the x-ray?"

Mark shrugged and rubbed his eyes in frustration. "This is one of the reasons we use the North Dakota hospital. There is protocol there for Blackstone to get information. I understand why Frank brought Daniel here, but it sucks not knowing anything."

"Yeah, I bet. I'm sure everything will be okay, and regretfully, we aren't the only ones in this hospital."

Mark moved the drone pictures around on the table and studied them.

"I knew this fight was going to be endless." He sounded beyond beat. "I knew, we all knew, we'd lose some of our people, but we were prepared for everything we possibly could be. The cartel are like rats. Every time you stamp out a pack, more just keep coming back. We spent nearly a year coming up with a strategy that would work while we were in enemy territory. Blackstone counts on having the element of surprise," he picked up a photo and showed it to me, "so how in the world do they know what we're doing before we even get there?" I opened my mouth to speak, but he held up his hand. "And don't tell me we have a possible leak somewhere."

"I promise you, Mark, I'm doing everything in my power to prove otherwise."

Mark dropped the photo he was holding and sat down on the couch, his face in his hands.

"They're picking us off. Half of North Rock is fighting for their lives in North Dakota, or missing, and who the hell knows if they are alive or not? Now Daniel, if he even makes it, will have months of recovery. John sounds like he has jacked-up ribs." He threw his hands into the air. "Our teams are being held together with Band-Aids and gauze."

"It looks bad right now, Mark, but give me time. I'll figure this out. This is what I do. If there is something here to be found, I'll dig until I find it."

Mark nodded a few times. His face looked defeated, he was pale, and there were dark circles under his eyes.

"How much longer until Mia arrives?"

"She should be any time now." He stood and shook his arms as though to relieve the stress. "All right, we'll be in the other room. If you get burned out, or need anything, you know where we are. I'll let you know if we hear anything."

Mark's words bounced around in my head again. As much as I didn't want to go there, the reality was that Blackstone had had a leak before, and money was definitely the root of all evil. I woke my computer back up, opened a fresh web page, and began to look into all of the North Rock Team's lives.

I madly flipped the page in my notebook and began to draw lines on how each soldier was connected to the other. Some were friends before they were recruited to North Rock, and some had never met. Then I began to look into the rookie who was killed. As I read through his records, I noticed he had taken the last test twice before he graduated. I pulled out my red pen and circled his name. That test was only supposed to be taken once. I sent a quick email off to my father asking him if anyone had ever taken the test twice, and if so, who, and why there would be exceptions.

I tossed my coffee cup in the trash and glanced out the door to the other room and then back at the time. I joined the others just as the doctor came through the door. He stepped back to let me by, and the others jumped to their feet.

"First, I want to thank you for being so patient with my team," the doctor addressed us. "It was a complicated procedure. Daniel had an open compound fraction of the femur, but thanks to the splint that was applied in the field, I was able to repair it. He also suffered a head injury that caused some swelling to the brain, and we're watching carefully to see if the swelling decreases. Right now, myself and Dr. Tahoe don't feel surgical intervention is needed. Rehab will be extensive, but he should have full mobility in the months to come. All things considered, he should make a full recovery. It's a good thing your men are trained in first aid as well as they are. They should be commended."

The tension in the room evaporated with sighs of relief and some tears.

"Excuse me, Doctor." I caught him just as he reached for the door handle. "John Black went in for x-rays hours ago, and he hasn't returned. Do you happen to have an update on him?"

"No, but I'll send someone out to speak to you and let you know."

"Thank you. I'd appreciate that." I turned back to give Sue a big hug and noted that Cole sat down with a thud, I'd bet for the first time today. His father's injuries sat pretty heavily on his shoulders.

I could relate to the type of stress they were feeling. There were many types of stress, but the stress a soldier faced each day to ensure our freedom took a special kind of courage. I could remember my mother would sit and worry about my father's return, and as I got older, I joined her in it. You couldn't know what it was like unless you'd lived it.

"Excuse me, are you all with John Black?" A tired-looking nurse with wrinkled scrubs appeared in the doorway. Cole jumped to his feet and stepped forward and said we all were.

"Should I speak to one of you or all of you?"

I shot a quick look at Cole, who immediately took charge and said, "We are all his family, so you can go ahead." Cole stepped over and stood next to me, and I appreciated his support.

The nurse removed her mask and twisted it between her hands. "Mr. Black was admitted into ICU, and it can go either way at this point."

My hand flew to Cole's arm as the tension in the room grew once again.

"What?" Mike questioned. "He went in for x-rays on his ribs."

"Yes, he did, and four are broken." She swallowed hard and looked around at all our faces then quickly continued, keeping her eyes on Mike. "But there is also a large cut on his calf." Her face grew flushed, and her words came faster. "He was disoriented and running a fever at first, then his blood pressure spiked, and his pulse oxidation decreased dramatically. He required supplemental oxygen through a nasal cannula. We didn't know what was going on at first, then we realized it was an infection in the cut in his calf. We ran bloodwork, and our suspicions were confirmed. He has sepsis." Her eyes went to me. "What that means is that the infection got into his bloodstream, and that can be fatal if not treated right away. So, we immediately started him on strong IV antibiotics."

She glanced around the room once, and when she got back to me, her shoulders sagged. "Look, I'm really sorry. I was under the impression you had been updated on his condition. From here on, I'll do my best to keep you informed." Her gaze slid to the floor, and the entire room went still as if someone had hit the pause button. "Only time will tell if the antibiotics are working as they should. My name is Lily. If you need any more information, just ask at the desk. I'm sorry I can't be more forthcoming."

"Well, if all goes well, how much longer until we can go and see him?" Cole cut in. I felt weightless at this sudden change in what was happening.

"It's touch and go at the moment, you understand." She wrung her hands again and smiled. "Look, when we're sure he's stabilized, we'll let you know. If all goes well, then we will allow a few of you in to see him."

"Thank you." Keith offered a hand politely.

I felt their eyes on me, and Savannah was suddenly at my side helping me to sit. "I'm sure it's going to be all right, Sloane. We all have to think positively. John is strong, and there is no way anything is going to take him away from us." Her defiance almost made me smile, and I took her hand but couldn't bring myself to say anything. My throat felt as though someone was squeezing it. I just smiled a little and nodded.

"I think it's time we called John's parents," Abigail said softly as she removed herself from the room.

Mike, Mark, Keith, and Cole were all huddled at the other end of the room. I wondered what they were talking about. When Cole caught me looking, he said something to Keith and left the group to join Savannah and me.

"Be strong, Sloane. That guy's a born soldier, no fucking—" Savannah glared at him. "Oh, sorry, no damn infection is going to take him down."

"John always said if he was going to die, it would be on his mountain," Mike chimed in, "so not today, Satan."

They all seemed confident. I guessed you had to be when the worst was always staring you in the face, and they'd been through a lot lately.

I couldn't take the tick of the clock on the wall any longer. I needed to move and needed a change of scenery. The blue walls were mind-numbing. As I stood, Mike stood with me, almost as if he was watching me.

"I think I just need to go downstairs and get some fresh air."

"Great. Me too." Mike followed me out of the room.

I didn't know Mike, but the few times we had spoken, he seemed kind enough, and if John liked him—well, I knew he must be a good guy. Once in the elevator, he looked down at me and smiled through his own worry.

"I hear they have really good chocolate chip muffins at the coffee stand in the lobby."

"Oh, yeah?" I tried to be kind, but my head was with John.

"Well, Mark's had three already, so I'm guessing they must be great." He laughed softly, but it stopped short when the doors opened, and screams filled the tin box we were in.

"Mrs. Black?" Mike stepped forward, recognizing John's mother. "Is everything okay?"

As I stepped around Mike's massive body, I caught Kelly's frantic eyes as they swung from me to Ellie, who was in the middle of a meltdown in the main lobby of the hospital.

"Sloane, thank God you're here." She tried to calm Ellie down. "Oliver went looking for Cole, and Ellie must have fed off our tension. We're so worried. Have you heard anything about John? We can't take not knowing. What happened?"

"Mike," I quickly addressed him, "could you take Mrs. Black aside and let her know what's going on while I talk to Ellie?"

"Of course." He glanced at me, completely confused as to what was happening, but did as I asked and walked Kelly to a nearby table to fill her in.

"Hi, Ellie. I'm Sloane, a friend of John's. He told me you went looking for pebbles the other day. What color were they?" I frantically searched for a memory for her and remembered hearing about this at the dinner table. I knew from past experience that brain injuries involving the temporal lobe resulted in difficulty or the inability to access long-term memories from after the accident.

Ellie whirled around, tears streaming down her face and terror in her eyes, but I could see she had heard me by the way she quieted down. Her chest heaved, and she kept clasping her hands together.

"John told me about the pebbles and how much fun he had with you. How many did you find?"

"Seven," she huffed at me, and the red in her face seemed to fade away.

"Seven, wow! I could have sworn John said five."

"No, it was seven. John tried to get me to put two back, but I didn't." She shrugged.

I glanced over her shoulder at Kelly, who was watching us she mouthed a *thank you* with a hand on her chest, relieved she had a minute to focus on her other child.

The elevator opened, and Oliver came rushing over when he saw me with Ellie. "I'm sorry, Sloane. I just heard that Ellie was having a hard time down here."

"No, we are all good here. Ellie was just clearing something up for me." I almost welcomed this distraction, and I knew how much Kelly needed a minute for herself too.

Kelly and Mike joined us now that Ellie was calmed down and busy watching a show I had lured her to on the lobby TV. We all talked about John and what had happened and where things were now. I assured Oliver that the moment any of us heard anything, we would come downstairs. They both agreed it was best to stay in the lobby with Ellie. I knew they were torn, but they also were confident we would keep them updated.

Mike and I said our goodbyes and headed back upstairs. When the elevator door closed, Mike cleared his throat as though he wanted to say something.

"It's not my place to share something that isn't mine to share," I shuffled my feet on the elevator rug, "but thanks for helping back there."

"Sure thing."

It was hard enough to digest what was happening

with John, but then to walk into the storm Ellie brought nearly sent me over the edge. My head felt like it was about to come unglued, spilling in multiple directions. John, Ellie, the whole shitstorm with the cartel, and not to mention the fact that my face still felt like a swollen balloon. I knew Frank and my father were dealing with that situation back in Washington, and as much as I wanted to know what was going on, I frankly didn't care right now.

"Sloane?" Mike's voice stopped the whirlwind of thoughts in my brain, and I looked up to see him holding the elevator doors for me. "You okay?"

"Ah, yeah." I forced a smile and headed back to our waiting room.

Abigail and June took shifts to help Dell with the kids and did their best to keep Sue and me occupied as the time rolled on. Mark insisted on making sure we ate. For a man who needed a lot of taking care of, he sure was great in situations like this, or maybe he was feeling better because Mia had arrived. Either way, it was nice.

My email sent a vibration through my phone, and with a foggy head, I saw my father had responded to my email.

"The test can only be taken once," I whispered under my breath. "Interesting." I sent a quick response thanking him, then I tried to get my mind back to work.

"How long has it been?" Sue finally broke the silence.

"Three hours and fifteen minutes," Cole and I said in unison just as the door opened and Nurse Lilly walked in.

"Hi, folks. Thanks for being so patient. I've got good news. Daniel is in recovery, and he did just fine through his surgery. His doctor will update you on exactly what was done in surgery later, but you can see him soon." She stumbled while looking around at our group. "But one at a time, please. As for John Black, I'm pleased to pass along that he is now stable."

The whole room broke out in cheers, and the relief was evident in their smiles.

Lilly held up her hand for us to listen. "He gave us concern for a while there, but he is strong and in excellent physical condition, and that helped a lot. He'll have to spend about week in hospital on IV antibiotics and, if all goes well, he can go home. But," she turned her pointed gaze to Cole, who I was sure she heard was the team leader, "he must rest. No work or heavy lifting. His body needs time to heal."

"You have my word," Cole promised as Abigail nearly plowed us over to share the news with John's parents downstairs.

"Can we see him yet?" I was nearly weightless with the news.

"He's still in intensive care, but once he's brought down to his room, and as soon as he's ready, two of you can go in."

"His parents." I nodded to Cole. "I'll wait. They really need to see their son."

He reached out and gave my arm an understanding squeeze before he tuned in to Mark.

Sue went off to visit Daniel in recovery, reassuring Cole he would be next. She returned in happy tears and hugged Cole briefly before he left to pay Daniel his own visit. I would have liked to be a fly on the wall in that room, as I'd heard about how Daniel switched places with Mike before it all happened. I imagined Cole would have a few things to say on the subject.

"I'm sure you'll get to see John soon." Mike leaned into me. "We all knew he was too tough to lose that easily." He shifted before he said what I suspected he really wanted to say. "Ah, I just wanted to say how well you fit in at Blackstone. You can keep confidences, and I respect that."

"Thanks." I tried to sound thankful for the compliment, but my head was still stuck in a panic loop. I wasn't prepared for all this to happen. Daniel, John, Ellie's meltdown, and now Mike knew a secret John wouldn't be all right with.

"Sloane?" Sue's warm touch pulled me from my internal chaos. "I think John would really like to see you now."

"Really? Thank you." I forced a smile and swiped my shaky hands down my shirt. I headed out the door and down the long hallway then stood outside of room 506. My hands were cold, so I tried to warm them against my legs before I pushed the heavy door open and stopped short.

I wasn't naïve. I knew he would look pale and tired, but I wasn't prepared to see him hooked up to a machine, with an IV stuck in his arm and bandages wrapped around his midsection. His gown was hiked up like he had just been examined. It was a shock to see him this way. I was terrified to approach the bed but forced myself to move.

His eyes fluttered open, and he squinted to see who his third visitor was.

"Hi," I barely whispered and fought the need to cry. Today had been an emotional roller coaster, and the fact that I knew he'd eventually return to that hell didn't help.

He shifted and pressed his finger against the button to raise his bed. Once he got comfortable, he motioned for me to come closer. My feet betrayed me, and I couldn't get them to move.

"Sloane," he cleared his throat but sounded extremely groggy, "come here."

My traitorous feet finally gave in, and I went to his side. He tried to motion for me to lie next to him, but instead I held on to his hand and pulled the chair next to him. We stayed like that for a while, and then he drifted off to sleep, and I was left with the horrible beeping sound of the heart monitor.

THIRTEEN

JOHN

As the heart monitor faded from my consciousness, I slipped into a more pleasant memory from my childhood.

"John!" Ellie popped up from behind a rock covered in mud with a shit-eating grin. "Whatcha looking at?"

I rolled my eyes and jabbed her in the ribs as I moved to join her behind the rock. "Just scopin' the Maverick boys, waiting for the perfect moment to attack them." I showed her the homemade mud balls I'd made earlier.

"Maverick boys," she narrowed her gaze in on me, "or Maverick sister?" She giggled, and I jabbed her side again. She yelped but continued to laugh.

"Shhh," I warned and waited for the little shits to move closer. Tyler, Elliot, and Josh were the new kids on the block and thought they owned the woods around our property. It was time to set things straight.

"Look, there's Bethany," my sister whispered over my shoulder. "You have a mud ball for her too, right?"

"Yup," I lied and shook her hand off my shoulder.

"I'll get Elliot and Josh, and you take out Tyler."

"And Bethany?"

"She's all yours," I muttered.

"Yes." She moved into place, and we both waited.

"One," they came closer, "two," they stopped like they always did to claim their space, "three." I stood and biffed the mud ball with all my might at Elliot's back.

"What the hell?" He whirled around when Ellie stood and nailed Tyler and Bethany square in the face. Both kids fell to the ground with a cry. I nailed Josh in the neck and high fived my sister, who was very pleased with herself. We hopped to our feet and bolted back to our own yard. We didn't miss a beat as we climbed the ladder to the safety of the barn's loft. Ellie dropped down on the hay in a fit of laughter, and I joined her. We laughed until our stomachs hurt and we were out of tears.

"We showed them!" She giggled as she pulled pieces of hay out of her muddy hair.

"We did." I high fived her and turned on the

Christmas lights Dad had let us hang up once he discovered we used it as a clubhouse.

"John." She rolled onto her knees, her expression serious.

"Yeah?" I moved a chicken out of my way and sat on the ledge to let my legs dangle over the open double doors.

"Will you promise me something?"

"'Kay."

"Promise me that no matter what happens in our lives, we'll always be a team."

I glanced over and saw her arms were hugged around her knees and her chin rested on their bony tops.

"Of course. We made that pact years ago. Why are you bringing it up now?"

She shrugged, and her mouth drooped into a frown.

"I know Bethany and a few other girls are starting to look at you differently, and that's fine, 'cause boys are doing the same to me. But you're my brother, and I want to make sure that we come first. You know?"

"I know." I understood her fear. It had always been the two of us, and the idea of anyone breaking that up was scary. "We're one person," I laughed lightly, "until you decide to be independent."

"Sounds like me." She grinned.

"You can't break up a twin bond, Ell. It's scientifically proven," I reassured her.

"Twins before anyone else." She beamed.

"Twins before anyone else," I repeated, knowing I'd take that promise to the grave.

Pain jolted me awake, and it took me a moment to clear the fog that hung heavily in the corners of my mind. I couldn't seem to move my left arm, so I forced my eyes open and blinked away the blur. Her sweet scent found its way into my nose before it registered that she was at my side.

"Hey," I whispered and ran my hand through the silk of her long hair. Everything hurt, but Sloane being here made up for it big time.

She moved to sit up then winced and rolled her head around for a second. The fatigue on her face vanished as she looked up at me, and concern took its place.

"Hi." Her tone sounded strange. "Can I get you anything?"

I shook my head and tried to take her hand, only to have her stand up as though she was unsure.

"What's wrong?" I croaked and begged my head to keep up.

"I just..." She trailed off.

"Just what?" I shifted uncomfortably. *Fuck me, everything hurts.*

"I am a strong woman, John."

"I know." The room tilted a little as a sharp pain jolted through my center.

"Who has been up against some of the roughest men in Washington."

"Yes, you have."

"Not to mention being attacked in my own home," she went on, "but there's something about seeing the man you love fight for his life with no warning. There was no warning."

I paused mid-wince at her words. The word "love" bounced around the room, but she didn't seem to notice, so I didn't point it out…yet.

"You were standing there in the hallway talking to us," her arms moved about as she told her story, "then you were gone, whisked off for x-rays, but you didn't come back. You didn't come back."

"I know it must have been scary, but—"

"Scary?" She laughed as tears trickled paths down her cheeks. My stomach twisted at how much she was hurting. "Scary is finding out your Blackhawk went down after two RPGs blew into it." She sniffed and dried her soaked cheeks with the back of her hand. "This," she waved her arms toward me, "is frigging terrifying." I nodded to show I was listening. "You had some possible broken ribs."

"Yeah."

"You had a bad cut on your leg, and they said you went into some filthy water. You should have known better."

"Yeah." She was right. I knew better, but it didn't matter at the time.

"I know Daniel was in rough shape, but what about you?"

"He has a family—"

"What are Kelly, Oliver, Ellie, and…" She stopped herself.

"And?" I questioned with a smile, which further pissed her off.

"Tripper," she fibbed terribly. "They are your family, people you should care enough about to come home to. You're just as important as Daniel."

"I care about my family and my own life." I fought the wave of nausea and the black that hovered. I would not allow myself to pass out. "But that wasn't what was running through my mind while I hauled Daniel through that jungle." I reached over and grabbed hold of her arm a little more roughly than I intended to. "Please stop moving for a moment." I blinked back the black spots.

"Oh," her face fell when she finally tuned in to my hurting state, "I'm sorry." She sat next to me with a sigh.

"And I'm sorry I scared you. I acted on instinct. I know you understand that, being the daughter of a general." My mouth was like sandpaper. "Just like I know you're not mad at me. You're worried about me."

"Maybe," she huffed, and more tears leaked out.

"Look," I buzzed the nurse so I could get the hell out of here, "our mission got railroaded, and Daniel was in worse shape than me." Her face made me try harder. "Daniel's been like a father to me since I joined. I don't get to share this side of my life with my dad, so to have Daniel be that for me is pretty important." I clicked the button again, feeling worse as the seconds ticked by. "I ignored my leg and my ribs and whatever else and did what I needed to do to get us the hell out of there."

She started to cry, and I had to believe it out of relief more than anything else.

"Sloane," I rubbed her leg, "you gave me a reason to come home, a reason to care and not be reckless. I came home because of you."

"You almost died, John."

"But I didn't." I kissed her hand. "I didn't die," I repeated to reassure her.

The door swung open, and the nurse walked in, but I glared at Mark, who stood behind her. He'd caught the door with his foot and flashed me a wicked smile.

Oh, shit, here we go.

"Good morning, Mr. Black." The nurse started to change out my IV bag. "How are you feeling this morning?"

"I'm good. When can I go home?"

She laughed, and Mark moved into the room, looking around like he was admiring the decor.

The room was yellow, with muted salmon-colored furniture. There was nothing to look at.

"You're here until Sunday, Mr. Black," the nurse informed me, "and after that, you're on bedrest for another thirteen days."

Mark slowly turned and joined Sloane.

"I feel fine," I muttered.

"John," Sloane warned, knowing that was a lie. "He's

in pain, and he looked like he might be sick a few moments ago."

"I see." The nurse shot me a disapproving look. "I'll get you something for that and the pain."

I wanted to argue, but the nurse left, and Sloane rushed to join her, I was sure to embellish more on my condition.

Mark's shit-eating grin loomed over me.

"What?" I closed my eyes as another dizzy spell took over.

"Mm, nothing." He started to lift the side of the blanket, and my eyes flew open. "I heard you have a hose stuck in your twig."

"So help me God, Lopez," I growled.

"Someone's fussy?" He laughed. "Does it sting when you pee?"

"Die."

"Nah, I'm good." He sank into the chair in the corner of the room and checked the time. "Ten minutes until they serve you lunch."

"Knock, knock." Savannah popped her head in the door holding a bag. "Okay to come in?"

"Sure." I shook my head, hating all the attention. I just wanted to either get the hell out of here or sleep.

"Mia pulled some strings with a friend, and we thought you might like some food from home." She started to pull out some containers. "Soup, rolls, tea, just a few things to make your stay a little nicer."

"Thanks, Savi." The idea of food made my stomach roll, but the offer was very kind. "How's Daniel?"

"He's fine. He'll be a while recovering, perhaps a little longer than you, but I'll let Cole fill you in on the rest." She reached behind her and smacked Mark, who was already into the rolls.

Sloane came in and sat on the edge of the bed, still looking a million miles away.

"Okay, Mr. Black, I have some anti-nausea and pain meds." The nurse stopped when she took in my company. "One of you needs to go. Only two guests at a time. I'm sorry."

"That one." I pointed at Mark, who was stuffing his mouth with a second roll.

"You're so cold." Food rolled around his mouth.

"I should go too." Savannah gave me a hug. "I'll be back with more food."

I waved a goodbye and waited for the nurse to inject the goods. I hoped they'd hit fast.

"This will help. Now, get some rest." She eased the liquids into my IV then left.

Sloane moved up the bed and ran a hand through my hair. "Can I get you anything?"

"No." Warmth spread through my body, and I felt heavy. The top of my head started to prickle, and my mind slowly let go of the room. "Say it to me again?"

"What?" she whispered as she turned off the light next to the bed.

"That you love me." I gave in to sleep remembering my Delta days.

"My feet fucking kill," Dimitri bitched as we finished the last leg of our twenty-mile hike through thick terrain with a forty-five-pound pack strapped to our backs.

"You're fine," I muttered and grabbed Tony's arm as his legs gave out again. Delta Force training weeded the weak from the strong and the undetermined from the determined. A good part of it was mental. Harsh, but true. I knew that when faced with the challenges a Delta Force soldier would come up against, you'd better be the best of the best. Or you'd die.

"Come on, Tony." I bent down and used what little strength I had left and hoisted him over my shoulder. My knees shook, but I took a moment and cleared my head.

"Really?" Dimitri snickered as he hobbled along. "You'd think we were in a movie or something."

I whirled around and glared down at the bastard who had been riding my ass since we started training.

"By all means, then," I held out my arms and felt Tony fight for balance, "you can be the star in it. If you want to carry him, you can."

"I'm not carrying him and his extra weight." He indicated Tony's pack. "We're pushed for time as it is."

"Then shut the hell up and get back in line."

The rest of our unit followed in silence. We were all exhausted and had little patience for Dimitri and all he'd put us through. Multiple times we'd had to stop and help him out, but the first time someone else really needed help, he was willing to leave them in the woods just to finish on time. His type was not cut out for the Army.

"Ten minutes," Waters chimed in, "and we have two more miles to go."

"So, pick up the pace." Dimitri hit my arm as he hurried by. "You can be the hero, but I'm finishing this test."

"Whatever," I hissed and watched more than half of the unit race after him.

"Not worth it." Tony tried to sound coherent. "Drop me." I shifted a bit to relieve my right shoulder.

"I wouldn't drop you in battle, so why would I do it now?"

"You won't make it in time." Waters' voice came from the side. I hadn't noticed him because of Tony's legs.

"I don't care," I nodded toward the finish line ahead, "but you should go. This was my decision."

Waters shook his head and stayed close. "If I ever have to fight in a battle for my life, Black," he looked over at me, "I would want you with me."

I lifted my fist to give him a bump.

My mud-soaked boots crossed the line with thirty seconds to spare. I handed Tony to the EMT who was *waiting on the sidelines and dropped my pack with a thud. I ignored the cheers from the rest of the unit, grabbed my canister, and headed to a quiet spot. I usually loved the brotherhood of the Army, when you were in the right company. Other than Waters, my unit was disappointing. Perhaps in time their mind-set would change, but if it wasn't in them now, I highly doubted it would ever change.*

An upside-down bucket seemed like a good place to sit. It was in a shady spot and a short distance away from everyone else. I sat down and chugged about half of my water then closed my eyes, happy the testing was over. I knew I had done well, and it felt good.

"Black." My commanding officer waved me over. Damn. I pushed back on my tired knees and made quick work to join him.

"Sir," I greeted with a curt nod.

"I'm not going to drag this out. We don't need to evaluate you any more. You have proven yourself time and time again. Welcome to Delta Force."

Holy shit.

"Thank you, sir." I reached out to take the hand he held out. "I won't let you down."

"I know." He granted me the first smile I'd seen from him.

As I was about to leave, his gaze moved over my shoulder, and I turned to see a general standing by an SUV. He stared right at me and gave my

commanding officer a nod before he got back into the
vehicle.
What was that about?

"He's been out for a while." Sloane's voice brought me back to the present. I tried to pull myself up from the depths as I felt someone touch my arm.

"He needs his rest, and this will help. We'll move him later."

"It's only been four days. Are you sure he's okay to be moved?"

I was sucked downward again, and as I let myself go, images of my time in Delta flashed before me like a flip book.

"My leg!" Waters screamed into the dead of the
night as rain pelted our faces. Chaos and panic
surrounded us like a thick blanket of fog. We had
done this jump thousands of times, but this time the
chopper had swung up to the side to avoid being hit
by incoming fire. Waters lost his grip, and the rope
had tangled around his thigh as he jumped. He was
now hanging upside down, staring death in the
face.
"Black!" His red face desperately pleaded as his
bulging eyes latched on to mine. He dangled sixty feet
above the ground, a perfect target for those below.
I knew the rest of the team had landed and were
moving into their positions by now.

"Shit!" Waters flexed his stomach at the sound of the bullets that were randomly being sprayed into the sky. I hated those assholes!

I only had one choice. I reached out, grabbed my rope with my knife in my mouth, and slid down to where he was.

"Quick, Black. I need my leg!" he screamed.

I clenched my rope and kicked my feet out hard, and as I slammed into him, I wrapped my legs around his stomach, and with a quick swipe of my knife, I cut the rope that held his leg. We both dropped like rocks. I couldn't use my feet to control my speed, and he was upside down and couldn't control the speed with his arms.

The sound was haunting as the rope zipped through my gloves, and we picked up momentum as we fell. In one last desperate effort to save our lives, I shouted to Waters to squeeze the rope with all his might. I did the same, and just before we hit the ground, we were able to cut our race toward death in half.

Whack!

We hit hard. The air jolted from my lungs, and I blacked out for a half a second. The moment my head cleared, I was on my feet and grabbed Waters to check him over.

"How are we alive?" Waters started to laugh.

"Don't ask questions we can't answer." I joined in on the laughter in a need to shake off my adrenaline rush.

"Together to the end." Waters smacked my shoulder, then we both hauled ass deep into the desert to join the others.

Later that night back on US soil as we piled out of the chopper, I was stopped by my commanding officer, who was waiting on the tarmac.

"General Mac wants to see you, room three."

Oh, shit. I knew I was probably going to be grilled for what happened. Swiftly, I moved inside and told the soldier at the desk I was there at General Mac's request. He indicated a chair outside a closed door. I took the seat and rested my head in my hands. I really needed some time to rest so I could digest the last mission. There was protocol for what happened, but if I'd followed the rules, Waters would have lost his leg or worse.

"Tell me about Black." A voice came from the other side of the door and stopped my thoughts.

"He's a born Delta member," General Mac replied in his distinctive voice. "Mentally unbreakable, smart, he's liked by all, and on this last mission he risked his own life to save one of his men when his leg got tangled up in the jump rope."

"Impressive." There was a pause. "Not many of them would do that."

"My thoughts too."

"I've been searching for the right person to complete my team, and I think Black would be the perfect fit."

I leaned back and rested my head on the cool tile so I could hear better.

"You're going to have to ask Frank. He's had his eye on Black, and Waters too, for that matter."

I heard a light chuckle before the voice spoke up again. "I think we can come to an understanding."

General Mac appeared in the doorway, and I jumped to my feet out of respect.

"Black, this is General Logan. He would like to speak to you."

"Sure thing." I gave a nod and wondered if he was related to the Cole Logan I'd heard about. He was legendary and one of the youngest men of my generation to make Colonel. His reputation was well known, but not many people had the pleasure to meet him in person.

"Please call me Daniel. Would you mind if we stepped outside?"

"Not at all." I followed him outside, curious as to why he wouldn't want to talk there.

"I don't like stuffy offices." He seemed to read my mind. "I prefer to conduct my business outside with a clear head."

"I'm not complaining, sir." I shot him a friendly smile and liked how at ease he made me. We stopped at the edge of the property where the grass ended and the trees began. An owl could be heard in the background over the partying that was beginning to pick up since our mission was successful. I crossed my arms

behind my back and stood waiting to hear what this man had to say.

"Have you heard of Blackstone?"

I thought for a moment.

"No, sir, I haven't."

"I guess that's a good thing." He chuckled to himself.

"What about Eagle Rock?"

Now that, I had heard of.

"Yes, I do know about Eagle Rock."

"Well, Blackstone is its brother company. My son Cole Logan has taken the team over, and we are looking to fill the last spot."

Son? Well, that made sense.

I had waited my whole life to be a Delta solider, but nothing prepared me for this. Soldiers would sell their souls to be asked to join one of those teams. It was an impossible dream that only a few earned.

Daniel turned to look at me, one hand on his chin while he spoke. "I was there the day you finished your training and made Delta. What you did in training, risking your chance at running out the clock, that's not something you see every day."

"No man left behind."

"Yes, in the field that's true, but you were fighting for a spot on a Delta Force team."

"Mission or training, it shouldn't make a difference. A life is a life. A brother is a brother. If they're hurt, you're hurt, your team is hurt. If we don't stay true to *that in training, how do we know the person will have our back in the field?"*

He studied me for a moment before he nodded. "You've been on this team for just over a year, and you're still quick to move when someone is in trouble." He waited a beat to let me know he knew about what had happened this morning. "And I know you went through hell and back for a spot here, but I think you'd be a great fit for Blackstone." I cleared my throat and tried not to smile. "If you're interested, we can meet tomorrow and go over the details. I understand a fresh head is important with an offer like this."

I didn't need to think about it, I knew it was what I wanted.

"No need to wait, sir. I'm in. Thank you."

"Daniel," he reminded me, "and I'm happy to hear that, and my son will be too. He's had his eye on you for the past thirteen months." He turned away and took a couple steps when I called out.

"Daniel." I tested his name, but it felt disrespectful. "Sir, Waters is a damn fine option too."

He smiled and pressed a finger to his mouth as if it was a secret. "That's why Frank has added him to Eagle Rock."

"Sir?"

"We don't let the best of the best slip through the cracks, Black. Welcome to the team."

A chopper suddenly took off, and wind whipped the

loose dirt around us. My lungs filled, and I fought to breathe.

My eyes jolted open, and I gasped for air. It took me a moment to realize where I was. Still in the hospital, but the colors were different? Did I get moved to a different room?

"You couldn't have let me have this one moment." The annoyed voice made my head jolt over to the side to find Daniel sucking down a juice box.

What the hell?

"Why am I here?"

"Sue thought we'd like to be bunkmates." He rolled his eyes before he stuck the straw back into his mouth. "By the way, you talk in your sleep."

FOURTEEN

I'd spent the last ten days working inside these hospital walls, and for all ten days I'd been listening to the endless banter between Mark, John, and Mike. Mark's favorite thing was when John would wake from a nap. He'd jam that stupid Furby in his face and watch him jump. I couldn't wait for that toy to disappear, but they seemed to know where it was at all times.

They were such great friends, and it warmed me to hear them keeping up John's spirits, toy or no toy. But Keith and Cole, on the other hand, were a lot less chatty. I didn't blame them. While the guys joked and carried on, those two had been in constant communication with Frank and North Rock. Things were not good.

Sue refused to let Daniel work, and the poor man was going crazy. I knew he'd soon start crawling the walls. I felt bad for him, but I understood his health was much more important right now. Sue was on him like a cat on a light beam if he so much as moved.

"Excuse me." The day nurse scrunched her face in an apology as she once more needed me to move. It was probably for the sixth time today.

"I'm sorry." I lifted my laptop and shimmied out of the way. Daniel reached out and tugged me to him.

"I will give you a twenty if you share an update with me, anything at all."

I laughed and shook my head. He was like a caged animal dying to be let loose, and I felt for him.

"I'm sorry, Daniel." But I tilted my head at Sue, who was pretending to read but really watching us. "She will have my head if she thinks, for one minute, I've given you food for thought, any kind of thought." I smiled in sympathy at him.

I glanced over at Mark, who was trying to peek under John's blanket. We watched as Mark got a punch in the shoulder for his effort, and then we laughed out loud at John's outrage.

"Look, Daniel," I patted his hand, "I promise if I find anything, I will sneak it to you when Sue isn't around and you can help to find the answers. I know you know a lot more than I ever could about the cartel and how they work." I saw his face relax a little. Typical Blackstone man. He needed to know he was in control of something, even if it was from a hospital bed.

"That's right." His shoulders relaxed back into the mattress. "I would appreciate that."

"You have my word."

The door swung open, and the doctor came in with a chart in his hand. He smiled at the room then immediately looked down at the chart once he took in the two sets of steely eyes directed at him in anticipation.

"As much as it's been a pleasure having you all here." He gave a pointed look to Mark, who hadn't so much as taken a breath since he walked into the room. "Mr. Black, you are free to leave."

John's face lit up as he sucked in a deep breath of air. His gaze then latched on to mine.

"Free," he mouthed.

"Ah," Daniel cleared his throat, "what about me, Doctor?"

"Sorry, Mr. Logan." He walked over to the bed, and Sue stood and joined him. "You will need to stay approximately another week. You simply aren't ready for discharge yet." He took a few minutes to update Daniel and Sue on his condition, ending with the need to be patient.

Once the doctor went over the paperwork with John and he got the green light to ship out, he took the time to give Daniel a little pep talk before the nurse pushed him out the door to freedom.

"Can you pop a wheelie?" Mark held the door for the nurse as they went into another hallway.

"Why are you still here?" John snickered but playfully swiped at him as they moved down the hall.

"Mia is visiting a friend downstairs." Mark tucked his hands in his pockets as he strolled beside me. "So, I thought Sloane might need my help getting you ready."

"How kind," John grumbled.

I struggled to balance John's bag, my work bag, and his paperwork. As soon as we got to the elevator, it dawned on me that I forgot my phone on the chair back in the room.

"Shoot," I hissed and handed Mark my heavy load. "I'll meet you in the lobby. I forgot my phone."

"You sure?" John caught the closing door.

"Yeah." I turned on my heel and raced back toward the room. I quietly opened the door so as not to startle Daniel, who was already in a foul mood with his bunkmate leaving. I spotted my phone, and just as I scooped it up, I felt the three cups of coffee I'd had hit my bladder. The drive back along the winding roads of Montana's mountains went through my head, and my legs clenched together at the thought.

"Sorry," I whispered to Daniel as he opened his sleepy eyes. "I just need to use the restroom."

"Of course, dear."

I rushed into the restroom, seeking relief. I heard footsteps out in the room as I stood to wash my hands and hesitated, hearing his angry voice.

"I have never been this mad at you in my entire life." Cole's voice froze me to the spot.

"Son—"

"No," he interrupted, "you will hear me out. You have always been a smart, methodical man. I've always held you on a pedestal. Never once did we go into a mission without knowing plan A, B, C, and God forbid, option D."

I tried to be very quiet, knowing I shouldn't be hearing this; it wasn't for me. It was their private moment, but I wasn't sure what to do.

"I'm so sorry," I whispered and leaned my back against the wall.

"What you did," Cole nearly shouted, "that decision was not in the plan. If any of us did that, we would be kicked off the team without even a thought. Why?" He stumbled on his words. "Why in hell would you make that call? Why the sudden change in plan?"

"I thought I had more knowledge of the southern side then Mike did. I had no idea that we'd be shot down."

"You both were almost killed!"

"Yes, I know that, and when we were spiraling in the air like a spin top and the ground was racing toward us, all I could think about was I'm glad it was me and not the man who had just had a baby."

"And what about John, Dad? He had no say in what you did. We all know the risks we take. The risks you have drilled into our heads over and over again!" Cole growled. "That's why we have protocols in place. That's why we practice our plans, review our maps, plan for the worst.

But we can only do that when we are all on the same God-damn page!"

"I'm sixty-three years old!" Daniel shouted and made me jump. "I'm sixty-three, Cole. I know the rules, I knew the risk of what I did, but I did it because…" He paused. His voice quieted. "I know what I did was wrong, but it was a calculated risk, and I was with one of the best soldiers we have."

"That hardly makes it right, Dad, and…" He stopped as the door opened. Sue's voice could be heard as she spoke to someone in the hall. "Oh, hello, son. I only left because I thought your father was sleeping."

"I was resting," Daniel sounded grumpy, "but you two can just stop your hovering and let me sleep now."

As things got quiet, I waited for a few more uncomfortable minutes then quickly washed my hands and stepped out into the semi-darkened room. I quietly fled out the door and down the hall to the lobby.

John looked happy to see me. "Mark went to get the car. We dug the keys out of your purse. Hope you don't mind. I can't wait to see the back end of this place."

Mark helped us get loaded up and waved us off as we started the short drive to John's parents' place. John fell asleep once we hit the road, and I let my mind drift back over what I had heard in Daniel's room. I felt off, and I wasn't sure how to navigate it.

When I stopped at a traffic light, I glanced over and studied his face. The lines that normally gave away his daily stress were smoothed out, and he seemed at peace. He was such an attractive, strong man, one who apparently held a large piece of my heart. I still couldn't believe I told him I loved him without even realizing it. It wasn't exactly how I saw those three little words being uttered, but my subconscious apparently had other plans.

I reached back for my purse and stuck my hand inside to fish out my lip gloss and jumped at something furry that bit my finger. I swallowed back my curse. I hated that fucking toy!

If John wasn't just released from the hospital, a full-out assault would be happening right now, but as for Mark…game on.

John jolted awake when we turned off and hit the icy gravel that led up to farmhouse.

"Damn drugs," he muttered and coughed to clear his sleepy throat. Tripper was waiting on the porch for us when we pulled into the driveway.

"Savi said she dropped Tripper off this morning. Said he missed you." I opened my door, only to hear him mutter.

"You mean he missed *you*." I laughed, and he scowled at me. "You stole my dog, Sloane. He was a guy's dog until you puss-a-fied him."

That made me laugh harder as I grabbed my bag from the back seat.

"Don't blame me for being the one who's always at the house. Maybe you shouldn't leave so much."

My face fell at my own comment, but right before I forced my smile back, he caught it.

"Welcome home, John." Kelly grabbed her son and wrapped him in a hug as she kissed his cheek. "You're looking good."

"Of course I am," he joked and reached for my hand after Kelly granted me a hug too. "Where's Dad and Ellie?"

"Dad's in the field. He thought you were coming a little later on, and Ellie's in her room. We'll give her a bit before we tell her you're here."

"Okay, just let me drop my stuff, and I'll go help Dad."

"No," Kelly and I both said at the same time.

He lifted a sexy eyebrow with a smirk. "Just because I'm under house arrest doesn't mean I can't do anything."

"That's exactly what it does mean," I shot back. "Don't forget I have Cole's number. It just takes one text, and your ass will be back in the hospital or under Savannah's eagle eye at Shadows."

"You wouldn't."

I had taken the liberty of talking with Cole about where John would go to recuperate. It took some time, but I convinced Cole that he would be better off at his parents' than at Shadows. I still wasn't sure how John felt about it. He had said very little but had listened as I explained how important it would be for his parents and sister to have him close after what had happened. I knew that would reach him more than anything. I watched as Tripper started to lick John's face. It was obvious it had been a good decision to bring the pup here. John was happy. I leaned down and mauled the fur ball a bit, glad he was here for John.

"Wouldn't I?" I eyed him over Tripper's head as I began to tickle his ears, and he positively swooned and his tongue fell out of his mouth in delight. "Hell-wo, big boy. Who's my little fluffer puppy?" His tail wagged so hard he could barely stand up as he leaned into me. John tried to pull him back to him, and he growled a little with jealousy, fighting for more of my touch.

"You're a she-devil," he hissed.

"Remember that before you try to do too much."

"That's right, John. You listen to what Sloane is saying. She knows what's she talking about." Kelly's face positively glowed as she looked up at me. "Now I'm going to make you a nice healthy snack."

John groaned at me. It was obvious I was delighted that I had his mother's support.

After we got settled and I made sure John's medication was ready for the week, I took a quick shower and changed into some warmer clothes.

He insisted he could unpack and look after himself. So, needing something to do, I eyed my laptop and wondered if I could dive back into my work for a bit. Before I did that, I decided to check things out downstairs first.

At the top of the stairs, I heard Ellie in her bedroom.

"Knock, knock," I called gently, and she twisted on her bed to see who it was. "Hi, Ellie, I'm a friend of John's. I just wanted to say hi."

"Hi," she said quietly.

"I'll be staying at the house for a little bit. Your mother will need some help, so I thought I would let you know."

"Okay."

I looked around her room and noticed all the magazine pictures on her walls. "I really like your room. Are these pictures of all your favorite things?"

"Yes, ah, thanks." She smiled hesitantly then looked down at the magazine she had open on her bed.

With a wave, I left her and headed down to the living room. I heard noises in the kitchen, so I popped my head in.

"Hey, Kelly," I stepped forward, "can I help with anything?"

"Oh, my gosh, yes, please." She handed me a knife. "Could you chop this up fairly fine?" She rushed on, "My sister called, and now I'm behind schedule. I was supposed to drop her package off this morning." I could tell she was stressed over something.

I started to chop the onion and waited a moment to see if she would say anything further. When she didn't speak up, I did what I did best. I got her talking.

"Where does your sister live?"

"Sulema lives just outside town. She owns her own

business, and I was supposed to pick up her order and drop it off, but Ellie had a hard morning, and once that happens, it's like my entire day just falls apart. I forgot to pick it up for her."

I glanced around the kitchen and spotted a cookbook flipped open to a recipe for spaghetti.

"Here's a thought. Why don't I make my mother's recipe for spaghetti since I know it by heart, and you go drop off your sister's package?"

Her hands stopped what they were doing, and she placed one on the counter almost as if to ground herself.

"You know, Sloane," she kept her head turned away, "I keep telling myself that the next day will be a little easier, but it never happens." She sighed. "Today, I was so happy that John was coming, I just wanted to prepare for him, make him a nice meal, enjoy having him home. You know?" I looked at her and nodded to show I understood but didn't speak. "I wanted so much to do one simple thing for my sister, to allow myself to be normal, but with Ellie, well, now I've let her down. I can't help but wonder if I'll ever be normal again." She turned back to the counter and lifted her apron to wipe at her face. I reached over and gave her a hug.

"Kelly, please let me do this for you. I'd really like to help. Ellie will be fine. I'll keep a close eye on her, and John is here."

She stood straight and wiped her hands on her apron then removed it and placed it on the counter. "You are such a good person, Sloane. You show up here like a breath of fresh air, and now you make such a lovely offer." Her hand moved to cover mine. "Yes, you know what, I would really appreciate your help."

"I'm happy to be able to." I watched as she cleared her throat and her shoulders straightened again. I had to give Kelly props. She was doing a much better job at holding herself together now that she was attending the meetings. I wasn't sure how often she actually went, but accepting help was progress, and it was nice to see.

She hesitated as she went to leave, but I assured her again that Ellie would be fine. She was still in her room, and I would call Oliver or John if she needed something.

Once I got all my ingredients in place, I hooked my phone up to the speaker and quietly played my favorite playlist. It was a crazy mix of Chris Stapleton, Justin Timberlake, Billie Eilish, Hudson Rainer, and Kaleo. I'd always loved music, but I could never find one genre that called to me. I dabbled in them all. There was no reason to limit yourself, after all.

Once the pasta water started to boil and the sauce was well on its way, I spent time chopping the pancetta before I tossed it in the cast iron frying pan.

"You're cooking?" Ellie was standing in the doorway of the living room holding a book.

"I am." I chopped up another onion and wondered how long she had been standing there before she said anything. "Would you like to help?"

She hesitated and looked out the window as John

walked into sight, and we both watched as he joined his father near the barn. She nodded.

"Can you wash your hands?" She headed over to the sink, and when she was finished, she waited for her next instruction. "Here," I unrolled the dough for the French bread, "watch me." I pulled at the side of the dough and folded it into the middle over and over. "Now you try."

Slowly, she started to knead the dough, and after a few tries she became more confident and picked up the pace.

"If it feels a little sticky, just do this." I held my hand over the dough ball and let the flour slip through my fingers.

"Ellie, do you remember my name?"

Her lips pressed together as though she was attempting to pull it from her foggy memories. "S-S-So," she tried.

"Sloane." I helped her out. "Do you have a flip book?"

"No, I don't think so." She folded the dough again.

"We should make you one."

"Like a craft?"

"Exactly."

"I love crafts." Her face lit up.

"Me too."

I wiped my hands and pulled my phone free. I opened the camera and flipped the camera to face the two of us.

"Ellie, will you smile at the camera?" To my surprise, she came up and smiled over my shoulder. I snapped a photo of us and one of her kneading the bread.

Oliver stomped dirt from his boots before he came

into the kitchen. He stopped short with surprise when he saw Ellie helping me.

"Kelly needed to run to her sister's," I kept my voice light, "so I offered to help out. Ellie is making the bread, and I'm just finishing up the sauce for the pasta."

His smile grew about three sizes as he shrugged out of his jacket and hung it on the peg inside the door.

"I'm starving." He closed his eyes and took a deep breath in through his nose.

"Good," Ellie chimed in. "Wash your hands, Dad."

"Yes, dear." He scuffled a laugh and did what his daughter ordered.

Once the table was set and the sauce prepared, I eased the pasta into water. I grated some fresh parmesan and put it on the lazy susan in the middle of the table. I glanced out the window at John, who was now under his father's truck.

"Seriously?" I grumbled under my breath and snapped a photo of him not doing what he promised.

"You didn't actually think he was going to listen, did you?" Oliver laughed behind me. "John does what John wants. He knows his limits and will calculate the risk of whatever it is he's about to do."

I eased into a chair with a huff and watched Ellie as she concentrated on her task, ignoring us. When she finished, I helped her put the bread in the pan.

"Thank you, Ellie, for all your help. Now, why don't you look at your book while we wait for dinner?"

After she went into the living room, I turned to Oliver.

"Between you and me, Oliver, do you know what John actually does for a living in the Army?"

He poured me a glass of red wine before he opened his beer.

"If someone was to ask me, I'd just say he's in the Army, but I know better." He took a draw from his beer. "You don't get broken bones, staples, and fractures from working in an office. I know what he does is dangerous. I can see it on his face when he comes home after disappearing for weeks on end."

"Does it not bother you?"

He shrugged with a sigh. "When Ellie wasn't around, John was independent, always wanted to be alone with his thoughts and do his own thing. He's strong as an ox and is very disciplined. So, when he joined the Army, I wasn't surprised. In fact, I was waiting for it."

"Did he ever share any of it with you?"

"Oh, yeah, at first he did." He nodded. "He lived and breathed the military life. He wasn't born to be a farmer's son. He was born to lead and fight. But the stories of his wild adventures and friendships stopped when he tried out for Delta. That's when he came back, explaining he got a position in an office. We both knew it was what he needed to say, and I knew it was for all of us, for our protection." He pulled back the curtain a little more and saw John cleaning off his hands. "I hate what his sister's accident did to this family." He turned to me. "It was as if a bomb went off, and we all got shot off in different directions. It's only now that we are beginning to find our way back."

"Time has a funny way of redirecting life back on course after something tragic has happened."

The door opened, and John came in, dusting some dirt off his coat. Oliver looked at me and smiled. "Yeah, it sure does."

FIFTEEN

JOHN

I lost track of Sloane, who had become quiet during dinner. She'd slipped out just after the kitchen was cleaned. Ellie happily bragged about her bread-making skills at dinner, and I still couldn't believe she'd helped. Normally, she would have just stood back and watched us go about the process of everyday living. I'd noticed Mom was a lot calmer when Sloane was around, and even my father seemed to smile more easily. There was no denying that she was good for them as well as for me. I certainly knew she was good for Ellie, but I knew I needed to make sure my family didn't rely on her too much. That wouldn't be fair, and I wouldn't want to run the risk of smothering her either.

"I'm going outside for a bit." I kissed Mom on the cheek, and her face twisted into a smile.

"Oli said she was outside by the horses."

I laughed. Even with the chaos of our lives, my mother could still read me like an open book.

I stepped outside where, to my surprise, Tripper was still on the porch.

"Hey, boy." I patted his head and rubbed his ears the way he loved. "Where's our girl?" His ears perked up, and he let out a whine.

Darkness draped across the yard and cast deep shadows around the farm equipment. There was a time when I would spend hours hidden away, invisible to the naked eye, pretending I was running from the enemy. My mission was to get across the field without our dog spotting me. Apparently, I was training for Blackstone at seven.

Tripper growled and poked my hand with his nose to get my attention. I followed his line of sight and spotted Sloane up in the loft.

"Good job." I gave him another pat. "Stay," I ordered as I made my way across the driveway toward the barn.

The cool air dipped into my jacket and made me shiver. The promise of snow could be felt in the air, and according to the weather report, we were in for a storm.

Doug stood above me and pecked at the ladder for me to come up. In a few strides, I brought myself to his level and twisted to stand then flipped on the twinkle lights and the warming lamp. A calming hum filled the space as I scooped up my beloved rooster and gave him a pat.

"How are the hens, Dougie?" I kept my voice quiet so as not to startle Sloane.

She snapped out of her daydream and looked back at us as I came up behind her.

"Oh," she quickly dried her cheeks, "I didn't hear you come up."

"Tripper outed you." I tried to make her smile, but something was clearly bothering her. I shrugged out of my coat and tossed it aside. I often ran hot.

"Yeah," she sniffed, "he wasn't happy when I told him to stay."

Sitting across from her on the ledge, I balanced Doug on my thigh and saw she must have been upset for a while.

"What's going on?"

Her head dropped forward, and to my surprise, she smiled. It wasn't necessarily a happy smile, but still. She ran a hand through her hair and let out a long breath.

"Something just hit me, and I'm still trying to process it."

"Like?"

"Like something personal." She drew her legs up and rested her chin on her knees.

"Well," I looked out over the property, "Doug, here, is who I talk to when things get personal." I held Doug up as an offering. He clucked, annoyed to have been moved from his warm spot on my leg.

"Thanks, but I'll stick to Tripper." She eyed my buddy and held up her hands, not wanting to accept my feathered pal. Then she laughed softly in an apology, and we fell back into silence. I hated that something was bothering her. I normally wouldn't pry, especially into a woman's head, but this was different. Whatever was bothering her was now bothering me.

"Hey," I shook her foot, "come on."

She sniffed again and closed her eyes then physically shook herself as if to shed the feeling.

"I grew up in an Army household. My father spent lots of time away. There was always a piece of me that left with him, and I never felt complete until he came home."

"I can understand that."

"I know how hard it was on me as a child, a child who thankfully didn't know the awful dangers. Only now I can imagine what it must have been like for my mom." She rubbed her arms. "It's very different. You know? How a child misses and worries about their father versus how the mother must have felt."

"Sure." I was curious where she was going with this.

She looked up and dried her cheeks again then seemed to have made a decision.

"When I went back to get my phone at the hospital, I overheard something I know wasn't meant for me, but the situation was what it was."

"What situation?"

"Wasn't meant for me to hear, so it wasn't meant for me to repeat." I could see she wasn't going to share.

"I respect that." I waved for her to go on.

"I heard a little of what went down on your Blackhawk, before it crashed."

Shit. A heavy pit landed in the center of my stomach.

"I guess," she sniffed, "something inside me realizes how the tables have turned. I'm not the child sitting on the front step waiting for her dad to come home anymore. I'm the woman in the living room hearing that your chopper went down and knowing that you're okay, but you still need to get out of that place."

"Sloane, I know it's scary—"

"Oh, but you don't," she shot back and jumped to her feet. "You don't, John."

I moved to stand, setting Doug on the floor. She held up a hand to stop me when I took a step toward her.

"You're the one leaving, and I'm the one watching you go."

My shoulders sagged with a familiar heaviness. "Yeah, that's true. It's why we don't like to date, why we don't like to fall in love. But, Sloane," I pulled her to me, "try understanding what it's like being the one who walks away. The one who has to turn their back on those we love. We have to go and play the game of life and death with ruthless killers. But I know how important the work we do is. I know that, but I also know how important it is coming home to you, to someone I love." I brushed a tear away from her cheek with the back of my finger as my words sank in. "When the chopper was going down, your sweet face was in my head, and when we finally hit the ground and I still had a heartbeat, it was you I thought of. Getting back to you."

"I was so scared." She pressed her forehead into my chest. "When Frank shared what had happened, it was like someone was squeezing my chest, and each breath made it tighter and tighter."

"I'm sorry," I kissed the top of her head and wrapped my arms around her, "and I'm sorry you heard what happened like that."

We stood there for a while. She needed my strength, and I needed her comfort. She smelled like home, and I buried my nose further into her neck and drank in her scent. I never thought I needed a woman. Until I'd met Sloane, I was content to be alone. Figured I'd be married to the job forever.

Whoa, where was I going with this?

"Oh, wow," she whispered and pulled out of my hold, "it's snowing."

Little flakes of white fell from the dark sky and started to blanket the field.

"You know what they say about the first snowfall of the month?"

"What?" Her eyes looked intensely blue against her gray sweater. All I now wanted in this life was to be able to stare into those pools of blue and know they were for me only.

"You're supposed to kiss the one you love to keep them close forever."

Her tongue darted out and licked her bottom lip. I

instantly grew hungry but reined in my desire to ravish her. Instead, I threaded one hand into her cold, silky hair, and the other slid down her side to her hip to settle on her bottom.

"Keep me close forever, then."

Her words warmed me from the inside out. I didn't waste any more time and sealed my lips to hers. The moment I did, her body relaxed, and her arms wrapped around my neck. We were lost in each other. I didn't care that we were on display for the world to see. I had fallen for someone, and for once in a very long time, I allowed myself to be happy.

I slipped my hand into my pocket and tapped my phone that was set to play one of my favorite songs.

"Dance with me," I whispered against her lips.

"But there's no—" She trailed off when the speakers switched on and Brothers Osborne's *Love the Lonely out of You* began to play. "Oh." She smiled up at me and allowed her arms to drape over my shoulders. We slowly moved about. The snow acted as a privacy curtain, letting us have a moment that was just ours. When the chorus came, I whispered the last part into her ear, and she held me tighter. Whether we both realized it or not, we were lonely, and sometimes it took a person coming into your life for you to see that.

Our shadows cast out across the snowy ground. It wasn't often that I would ever take the time to stop and really take in something so intimate, but it was obvious to me that we truly belonged together.

When the song ended and jumped over to a Chris Stapleton song, I removed her arms and nodded for her to follow me. I opened the old leather trunk my grandfather used when he was young and pulled out a bunch of blankets. I laid them on the hay like I used to do as a kid and made us a makeshift bed.

Ellie and I would spend most of our summers up here. Sometimes we would pretend we lived in the boxcar of a train. Our favorite thing was to go up there whenever there was a storm. We both still loved storms.

"Come here." I pulled her down and waited until she tucked herself in beside me. The way we were lying, we could see the outside, and we watched as big, fat snowflakes drifted past the light of the open loft doors.

Her hand inched its way up my shirt and started to outline my stomach.

"You're so warm."

"I guess that's why I love the cold so much." I sighed, loving how she felt next to me.

"I love the cold too, but I'm never as warm as you are right now."

I moved the blankets up higher before I flipped my body over top of hers.

"Maybe I can help you with that. I have plenty of heat to share." I grinned.

"Yes, please." She used her leg to brush by my growing erection before she undid her jeans. "They say the best way to stay warm is to be skin to skin."

"That they do." I pulled my shirt over my head and

shimmied out of my jeans while she stripped down to her panties and bra. I slowly dragged my fingers from her ankle up to her thigh, and continued to her stomach, then I flattened my hand out and felt her muscles twitch and tighten. I dipped my thumb down and found her greedy bud swollen and ready.

Her hands covered her face, and she granted me a soft moan.

"Sloane, let me see your face." She dropped her hands and bunched the blanket in her fists.

I continued to massage her until she was slick and ready. Her legs squeezed my sides and drew me forward.

"Hungry, are we?" I chuckled. "Me too." I dragged my tongue from the bottom of her opening, between her folds, and blew a stream of warm air across her sensitive skin.

"John," she half laughed and cried a plea for relief.

I glanced up at her nipples that were tight little peaks. Her body was ready, and as much I as wanted to play and explore, I wanted to give her what she wanted.

Pushing two fingers inside her, I hovered over her and watched her wild eyes as they latched on to mine. The moment I did, I knew I couldn't hold out any longer.

I pulled free and held the base of my erection and sank ever so slowly into the woman who had flipped my life upside down. Her back bowed the deeper I went. I didn't stop until I was fully in. She was warm, tight, and soft. If I could live anywhere in the world, it would be right here.

Sloane suddenly reached up and pulled herself to straddle me, so we were both sitting upright. She held on to my neck and let her hair fall like a curtain around us. Her smile touched her eyes, and the skin on her chest blushed bright pink.

Slowly, she started to rock back and forth and from side to side. I moved my hands down her back and anywhere else I could reach.

"Meet me at the peak?" I grinned at my reference to our approaching orgasms.

Her pace was too slow, and I started to feel like I was losing self-control. With both hands, I held on to her hips and thrusted deeper, which forced her forward to bend over my shoulder with a throaty groan.

I repeated the action a few more times until I felt her shake and moan through an orgasm. I licked her neck and nibbled on her ear and picked up the pace again.

Hot licks of anticipation lashed at my skin, sweat broke out across my back, and with my last deep thrust, I held on to Sloane with all my strength and bared my vulnerability.

A sea of colors and sounds filled my head, which seemed to go on forever. I rode the wave without a care in the world.

When I came back, she was putty in my arms. I carefully laid her next to me and wiped her silky hair off her forehead.

"Hey," I kissed her mouth and felt her chuckle against my lips, "you know you can give a man a complex laughing so soon after sex." I pretended to scowl.

"No," she laughed harder and shimmied to sit up on her elbows pointed at something, "I'm thinking we just scared the shit out of Doug for life."

I tossed my head back and laughed with her. "Trust me, the things I've seen on this farm, they all owe me."

She covered her eyes and laughed harder. "Thanks for that visual."

"Anytime, babe." I twisted so I leaned up against a bale of hay, thankful for the blanket behind me. I gently guided her to sit between my legs and wrapped a blanket around her body then wrapped my arms around her shoulders, giving her neck a kiss.

The snow came down harder now, collecting a small amount along the edge of the doors. Sloane yawned and rested her head on my arm.

"Are we crazy?"

"It depends on who you're asking," I joked.

"Can we even do this?"

"You mean date?"

"Yeah, I mean, I know the others have, but their situations are different. Will it even be allowed?"

"I'm guessing, since you're already vetted, and Frank knows you well. I mean, you're living at Shadows, and you're working for us. I think it's safe to say yes."

She nodded with another yawn, and I knew she wasn't long for this world. Then something hit me, and I struggled to find the right way to ask.

"Sloane?"

"Mmm?" she murmured.

"I think the bigger question is, would you leave your life in Washington to live at Shadows with me?"

I held my breath, unsure whether I was asking something too soon.

"Would *you* leave Shadows to be in Washington with me, John?" She shifted to get more comfortable while I digested what she was asking of me. We both stayed quiet and watched the storm in front of us, wondering who would speak first.

I think I would leave, and that scares the shit out of me.

/ # SIXTEEN

"Hey," Oliver stood in the doorway of the study, "I thought you might like something stronger than tea." He set a cup of coffee on the desk and glanced at my computer screen.

"Thank you. I needed this."

"You've been in here a lot the past couple of days."

"Yeah." I nodded and pulled off my glasses to rub my tired eyes. "I found something that has nagged at me since. It keeps leading me back to the same person, but I'm not sure why."

"Well," he in the sat on the edge of the couch and hung his head as he thought, "maybe that person is trying to tell you something?"

"Maybe." I shrugged. "The only problem is he's dead."

"The dead can still speak." He smiled. "You just need to open yourself up for the signs."

I moved my gaze back to the computer screen and pulled my notes free. I thought for a moment, and things suddenly started to click. The change in my expression must have been obvious.

"Run with it, dear." Oliver gave my shoulder a pat as he left me alone to follow my new train of thought.

It wasn't until eleven that night that I climbed onto the couch. It was as if once I started to follow more clues, I couldn't stop the flow. I wasn't sure when I passed out, but my phone rang at 4:45 and jolted me awake.

"Hel—" I cleared the fog away from my throat. "Hello?"

"Hey, honey." My father's voice made me swing my legs in front of me. "I got you cleared, but you'd need to leave in fifteen to make the flight. Can you do that?"

"Yup, yes." I shut my computer and slipped it into my bag.

"You were right, and I do believe you're on to something. Your gut has never steered you wrong, so go with it, but if you get into trouble—"

"I'll call, Dad. I promise."

"Text me when you land."

"Will do. Thanks!"

I tossed the phone in my bag and quietly rushed upstairs, careful not to wake anyone. John's room was empty, but I didn't have time to wonder where he was.

My luck, he was out working on some crazy farm machinery, like he was forbidden to do.

In record time, I showered and packed enough for three days and hoped that if I needed to stay longer, I could find a laundromat.

A cold gust of wind shot down my jacket as I pushed my suitcase out the door and onto the porch. Holy sweet hell, it was freezing! I checked the time and saw I was cutting it close, but I had to say goodbye. The spotlight helped me locate Tripper staring up at the loft in the barn. I made my way over and thought about the last time I was there with John a week ago. Both of us had pretended we hadn't asked the other to move in with each other. Truth be told, there was nothing keeping me in Washington. My brother was going to move closer to here, anyway. I just wasn't ready to admit anything to myself yet. John seemed too good to be true sometimes, and if we were allowed to date and we were meant to be together, we could revisit that conversation later. I had been burned too many times with men. I wasn't bitter or jaded, I was just realistic and cautious.

"John," I called into the frigid morning air. I swore my breath came out and froze in place. "Black!" I tried the name the guys used.

A dark figure appeared above me, and Tripper's tail started to wag.

"Sloane?"

"Can you come down real quick?"

He reached out for something and rappelled down the

rope like a friggin' fireman on a pole. But the pole was, like, twenty feet high, and he was still supposed to be in recovery.

Once his feet hit the ground, he turned on that sexy smile that always made my stomach coil into a warm knot.

"You're up early." He went to take a step toward me, but his eyes caught my suitcase in the middle of the driveway. "What's going on?"

"I found something." I checked my watch again and cursed the taxi for being late.

"Did you get clearance to leave?"

"I don't need clearance to leave." I lifted an eyebrow. "I'm not at Shadows."

"Sloane, the last time you left, you got yourself into trouble."

"Wow." I held up a hand. "First, I'm a guest at Shadows—"

"Hey," he took my hand and pulled me closer, "don't get snappy about the fact that I care what happens to you. I didn't mean it like that." He wrapped his big arms around my waist, and I rested my hands on his chest. "I just meant did you let Frank know you were leaving?"

"Of course, I did. Who do you think booked my ticket?"

"Okay." He paused, but I could tell he wanted to say something else.

"What?"

"Why are you pissy?"

"Because you're supposed to be resting, and instead, you're out here doing God knows what and rappelling down twenty-foot ropes. What if you fell or couldn't hold on?"

He tossed his head back and laughed. "I've dropped down from a lot higher and in a lot of worse situations." He kissed my lips quickly. "I'll be okay."

"You think?" I lifted my eyebrow at him again then let my smile turn into an evil one as a plan was hatched.

"What does that look mean?"

I shrugged as the lights from the taxi lit us up.

"I'll call once I've landed. I'll be in Missouri, Indiana, and possibly Iowa."

"When will you be back?"

"When I get what I'm looking for, I guess."

"Miss?" The taxi driver stood by the vehicle after he put my belongings inside.

"Coming." I turned back to John and gave him a long kiss. He held me tight like he couldn't let go. I didn't want to go, but I knew I had to.

"Be careful," he breathed into my ear then took a step backward.

"I will." I rushed to the taxi and was about to step inside when he called out.

"Babe?" He waited for me to look back. "What did that look mean?"

My evil smile returned and raced across my face as I laughed darkly into the cold air.

"Call you soon." I blew him a kiss before I shut the door and disappeared into the taxi.

I raced to make my flight and checked in just as my gate was about to close. I hurried to my seat and sent a quick text to John letting him know I'd made it.

I was surprised to find the flight was pretty empty. Maybe it was because no one wanted to go to Missouri in the winter. I smiled to myself and pulled up Mike's number and sent him a text. He was kind enough to give it to me at the hospital after Ellie's little moment and explained we were a family and if I needed anything to call him. My phone lit up on my lap, and I quickly sent it to voicemail. Frank could wait. I got my clearance to leave. The rest could wait.

Once we taxied and started our takeoff, I closed my eyes and let my mind slip into work mode.

———

"Miss." A man with a huge scar across his neck greeted me at the table with a polite nod. I had slept like a log when I finally got to my hotel, and somehow was able to flag down a cab despite the amount of snow that was falling.

"Greenburg, correct?" I settled into a chair.

"Yes, ma'am." He prattled off his rank and what tours he'd done.

"Please, sit." I motioned to the chair across from me. "I really appreciate you agreeing to speak with me today."

"With all due respect, it beats being in there." He

pointed to a cubicle where he was a call center support tech.

"What brought you here?" I knew, but I wanted to hear his version of it.

He pulled down the collar of his shirt to show me more of his scar. "Wrong place, wrong time, didn't clear the room right and paid the price."

"Honorable discharge?"

"Something like that, yeah." He rolled his eyes. "It was not how I saw my life going, but I got my girl pregnant, so here I am, trying to make enough to support us."

"That's very responsible of you."

He shrugged at my comment, and I could tell he wasn't good at taking compliments.

"I'm just going to jump in." I pulled my glasses on and twirled a pen around my fingers. "Tell me about training with Nick Stewart."

He closed his eyes. "That fucking guy," he muttered.

"Not a fan?"

"He was a spoiled brat. He came from money, and we all know with money comes power, whether you deserve it or not." He snorted.

"Go on." I started to jot down my notes.

"When you start off in the Army, everyone is equal. You earn your stripes with hard work and discipline. You earn the respect of those around you, and you recognize your rank and act accordingly." His thumb brushed across his nose as he twitched. "Not that way for Stewart."

"How so?" My pen didn't stop, but I kept my gaze on

him. There was a lot of hate in this man that simmered just below the surface.

"Look," he leaned forward and lowered his voice, "I'm not a snitch. I'm proud of what I've accomplished, but Stewart, he bullshitted his way to the top while we all carried his load. There's no brotherhood in that. That's all I know about it."

I was clear Greenburg wasn't going to open up much further, so I reached in my bag and pulled out the folder that held Stewart's autopsy report. I flipped it open and set it in front of him.

"I'm not asking you to be a snitch. I'm just trying to figure out who the guy was because he was dropped into a world that got him killed within a matter of weeks."

Greenburg eyed me then pulled the file closer and scanned the paperwork, while I studied his face for any remorse. None showed.

"Doesn't surprise me." He shut the file and pushed it toward me.

"Look," I rubbed my forehead and decided to take another tactic, "my friends are in some real trouble. Good Army men who worked their way up the ladder and earned their place just like you did. Something bad is happening here, and I need to understand who Nick Stewart was in order to help them. So, please, can you offer me anything?"

He cursed under his breath and seemed to make a decision. "Let me put it to you the way I see it. His parents have money, and they're good friends with the general who was overseeing our unit while we were training for the test."

I shifted in my seat as my neck heated. "Do you recall the general's name?"

"Even if I did, I'm taking that one to the grave."

Of course, he was.

"All I know is he failed the test, and the very next day he was being pulled from training to take it again."

"Did he ever say why he got to take it again?"

He smirked darkly. "He said his test got lost and that they needed him to do it again. Three days later, he was bragging about being picked up by an elite team. Normally, we'd call bullshit, but Stewart got what Stewart wanted."

"No one ever questioned him or confronted him?"

He chuckled lightly. "Nope."

"Why? Were you scared of him?"

"No, ma'am, not him."

"Oh, the general." I nodded at him, and he gave me an eyebrow.

"Okay," I sifted through my files and opened the last one to show him a drawing, "one last thing." I held it up. "Does this mean anything to you?"

He squinted at it before he took it from my fingers.

"Seven Webs," he muttered, and I could tell he was searching his memory. "I'm not sure. At first glance, I would rule out an Army tattoo. There isn't much to it."

"What if I told you it was used as a nickname for someone?"

He rubbed his bottom lip and thought again. "Nothing rings a bell, but I can ask around if you'd like."

"I would. Thank you."

Twenty more minutes went by, and I finally got him to give me the name of someone else to talk to, Mason. Stewart's bunkmate. I thanked him for his time and raced down to the coffee shop to grab a sandwich.

Just as I sat down, my phone rang.

"Hello?" I chased my dry mouth down with some water.

"Hey, you." John's voice sounded quiet. "How's it going?"

"Interesting." I brushed the crumbs from my fingers while I dug out my notebook.

"Good or bad interesting?"

"I'm not really sure yet." I pulled my phone away from my ear to look at it when I saw another call coming through. "I'm sorry, John, but I'm waiting on this call. I have to go. I'll call you back, okay?"

"Yup, no problem. Be safe."

"I will. Bye!"

I hit the button and connected to the new line. "This is Sloane Harlow."

"Miss Harlow, this is Mason Leaves, returning your call."

"Hi. Thank you for the call back." Again, another call came through. It was Frank, but I sent it to voicemail. He and my father both wanted to get a full report of what I was doing, but I didn't have the headspace for that conversation, so everyone could just hold on for a few days.

"I, ah…" I tried to think. "I wanted to ask you a few questions about Nick Stewart." I waited, anxious if he'd say anything. There was a long pause before he cleared his throat.

"What would you like to know?"

"He died a few months ago, and I'm trying to understand who he was."

"How?"

"Murdered."

"So, karma does exist." He seemed more amazed than anything else.

"I'm not going to beat around the bush here, Mason. He was working with some friends of mine, and things went very bad. I'm just trying to understand this guy a little more."

"Why? Do you think he was in on something?"

The next question fell from my mouth without thought when he asked that. "Do you think he would flip?"

"It's no secret that our unit despised that weasel. He was rich, entitled, but dumb as a post. He could barely remember his left from his right. He carried a little notebook around with notes of simple everyday things just so he wouldn't look stupid when he was given a command."

"Is that how he passed his test?"

"He never passed, but his parents got him pushed through because of their relationship with the general."

"General." I paused and waited.

"You seem real nice, Miss Harlow, but something like that, you'll have to find out on your own."

Damn. "Can I ask you one question?"

"You can. Doesn't mean I'll answer it."

"Was it General Csaba?" I wasn't sure if I wanted the answer or not.

There was another long pause, and my stomach crept into my throat.

"No."

I sagged into my seat and sighed with relief. I wasn't proud of myself for going there, but let's be honest, my father didn't have the best reputation.

"Thank you, Mason. I appreciate your time."

"Miss Harlow?"

"Yes?"

"Greenburg put out a text about you poking around about the general. You'd be wasting your time hunting down the rest of the men. They won't speak to you."

"Fair enough." I figured as much. Damn, I wished I had started with someone else.

The line went dead.

SEVENTEEN

JOHN

"Hey, man, just checking in." Cole sounded just as frustrated as I was being told to stay put. We could do nothing until we got word to return to Mexico. There had been very limited communication with North Rock, and the last we'd heard from Chamness was that they were missing another man. We were told that the four other team members in the hospital would not be returning to duty anytime soon, if ever. Frank mentioned something about filing the paperwork for their honorable discharges.

What the ever-loving fuck was happening here?

A selfish part of me was happy they hadn't been called out while I was on leave, but then guilt and rage filled the holes when I remembered I wasn't the one trying to survive in the bush being hunted by the enemy.

"When is Sloane coming back?" Cole asked.

"Tomorrow sometime." I neatly packed my duffle bag to prepare for my return to Shadows. I just needed to wait for clearance from Frank. "However, I think it might be more like three before she'll get here. She went flying down a rabbit hole, and I was warned to let her be because this is what she does best." I chuckled as I thought of Frank's face when I told him she still wasn't home. He told me a story about how she went rogue for weeks and didn't surface until she'd found something to prove her client's innocence. Scared her parents pretty good.

"Hang on one second. What?" There was a pause, and I heard a scuffled sound. "Livi wants to talk to you."

"Sure." I pulled my Army boots from the bag and put my snow boots in their place.

"Uncle John." Livi's little grown up voice carried over the line clearly and assertively, just like her father.

"Hi, Livi. How are you doing?"

"Well, thank you. Have you been practicing?"

I smirked. "I was going to ask you the same thing. Yes, I have. Have you been?"

"Of course. How are you feeling? Are you sure you're okay to…" She didn't finish her sentence because we had been keeping this secret for nearly four months.

"I wouldn't miss it for the world." I grinned and pictured her happy face. "Why do you think I rested up?"

She laughed. "Sloane's been outing you, Uncle John. She texted Uncle Mike and Daddy and told them you weren't listening to the doctor's orders."

Oh, is that so? Now I knew why she was smirking the night she left.

"Sloane hasn't been here for nearly seven days. She doesn't know if I'm resting and not following orders."

"When, Daddy?" Her voice muffled a bit as she spoke to Cole. "Can I stay on the phone until then?" She giggled, which made me miss home even more.

"How have the twins been?"

"Ugh, they were misbehaving the other day, so I convinced them to play a barrel roll game, and, well, you know those barrels that you guys use for your workouts?"

"Yeah, I do."

"You know the ones with the lids?"

I started to respond, then I caught what she was saying and burst out laughing.

"How long did you trap them for?" I loved this kid.

"Until Auntie Mia was looking for them. Butters gave them away."

"What did Daddy do?"

"Nothing until Auntie looked away, then he high fived me." I could hear her giggle again.

"Not everything has to be repeated, Liv," Cole said from somewhere.

"When it's funny, it should be, Daddy."

I chuckled but perked up when I heard Tripper and then wheels on the driveway.

"Sounds like they deserved it." I took the stairs three at a time and whisked past my mother, who was complaining about making dinner.

"What are you doing?" Livi must have sensed I was distracted.

"I see one of our SUVs coming up my driveway."

"Really?" She seemed interested.

I could picture her sitting at Cole's big desk chair while he was probably stretched out on his couch looking over a file. He loved when she came into his office. He was always so busy that he didn't get as much time with her as he'd like. He even went so far as to build her a little desk and chair so she could work alongside him. She used it sometimes but preferred to sit at his desk when she could.

"What the hell?" Mike, Keith, Mark, Savannah, and Mia all piled out of the SUV with bags in their hands. "Um, Livi, I have to go."

"Don't be mad, Uncle John. They have a good reason for it."

My mind did a circle as her words sank into my head. What was going on? Panic spread through me. The guys didn't know what Ellie was really like. I'd hadn't shared that, and it was a choice I'd consciously made.

I hurried out to the front porch and closed the door behind me, hoping Ellie wouldn't follow me.

"Hey, stranger." Savannah moved her tray full of something out of the way as she kissed my cheek.

"Hey, ah, what are you guys doing here?"

"We wanted to be here sooner, but we had some stuff to finish for Frank." Mike stepped aside to let the others in, and again I wanted to cringe. They'd never done this before.

"Do what, exactly?" I hugged Mia and welcomed Mark's slap to the shoulder.

"We brought food, groceries, booze." Keith held up a twenty-four pack of beer.

Mike followed Keith inside, and I mentally cursed the potential shitstorm that was about to happen.

"Look, guys, this is too kind, but really, I'm back tomorrow. You don't need to do this."

"Hello, Mrs. Black." Mark removed the tin foil on Savannah's famous lasagna. "Any chance you can heat the oven to three-fifty?" He wiggled his eyebrows at my mother. Christ, this was not happening.

"This, oh…" My mother's hands went to her face, and I could tell she was happy to see them all over. "What a treat!"

"Where's your pops?" Keith looked out at the barn.

"He'll be back any moment." I went to say more, but my attention was drawn by Mike, who motioned for me to join him in the living room.

I eyed Ellie as she appeared at the top of the stairs, listening to what was going on.

"I know." Mike's voice was steady as he bumped my shoulder. I tried to read his expression.

"Know what?"

"Look, John, when you were at the hospital, Sloane

and I went downstairs to get some air, and we ran into Ellie. She was, ah, pretty upset. Sloane took charge and was able to calm her. I get not telling us. We all have versions of ourselves we'd like to keep private, but this is different. You needed help, and you should have asked us."

My blood rushed through my veins, and the sound in my ears was almost deafening. I hated this topic. I hated that the moment it was brought up, I felt the noose around my neck tighten and the guilt rip through my body.

"I'm sorry about Ellie, John. I can't imagine how it must be for all of you. I'm also going to assume that was why she didn't stick around long at my wedding."

"I wanted to give my parents a break, and I thought I was ready. But she saw something that triggered her memory, flipped out, and had to leave. I wasn't about to ruin your big day." I spoke the truth and hesitated to go on, but I had to ask. "What did Sloane tell you?" I needed to know if the woman I loved had told my darkest most painful secret.

"When I questioned Sloane in the elevator, she clammed up and wouldn't answer me. Man," he grinned, "she had the best Blackstone line. Made me proud that you found our kind of woman."

The air rushed out of me, and for the first time in a very long time I felt like I could breathe. The truth being out there took away the tension in my stomach, and I almost felt lightheaded.

"Sloane did out you for rappelling down the barn, though." He laughed and turned me back toward the kitchen. "Like I said, you found our type of woman. They love us hard and will make sure you follow the damn rules."

"Yeah," I huffed in agreement.

"Look," Mike leaned into the wall and sipped his beer, "I don't know the whole story, and that's fine, but what I do know is the look of a man who's carrying a level of guilt on his shoulders. No matter what sequence of events led up to the accident, no one could have predicted that particular truck would have been there at the exact time Ellie was. What happens afterwards is what counts. Life's a bitch, and we're only along for the ride, so let that shit go before it eats you alive."

He was right, but it would take time to shed the armor I'd worn for these past years.

The scene in the kitchen felt surreal. My father was smiling and being served some garlic bread by Savi, and Mia was insisting my mother join him while they fussed around making sure that when I left for Shadows, they would be well taken care of.

I leaned against the wall and watched how my two families moved about as one. Laughter, playful insults, and horrible flirting on Mark's end happily bounced from the walls.

"What's going on?" Ellie slipped up next to me, with a careful eye on our company. Instead of being full of concern for what might happen, I just smiled over at my twin.

"Our friends are here for dinner."

"Oh, cool." She took a step into the kitchen and sat down. Not one person acted any differently, and when Keith handed her a plate, she took it with a thank you.

My parents both looked over at her, and when my mom's glossy eyes found mine, she mouthed, "Did Sloane do this?"

I shrugged because she may or may not have initiated the gathering, but I knew she was the reason for all of this.

I wished she was here.

"Hungry, Black?" Keith held up a plate for me.

"I am." I pushed off the wall and joined my family.

The cold found its way inside my lungs, and I relished the sting that settled deep down inside my chest. A part of me felt guilty for having a good time when North Rock was stuck in a humid hell, but sometimes you just needed to let loose and clear your head.

"This is gonna hurt like a son-of-a-bitch." Mike grinned and held the frozen leather between his fingers. "Ready?"

"Bring it, like your sister did the other night," Mark taunted him as I shook my head at Keith. I knew he understood what was about to happen.

"But wait." Savi popped her head up and lost her formation *again*. "Which sister?"

"Which sister?" Mike hissed.

"Well, yeah." Mia joined in and spoke to Savi. "One and Four have the looks for sure."

"But I can see Three being more Mark's type."

"Yes," Mia pointed to Savi, "I can see that too."

Mike stood and rubbed the spot between his eyes. "No more wives in the game."

Savannah made a run for Mike while Mia bolted in the other direction. Savi slipped the ball out of Mike's hand and tossed it to Mia, who ran like the wind down to the spray-painted line and tossed it on the ground with her arms in the air.

"Power of distraction, ladies!" She high fived Savannah, and Mike and I let our heads fall with defeat.

"This is your fault," Keith hissed at Mark, who looked thoroughly entertained by his wife.

"She's so fucking hot right now." Mark raced over to Mia and scooped her up with a kiss.

"No more Mark either," Mike muttered behind us.

"Where is Cole?" I joined Mike on the fence when I felt my phone go off. I held up a finger to him and started down toward the patio.

"Hey, babe, I was starting to think you forgot about me."

"Never." Her laugh turned into a yawn. "Sorry, but I needed to clear something up, and I finally got the answer I was looking for. I'm in Nebraska tonight and then

Casper, Wyoming tomorrow, then hopefully tomorrow or the next day I can come home."

Warmth shot through my chest. I loved that she wanted to come back, not to mention she said the word *home*. "Do you have a lead for us?"

"Maybe, but I just need one more thing to connect the dots."

"You want to talk about it?" I would talk about the weather just to hear her voice right now.

"I wish you were here in this bed with me."

I closed my eyes and pictured her in bed under me. "Oh, you have no idea how much I wish I could be." Suddenly, I remembered something. "What about the next best thing? Mom and Ellie will be in Casper tomorrow for a specialist appointment."

"Really?" That seemed to perk her up some.

"Yeah. Why don't you see if you can meet up with them for lunch?"

"I'd love that. I'll text her once we hang up." There was a long pause before I heard her shift in her blankets. "John?"

"Yeah?"

"Nothing is holding me there."

"Holding you where?"

"Washington."

Oh!

"Are you saying you'd move here?" I held my breath and pressed my lips together for her answer.

"If I had a reason to stay, I would."

"Am I not enough of a reason?" I grinned like a sixteen-year-old boy who just had his first graze with a boob.

"Add Tripper to the pot, and then it would be enough," she teased. "But, John, I want you to know something."

"Okay." I wished she was here. I wanted to get my hands on her to hold her, stroke her, make her eyes do that thing they did. My body ached for her touch. I forced myself to focus on her words.

"John, I'm not looking to get married and have children right now, you understand. I love what I do and don't want to have to put things on hold because of a wedding or even to have kids because they are what comes next after that band of gold."

I swallowed hard at her words, amazed that she was even voicing what I had run through my own head many times over the past few weeks. I turned and watched Mike run after Mark then body slam him into a snowbank. Mia and Savi were sledding across the icy driveway.

"John?"

"I'll make you a deal." I leaned my forearms on the railing. "Let me marry you, and the rest can fall into place whenever. There are enough kids at the house right now, and I'm not in a hurry for any either. But you have to let me make you mine officially."

"No," she retorted, but I heard her amusement in my offer.

"Yes, and I will give you a steel ring, not gold."

She laughed.

"Come on, Sloane, you know my charm will win you over."

"This is hardly romantic, John."

"Oh, you want romance?" I chuckled playfully. "Okay, I can do romance."

"Oh my God! And who said I would say yes to marriage?"

"Me, because," I changed my tone to a serious one, "if you love me even a tenth of how much I love you, then you would say yes."

Silence.

I waited because I wasn't joking. It was the truth, I loved her more than I ever imagined I could. If she needed a moment to let that sink in, then so be it. I wasn't going anywhere.

"I love you, John, and I never wanted to fall in love with someone in the Army, but that's where I am now. Just let me get through this, and we can talk. Okay?"

I smiled at Savi, who gave me a thumbs up, asking if everything was okay. I gave her a wave and knew Sloane needed time to process. Her life would be changed more than mine would be.

"Okay," I brushed the snow off my gloves, "I'll wait for now."

She let out a long sigh. "Why do I think something more is coming?"

"Have you ever heard of how Keith won over Lexi?"

"Not really, no."

"Well," I laughed a little, and Mark looked over, "let's just say we Blackstone men don't give up easily."

"I can tell." I could hear her smile through her words. "I should get some sleep. I'll call you after ten."

"Night, babe."

"Night."

EIGHTEEN

The last soldier from Nick Stewart's class never showed up for our meeting. A part of me wasn't surprised. The news had spread fast that I was digging. Problem was, they thought I was trying to uncover who the general was who was probably being paid off, but he was never my focus. Well, to be fair, now that I knew it wasn't my father, I couldn't care less.

But where lies were buried, guilty consciences were never far from the surface. I just wished I could have had three minutes alone with this guy to ask one question and watch his face as he answered. I found it incredible that these guys hated Nick so much that when I said he had been killed not even a flicker of remorse could be detected. Clearly, Nick had been a sore spot for all of them in the class, and it was obvious he was a source of resentment and anger for them when he had been accepted into North Rock right out of training. But aside from all that, regardless of how he got there, Nick had been killed by the cartel on one of his very first missions. Somehow the cartel were one step ahead of Blackstone, and that was what bothered me more.

How?

I rubbed my hands over my face and wished I could move just one step forward in this case. Something was there, most likely staring me in the face. I simply needed to mute the white noise to find out what I was missing.

"Am I happy to see your face!" Kelly wrapped her arms around me and kissed my cheek. "Ellie, come take a seat."

"Hey, Ellie, remember me? I'm Sloane, a friend of your brother's." I addressed her, but I could tell she was tired by the way her eyelids looked heavy. "How was your day?"

"Long." She took the water from the waitress and began to pull the straw out of the paper wrapper.

We ordered and made small talk. She told me how everyone had shown up at the house and brought food, and that John had eased up and really enjoyed himself.

"John has many smiles," Kelly beamed with pride, "and the one he had on when he and Mike came back from talking in the living room made an old one surface. I think I'm finally getting all of him back."

"That's so wonderful." I grinned at Ellie as she studied my expression. "What's on your mind, Ellie?"

"Nothing." Her gaze moved to the window.

"He has developed a new smile too." Kelly leaned back and played with her tea string. An interesting expression played over her face. "One I haven't seen before."

"Oh, yeah?" I loved hearing what made John happy. "When does that one come out?"

"When he looks at you," Ellie cut in, and I saw that same expression on her face.

I felt my neck blush. I wasn't embarrassed—more flattered, I supposed. "That's nice." I sipped my water for something to do.

"Mom," Ellie picked at her sweater, "I think John likes Sloane."

Kelly laughed at the innocence of her daughter. "I think so too."

"So," I tried to get the focus off of me, "how often do you have appointments here?" I ate about a third of my burger in one bite. Oh, my God. I had no idea how hungry I was.

"Four times a year. We don't have to see Dr. Leak, but he's been with Ellie since the accident, and when he moved down here, we followed. It was fine at first. I could visit my cousin, but now Ellie doesn't like going there, so it's just an in and out trip."

"They talk a lot about stuff that doesn't make sense." Ellie shrugged.

I glanced at the time and thought it might be fun for Ellie and me to go out. Perhaps I could give Kelly a little fun.

"Why don't Ellie and I go get our nails done and maybe go see a movie while you visit your cousin?"

Kelly's face brightened, but it quickly disappeared.

"No, I can't do that. I don't want you to think that every time I see you, I'm asking for help."

"I don't think that," I assured her. "It honestly makes me feel good to help. Plus, Ellie is fun, and I get all the dirt on John."

She laughed, but I could see she was still uneasy.

"Well, here's a thought. Why don't you call your cousin and see if she wants to meet you somewhere around here? We'll all stay close, and you still get to have some much-needed Kelly time."

"I-I," she stumbled, "I could do that. Okay, yes." She beamed with excitement. "Thanks!"

Once Kelly got her plans in order, Ellie and I headed out into the chilly early afternoon.

"What would you like to do first? Nails or movie?"

"Movie." She nodded. "I don't like the taste of the polish when I eat popcorn."

"Fair enough." I pointed in the direction we needed to go. "Let's head that way."

As we crossed the street, I noticed someone was walking straight for us. I gently took Ellie by the arm to avoid a collision, but the guy never even wavered in his step.

"Hey," I called out, "you almost pushed us into the street."

The bald-headed man turned to look at us, and the way he held eye contact made me uneasy.

"Sorry." He gave me a nod and rushed on to turn the corner.

I smiled at Ellie and shook my head with a laugh. "Some people can be rude."

"A lot of people are rude," she added.

We bought our tickets to see the second *Jumanji* movie and grabbed some junk food before choosing our seats. Just when the credits started, two men sat directly in front of us.

"Seriously?" I hissed, wondering why when there was more than half the theater open to them, they had to sit right in front of us. Another two man came and sat on either end of our row. It took me a moment to realize that this was no coincidence. The few other people who were in the theater were nowhere near us.

I wasn't a stupid person. I had been around enough crime to recognize that cold prickle of adrenaline that inched its way up your spine was your subconscious giving you a heads up something was very wrong.

The movie started, and I tried to even out my breathing. I focused on the first letter of each name in the opening credits and compared them to the names of people I knew. When the third name popped up, I noticed the man to my left glanced over for a few beats.

"Oh, my God," I whispered, but the last word got caught in my throat as the man I'd seen earlier on the street started to walk up the stairs toward us. He stopped at the end of the row and slipped by the other man and took the seat right next to me.

My blood drained to my feet as the rest of me tried to hold it together. I reached over for Ellie's arm, but she was already engulfed in watching the movie and didn't even notice what was going on.

"Miss Harlow," the man muttered, "Henry would like to speak with you."

Shit.

"Like I told Henry before, and like I'm telling you now, there is nothing I can do for any of you."

I was so scared that the heartbeat in my ears almost made me sick.

The leather from his jacket squeaked when he leaned closer. "I think by now you'd know that's not the answer he is looking for. So, why don't you use that pretty little head of yours and start thinking about a solution? Because he is right outside, and this time you won't have your Army friend to save you."

My frozen fingers squeezed Ellie's arm tighter to grab her attention. "Time to go, Ellie."

"What?" She looked around. "But the movie just started."

"I know. I'm sorry, but we need to go."

I hauled her to her feet and waited for the man to move out of my way.

"I wouldn't do that if I were you," he called after me.

"Who are they?" Ellie sensed my fear and took my hand and held on tightly.

"Not good people." I headed out to the lobby, but the place was dead. "What did they do, clear this whole place out?"

Even in my bubble of fear, I managed to steer myself in the right direction and spotted the front doors. I nearly dragged poor Ellie as I focused on our escape route.

Just as I stepped out the front, a door opened to a town car that was parked directly across from us. Out stepped Henry.

"Sloane." He fiddled with his cufflink, and it was then that I noticed a new scar that traveled from inside his shirt up across his neck to just below his ear. The new pink skin that covered it was highlighted by the sunlight amplifying his evil expression.

"Ellie," I pulled her back inside the lobby, "when I say run, I need you to run as fast as you can."

"Where do I go?"

"Anywhere, but far from here, okay?"

"I don't know." She looked at me, confused.

The assholes from the theater now blocked the exit on the other side of the lobby.

"Dammit."

I whirled around and saw someone open the front doors for Henry.

Think, Sloane!

The bathrooms wouldn't be smart. They didn't even have windows. There may be an exit in the kitchen, but I couldn't risk getting stuck in there. I moved my frantic gaze around the place and realized I only had one more option.

"Come on." I pushed the big black double doors open and pulled Ellie into a dark theater where *A Quiet Place, Part Two* was playing. The theater was fairly packed as we raced in front of the screen. Only a few dirty looks were thrown as we pushed through a sea of legs and I helped Ellie into a seat. I bent down next to her, ignoring a lady's rude comment next to me.

"Ellie," I whispered, "I need you to stay here."

"I don't want to."

I took her hand and pleaded with her. "I'm so sorry, but these bad men are here looking for me when we were supposed to be having a fun girls' day. I promise if you sit still, I will come back for you. Just promise me you won't move from this seat. Please, Ellie."

A scary part of the movie popped up, and she squeezed her eyes closed. "I don't like scary movies."

I took her head between my hands so she'd look at me. "I don't either, so go to your happy place up here." I tapped her forehead. "Be with John and find more pebbles."

Tears flooded my eyes when the magnitude of what could happen to Ellie hit me hard.

"Please, please stay put for me."

Her eyes squeezed shut, and she started to mumble something. I saw the bald-headed man walk through the side door and scan the faces of the crowd.

I ducked down. I needed to get the hell away from

Ellie. I peeked between some heads when I saw him turn to talk to someone. Pushing to my feet, I kept myself low, and as the crowd jumped at a scary part, I stood and raced past the men. I used my body weight and slammed into the emergency exit and burst into the daylight. It took me a half a second to realize the alarm didn't go off and another second to hear his voice.

"Why are humans so predictable?" Henry shook his head as he walked toward me. "I really wanted more of a fight from you, Sloane. You were always such a spitfire."

A series of emotions plowed through me, but the strongest was to lash out sarcastically. I blamed my father for my tongue. It got me into trouble more often than not as a child.

"Fuck you, Henry. Is this the part where you stuff me into the trunk and drop me off in a lake?" I popped my hip out and tried to look in control when really my bones shook so hard, they threatened to separate from my muscles.

"I tried to give you chances—"

"Chances?" I cut him off. "Chances such as in kidnapping me from my home?"

"You caused that to happen—"

"Spoken like a true abuser."

His lips pressed together, then he nodded at someone behind me, and before I knew it, the bald asshole had his hands all over me.

"Don't touch me!" I punched his arm as he removed my phone and handed it to Henry. I wanted to cry. Not in a million years did I think I would be face to face with these people again. The last time I spoke to Frank, he said things were fine and it was all taken care of.

If I thought for even a moment that Henry was still after me, I would never had agreed to take Ellie out. Let alone meet up with her and her mom or even go on this trip. I still struggled internally with what happened back in my apartment.

"Unlock it," Henry commanded.

"You think I have anything worthwhile in my phone? You know I work with criminals, right?" I dragged my eyes up and down him just to make my point.

"Don't push my limit, Sloane. You may be hot, but I like my women submissive."

Rage burned through me like never before. Here came my father's temper.

"Well, good thing for you I loathe everything about you. You assholes disgust me," I spat.

The bald guy behind me chuckled and mumbled something that sounded like "*She cat,*" and Henry glared at him.

"Okay." He rubbed his chin then threw my phone on the ground and stomped on it. And before I could react, he sucker-punched me in the stomach.

My entire body folded on impact as it drove me backward. I had never been punched in the stomach before, and I instantly knew I never wanted to again. Hot, blinding pain scorched my insides and made my head go fuzzy. Suddenly, I was hauled up straight and pushed against the dirty wall while his men formed a circle around me. Henry bent down to my eye level and proceeded to hike up my shirt as he kissed my cheek with his gross lips.

"No!" I tried to knee him, but he blocked the blow. "Get your fucking hands off me!"

"I don't know, Sloane," he moaned in exaggeration, "maybe I'll change my mind and go for the feisty chick after all." He chuckled as he came in for another peck.

"I'm glad your son is going to rot away in prison." I spat in his face. "The longer he's away from you, the better!"

"The fuck you say?" His eyes went from those I knew to someone completely different. "You little bitch. You think you're so brave, do you?"

"Braver than you," I challenged.

He leaned in and pressed his weight into my arms so I was pinned to the freezing wall. "I was brave enough to pull the trigger on a family who wouldn't pay their debt. I was brave enough to wait you out until you came home, and I was brave enough to find you here alone with some rent-a-friend." He pointed to the door of the theater, and I saw red thinking of Ellie inside.

Be an asshole to me, but don't you dare mention the ones I love!

"Now I'm glad the judge listened to me." I smirked through my lie. "I knew your son was guilty, just like I knew you were involved. All it took was my sad little eyes to convince him to convict your son." His face went red, and for once in my life I was pleased I could pull off a lie with a straight face. Sometimes in the courtroom, a bit of acting helped the case—not that I would ever lie in court. "I wish I was there when those doors slammed shut between the two of you."

"Bitch!" He ripped at my shirt and tore at my pants. My inner tiger came out, and I grew stronger, and even though I was horribly outnumbered, I wasn't going to go down without a fight. "I'm going to show you what I've been wanting to do since the day we met!"

"Screw you!" I managed to wiggle a leg free and lashed out at him.

"Watch out. She's a kicker," one of his men called as Henry felt between my legs.

"Help!" I screamed at the top of my lungs. "Please, someone help me!"

"You think anyone is going to help you? One look at the six of us, and they'll run like the cowards they are." He moved in close, and I felt his breath on my neck. I took that chance to bite down on his ear. He yelped and growled like a wild animal. I spat whatever was in my mouth in his face, only to get another punch to my stomach.

"She's scrappy." One guy laughed, entertained by the whole thing while I once again fought to suck in sweet air.

"Bitch." Henry felt around his wound and glared at me. "I should have finished you the day we left the courtroom."

"But yet, here we are." I coughed and blinked back the dark spots. *Stay focused, Sloane. Fight to the very end.*

"Boss," the bald-headed man looked over his shoulder, "I think we should move this along."

I felt my fight return, and sucked in the deepest breath I could muster, and…

The loudest, scariest cry I'd ever heard a human make stopped mine mid-scream. It took me a moment to realize I wasn't even the one who made it.

Ellie was wild, red in the face, and her arms were locked at her sides. Tears streamed down her cheeks while she moved forward like an unstable maniac. She raced toward Henry, and he jolted back, unsure what she was capable of.

The men jumped back too, and Henry looked around, realizing a lot of attention was being directed our way. Ellie sucked in a deep breath and started to scream again.

I tore free and spun around, breathing wildly. It was as though time stood still, and everything shifted like a movie trying to catch up while buffering.

Three men in business suits approached from the parking lot and called out, asking what was going on.

"Shut her up!" Henry yelled, but when one of the men went for Ellie, she covered her ears and screamed her incredible scream again in his face.

"Help!" I desperately called to the three men, and they started walking toward us. One of them pulled out his cell phone.

"Shit!" Henry waved his hands at the guys. "Get in the fucking car!"

One moment I was inches from being sexually assaulted, and the next I was nearly run over as the car squealed by, only missing me by a hair. I fell to the ground and crumpled into a ball. I may have fight in me, but dammit, I was human and not made for the mob lifestyle.

"Miss!" One man came to my side, and I jumped at his touch. "Sorry." His hands pulled quickly back like I had burned him. "Are you okay?"

Awkwardly, I moved to stand with shaky knees. He offered to help, but I shook my head. I couldn't stand the feel of any man's touch right now. I was too raw and emotionally fragile. I moved as quickly as I could toward Ellie, who was still screaming. I grasped her tightly around the shoulders and hugged her to me.

"Hey, there. It's okay, Ellie. It's okay. I'm going to take you to your mom now." I pushed her hair back from her face. "You can stop yelling." I tried to smile through my own tears and terror. I finally got her to look at me, and her screams faded away.

"Should I call the cops?" The man who had tried to help me held out his phone like he was unsure of his next move.

"No, my father is a cop." Another lie. "I'll call him. Thank you so much for helping, though. We're okay now, honestly."

"We should wait with you until he comes." He looked

concerned, but his friends were all for leaving, and they called out to him to go with them.

"No, I appreciate it, but you've done enough. Thank you." I just wanted to get Ellie back to her mother. "Really, you've done enough," I repeated and caught his look of relief as he turned and left with his friends.

"What was that about? Why were they doing that?" Ellie searched my face for answers.

"They were after me, not you. This had nothing to do with you." Tears spilled out of my eyes and ran down my cheeks. The adrenaline started to leave my body, and I could feel the impact of Henry's punches. "It's okay now. You saved me, Ellie. You did just the right thing."

"John has smiles, and I have screams." She nodded.

"I'm very happy for your screams." I laughed out loud, and she smiled back, uncertain. I knew I had to get us out of there now, before I let what happened seep in to freeze my limbs. Everything hurt inside, but mostly in my heart. I had almost gotten Ellie killed. John would never forgive me for this. This could end us.

With jittery hands, I wrapped my shirt around me and snatched up my broken phone before I took Ellie's hand and we headed toward a nearby coffee shop. My anger grew the closer we got to the safety of the street. When we turned the corner near the shop, and I saw people moving around like normal, it fired an unreasonable anger inside me. The realization that life was going on just a short distance from where I was in a parking lot about to get kidnapped, raped, and beaten to death made me realize how extremely fragile life really was.

"Ellie," I turned to her, "can I ask you for a favor?" I whispered as more pain registered. My tongue was dry, and my head throbbed. "Hey, Ellie, can you keep a secret just between you and me?"

"Do I keep it from Mom, Dad, and John?"

I am officially the worst human ever.

"Yes. Is that too much to ask?"

She thought for a moment, and with every second that passed, I felt guilty for my request. It wasn't fair to ask her to do this, but I needed time to mentally prepare for this to be John's last straw with me.

"I can do that."

"Really?"

"John and I have secrets, like I broke the lamp in the living room last month, not our dog." She pulled on an old memory, and I tried to act normal instead of explaining what I was talking about.

I felt a little of the weight on my shoulders lift. It wouldn't last, but it was nice for now. I guiltily hoped she would forget what happened and our deal, or at least hoped her version of the story wouldn't be too bad.

"Thanks."

"Are you hurt?"

"I'm okay." Third lie of the day.

I managed to clean myself up in the restroom and zip up my coat. Ellie was kind enough to give me a moment for myself and kept her back turned while I gathered myself. I hurried so my dirty-tattered shirt wouldn't be picked up by Kelly, who looked about ten years lighter when she walked through the front door.

"This may go down as one of the best days I've had in years." She hugged me, and I tried not to cry at her mothering touch.

"I'm so happy to hear that." I smiled through the storm inside me.

"Did you ladies have fun?"

"Yes," Ellie answered a little monotone.

"Great!" Kelly was on too big of a high to notice our fake smiles or the fact that you could see that Ellie had been crying. Or maybe that was a normal look for her these days. Either way, I felt the guilt seep through what little armor I had left. "Well, Ellie, say goodbye to Sloane. We need to need to leave before traffic gets too bad."

"It was wonderful to see you both." I slid out of the chair and slowly walked them to their car.

"I'll call you later."

"Actually, I managed to lose my phone somewhere on the way back. I'm going to try to get another before I head back to my hotel."

"Oh, no, I'm sorry honey. I'll let John know too."

"Thanks. I'd appreciate that."

Ellie gave me a wave goodbye, and I watched as they pulled away from the curb. Once they were out of sight, I covered my mouth to stop the sob that wanted to rip through from my core.

When I got back into the hotel room, I switched my

flight to the first one out in the morning. If I never had to leave the safety of Montana for the rest of my life, I would be completely fine with that.

I hit the pillow hard. I needed to rest my head.

———

Davie met me at the airport instead of Dell, and the drive was very quiet. I should have sucked it up and made small talk with him, but my mind was in a dark place, and I wasn't sure I could trust my emotions. He glanced at me a few times and made a few attempts to say something but finally gave up and just drove.

It wasn't until we pulled into a school that I broke through the fog that held me captive.

"Where are we?" I didn't need any more surprises right now. I needed my normal back. My nerves were shot.

"Sue asked if I could bring you here. Something about John."

Davie opened my door for me and offered a hand.

"Yikes, you're frozen, Sloane. I could have turned up the heat if you'd told me."

"Oh, that's okay, Davie. It's just been a long day. I think I'm just tired." I followed him into the front office, where we quickly checked in, and then he steered me toward a gymnasium.

The first three rows were all filled with the familiar

faces of Shadows, and when Kelly spotted me, she stood and made her way over.

"Hello again." She gave me a hug, and Ellie smiled at me then looked away. "I was so hoping you were going to make it."

"What is this?" I tried to sound cheery.

"No clue. Sue called me and said we needed to be at Livi's school at eleven."

A man came up and asked us all to sit. Despite Kelly's request, I stood. I explained that I had been on so many planes lately, and I simply needed to stand. I found a spot over by the wall and leaned into it with a sigh as my head pounded and I prayed this wouldn't be long. I needed a big glass of wine and my pillow.

"Thank you all for coming today," the man said clearly into the mic. I assumed he must be the principal. "These kids have worked so hard, and it means so much that you could make it. Without further ado, let's get the show started."

Three performances and one that was questionable enough that I worried I wouldn't be able to scrub from my memory later, and Livi took the stage. To my utter shock and surprise, John came in behind her carrying a stool and wearing—yes, it was a cowboy hat that matched Livi's.

I scanned the crowd and almost smiled as I saw Kelly holding on to Oliver's arm. Ellie was drawing in a book. Cole and Savannah were leaning forward in their seats. Sue was crying already, and Daniel, who I saw had been released from hospital, was holding his phone in position to record whatever was about to happen. Just before I moved my gaze to the stage, I caught Dr. Roberts watching me. I gave a polite nod, but he continued to watch me until Livi spoke into the mic.

"Hello, everyone. Thank you for coming." Her confident little voice bounced from the speakers, and my heart melted. "I'm Olivia Logan, and that's my uncle John." She pointed over her shoulder with a giggle. "I chose this song because my daddy and mommy sing it together when they put me to bed at night. It's my favorite." She grinned, and I could see Savanah barely was holding it together. Damn, even I was feeling it, and my eyes watered.

John scanned the crowd, and I wondered if he was looking for me. I thought of waving, but then Livi gave him the signal to start.

A country tune flowed from John's guitar, and before she sang the first word, I recognized it. *Fishin' In The Dark* by The Nitty Gritty Dirt Band.

Our well-spoken little Miss Olivia had a gorgeous twang and a velvet voice. I knew Savannah was a singer, but wow, this little girl had talent. And when the chorus came, John stepped up to the mic, and they sang in harmony.

And the dam broke.

Tears started to fall, and I tried to stop my chin from quivering, but it was useless. My emotions were already at the surface, and it felt so good to cry over something sweet instead of frightening.

John looked incredibly sexy in his dark button-up shirt, jeans, boots, and black cowboy hat. Olivia was in a jean dress, pink cowboy boots, and a matching black hat. Once the end came, the entire room erupted into a cheer that made my head hurt, but I didn't care. They'd blown the entire house away! I was in awe.

Standing outside in the hall, I felt someone step up to my side. It was Dr. Roberts, and while everyone was greeting Livi and patting Cole—who couldn't stop crying —on the back, I could feel his solid presence. Mark and Mike had flowers for Livi, and Keith gave her a bag of something. What? I had no clue.

"Paintballs." Doc Roberts answered my thoughts. "Keith made a deal that if she would sing for him in front of people, he would supply her with all the paintballs she needed to take down Mark's twins."

I laughed, loving how awesome everyone was.

"Do you want to talk about it, Sloane?"

"What do you mean? Why do you ask?"

He cleared his throat and rubbed his chin like he was thinking. "Did Savannah ever tell you about the time she was attacked by a fellow Blackstone member?"

"No." I swung around to meet his gaze.

"It's not my story to share, but my point of bringing it up is this. When people are hiding things, they don't always realize they give off telltale signs."

"I'm not hiding anything."

He reached out to touch my forearm, and I flinched. *Shit.*

"I'm tired. I guess I just need some sleep."

"My door is always open." He patted my arm and smiled warmly then stepped away as Kelly approached.

"Okay," Kelly beamed, "when was someone going to tell me that my son could do that?"

"There you are." John wrapped his warm, protective arms around me and kissed my lips. "I missed you." He leaned in and whispered, "You have no idea how much I missed you."

"Me too," I responded quietly. "You were amazing out there."

"Wouldn't have done it for anyone else." He laughed. "Something about that little girl that I can't say no to. We're all going to dinner. Hope you're up for it." He waved at Livi, who was now being mauled by her parents, and there was no doubt she loved every moment of it.

"It was okay." Liam shrugged, and Doc Roberts gave him an elbow to the ribs. "Sorry."

"So, what happened to your phone?" John asked.

"They took it," Ellie blurted, and I felt my blood pressure drop.

"Who took it?"

Ellie looked at me like she was trying to remember, and I felt like the biggest asshole for asking her to keep something quiet.

"Sloane?" John asked.

"Long story." I waved him off and folded my arms

over my stomach. "I'm so tired, and I really need some sleep. Do you mind if I skip out on the dinner?"

He studied me for a moment like he knew he something was up, but when Mia called out that they were leaving, he dropped the topic.

"Are you sure?"

"Yeah. I feel like a zombie."

"Okay." He hesitated but then called Davie over and asked him to drive me, as he was heading back anyway.

Fifteen minutes later, we were pulling into the driveway and I dragged my weary ass inside.

Not even a hot shower, Advil, or clean clothes could make me feel right inside. I poured that much-needed glass of wine then called my father.

"Hey, honey. You've been hard to get hold of."

"Chasing leads."

"Yeah." He paused. "You're up late."

"I could say the same for you."

"Are you okay? You sound tired."

No.

"Um, yeah." I fumbled on my words. "How's Mom?"

"She's good, busy with work. You know her. She likes to keep busy."

"Good."

"Sloane," he cleared his throat, "are you happy?"

"I am." I wanted to cry.

"Then why do you sound like you might cry?"

I covered my mouth and stopped the urge to tell him everything. "Just a really long last few weeks."

"Well, why don't you get some sleep and call me in the morning?"

"Okay." I swallowed down the knot in my throat.

"Love you."

I hung up and cried myself to sleep.

———

Morning. Damn, only five a.m. I had the scent of Henry in my nostrils.

Shit! I blew air out through my nose to rid myself of the smell.

John was next to me. His gentle snore let me know he was asleep as Tripper's nose poked me. He sensed I was awake. Every time I closed my eyes, I would smell Henry and see Ellie's terrified face. Sleep wasn't going to come back and visit me. The blinds were open, and I studied the darkness, picturing the one place that always brought John happiness.

I held the flashlight as I made my way along the path. No more than three minutes into my walk, I heard branches moving and snow falling. I wanted to crawl out of my skin or scream so loud I'd wake the house, but I didn't when someone in white Army gear blocked my path.

"Morning." He rested his hand on his weapon. "Beta Eight." He patted his name tag. "I didn't mean to startle you."

"It's fine." I let out the air I was holding.

"Everything okay?"

"Yup." I patted Tripper's head. "Just needed to get some air."

He waited for a moment with his face hidden from the moonlight.

"All right." He stepped back into the forest and disappeared as quickly as he appeared.

God dammit, they were good. I shook off my nerves and let their nearby security calm me. Ten more minutes, and I reached the bottom of the beast. I stared straight up but couldn't see the top, and Tripper made an uneasy whine.

"It's okay, boy." I patted his head. "I know what I'm doing."

I dropped my gloves and replaced them with some powdered chalk.

"See you in a few. It's all about feeling your way," I eased the toe of my shoe onto a small foothold and lifted myself up.

I would do anything to calm the wild storm that brewed inside me.

NINETEEN

JOHN

"Wow, Savannah, this looks amazing." I sipped my coffee and took in the transformed living room. The entire cathedral ceiling had black and silver balloons with long curls of ribbon, six feet long, twirling down from each one. The mini bar was now a "full station" bar complete with champagne flutes and a keg of beer next to it, which made me laugh. Savannah always thought of everyone. A giant silver and black cookie jar stood on a table all its own, and adjacent to it was a serve-yourself candy buffet for the kids. Abigail, June, and Mia were in the kitchen preparing all our favorite foods. This would be a night to remember and one we'd been anticipating for what seemed like years.

"Thanks." Savannah let the last balloon float to the ceiling.

"Dammit!" June yelled from the kitchen, and Savi shook her head. "Was this Mark? It feels like Mark!" She held up the Furby, and I saw Mark slip outside. "One of these days, it will find its way into the trash, young man!" she called out the side window.

"I hate that thing, John." Savannah half laughed, but I knew the woman hated it, therefore we loved it that much more. Besides, all the blame should be on Keith. It was his idea to bring it here and torment Mike. "Where's Sloane? She was going to help us this morning."

I nodded to Doc Roberts as he stepped into the room, hands in his pockets, and his lips a thin line. He seemed uneasy as he stood and looked at the decorations.

"She was up before me, so I'm assuming she went down to the Tin House and got lost in her work again."

"You two didn't sleep at the Tin House?" Doc Roberts asked. I shook my head, curious as to why he would ask that. "Does she often sleep at the main house?"

"Just the once, I guess."

Doc rubbed his finger across his bottom lip as he mulled over my answer.

"What's on your mind, Doc?"

"Not sure yet. I wonder…" He trailed off in thought.

"Anything you want to tell me?"

"She seemed a little off yesterday, and I just want to make sure she's all right."

"I'll go check on her."

I set my coffee down and headed down toward Tin House. The more I thought about what Doc had said, the more I had to agree she did seem extra quiet last night. I brought up Frank's number and gave him a call.

"Okay, Black just like I told Logan, I have no information on North Rock yet. I'm hoping you guys can ship out in a day or two, but nothing has changed in the last fifteen minutes."

It was no secret we were itching to head south, but painful as it was, orders were orders, and we had no choice but to obey. My gut told me there was more to what was happening than we were being told right now.

"I'm actually calling for a different reason. Have you heard from Sloane lately?"

"No, why? Should I have?"

"She just got back from her trip yesterday and seemed a little off. I just wondered if she had said anything to you."

"No, not a word, but now you mention it, she hasn't returned my last two calls. That's not like her."

"I'll make sure she calls you. I'm just heading down to talk to her now." I stuck my phone in my pocket and opened the door to the Tin House.

"Hey, Sloane, where are you?" I called and waited for a response. When she didn't answer, I took the loft stairs two at a time and checked the bathroom, but there was no sign of her anywhere. The towels were dry, and the bed was made, but I noticed she had changed. Her clothes were lying on the bed. I heard Tripper whine outside the door and raced down to meet him on the porch.

"What's wrong, Trip?" I leaned down and moved my gaze to his eyes and tried to read his thoughts. "Trip, do you know where Sloane is?" At the mention of her name, he started to whine again. He trotted down the path a few feet then turned back to look at me. "Okay, you've got my attention. Lead the way, buddy."

Tripper had spent a lot of time at Camp Green training and learning search and rescue techniques. He'd proven time and time again how smart he was, so I knew not to ignore his behavior. As we came around a bend, Mike was checking a camera and replacing the battery.

"Mike," I called as I jogged closer, "have you seen Sloane?" He heard the urgency in my voice and pulled out his radio.

"Beta Eight, step out." The soldier dressed in white and gray camo stepped out and removed his sunglasses.

"Have you seen Sloane Harlow this morning?"

"Yes, sir. I approached her at zero six hundred in this very spot to make sure she was all right. She seemed jumpy but fine. Said she just needed a walk."

"That's it?" I asked, confused as to why she was out so early.

"Yes, sir, but I did watch her head toward the bottom of the peak."

"Are you sure you don't mean to the east of the peak?"

"No, sir. She went south."

I looked at Mike, confused. There would be no reason

for her to head that way, as it was the hardest route. It was my route.

"Oh, my God." Mike covered his face with his hands, while Beta Eight disappeared back into the trees. I folded my arms and waited for my brother to spill it.

"It was supposed to be a surprise," Mike uttered in disbelief. "We had a deal that she wasn't supposed to climb without me there, and we always used ropes."

"Climb?"

"She wanted to feel the rush and release that you feel when you climb. She wanted to be able to share that with you."

Before his last words were out, I hurried past him and headed south at a flat-out run. Tripper raced ahead and beat us there. About eighty feet up from the ground, I saw her clinging to the cliff face.

"Holy shit." I turned to look at Mike. "Get a rope up there." As Mike raced off, I dug into the gear we kept at the base of the mountain and fastened my harness on. I didn't have time to do my ropes but knew Mike would drop us one. I began to climb.

I knew this side of the mountain like the back of my hand. No one but Mike and I had ever attempted to climb it free solo. Even with ropes, she would have faced many challenges.

Minute by minute, I pulled my way up the mountain, avoiding the slippery parts where the iced had formed. Internally, I cursed her for being so reckless, but this was not Sloane's normal behavior, and I wondered where it was coming from. I was confident Mike would never have put her on the mountain without proper direction. I forced all thoughts from my mind and concentrated on the climb. Just as I reached the forty-foot mark, I planted my feet and shouted up to her.

"Sloane? Just stay still. I'm coming up behind you." I heard her say something but couldn't make it out. I continued to talk to keep her calm as I made my way toward her. I was careful to keep a distance between us until we were at eye level.

"Sloane, look at me. Open your eyes." It took her a second, but her lids fluttered open, and I could see the sheer panic. "What happened? Any chance you can tell me why you're up here?" I coaxed. A tear slipped out, and she swallowed hard.

"Bad luck just seems to follow me these days."

I wanted to question her, but now wasn't the time. If her emotions were this raw, things could go south very quickly. I needed to keep her calm.

"Okay, let's get you down from here."

"I…" She squeezed her eyes shut once more. "I think my muscles are frozen."

"That happens when you're scared, but you've done this with Mike before, yes?" She nodded. "Then you know how to go back down from here."

"Yes, but about thirty feet ago. I've never gone this high."

I let out a frustrated sigh and focused on getting her down. I heard Mike's whistle and the sound of the rope as it scraped against the rock and hit my side. I grabbed the cleat that was fastened to the end of it and secured myself then inched closer and carefully attached the rope to secure her to me.

"Okay, we're both fastened tight. Now lean into me. We're going to rappel down together." I could tell by her lack of reaction that my words weren't getting through. She was like a layer of ice frozen to the mountain.

Having been in this type of situation before, I understood what was happening in her head. Slowly, I slid my hand over her back and my foot across her legs until I was completely covering her with my body.

With my lips close to her ear, I whispered, "Fear is the enemy, and courage is your weapon. Dig deep and look for your strength." She gave a tiny nod, but her eyes were still squeezed shut. "What do you see?"

"You." Her breath shot out fast, and I smiled before I covered her hands with mine and pried her fingers lose from the rock. She gasped but allowed herself to fall with me.

"Mike has us, Sloane. It's okay. He won't let us fall. Just move with my body, follow my lead. I've got you."

I continued to talk to her until the moment our feet touched the ground. She sagged against me, and I turned her around and pressed my mouth to her icy lips. I devoured her mouth, needing her to ground me. The desire to have my way with her was consuming, so I pulled away.

"I've jumped from planes, I've been shot, I've come

face to face with cartel, but that," I pointed up the mountain, "just scared the living shit out of me. What the hell were you thinking?"

"I wanted…I just wanted to feel free!"

"Then take a hike!" I was fuming. "Not scale the side of a mountain!"

"I never expected them to be there," she blurted. "I never would have put her in danger if I'd known, but one minute we were fine and having fun, and the next we weren't." Her hand flew to her stomach. "He hit so hard, I couldn't catch my breath."

I blinked at her. "Who hit you? What are you talking about?"

"Then I made her lie. I made her lie!" She hiccupped through a sob. "Every time I try to do something nice, it backfires. I'm like a black cat on the thirteenth floor."

I started to speak, but she burst into tears, and I just held her in confusion.

Mike appeared at a run, looking fit to kill, but when he saw Sloane, his expression changed. I waved him off, giving him the thumbs up that she was okay. I let her cry for a few minutes, knowing whatever was bothering her was big. As the clouds grew heavier, I felt her shiver with the cold, and I knew snow wasn't far away.

"Let's get you inside." I took her by the shoulders and slid my hands down her arms and tucked her close to my side as I led her back along the path to the Tin House.

I couldn't keep my eyes off her while I moved about the kitchen. She stopped crying, but she seemed to be back in that fog that held her trapped the last time something bad happened.

She was curled up on the couch in dry clothes under a warm blanket. Tripper was in his usual spot, nuzzled up to her. I handed her a hot cup of coffee and sat on the chair across from her, sipping my own brew.

"Okay, Sloane, let's start from the beginning. Tell me what's going on."

She brushed a tear away and took a deep breath to steady herself. "I was doing really good chasing up my leads, but the word spread quickly that I was digging, though I still managed to gather enough evidence to continue in the direction I'd been going." She shook her head as though realizing she'd gone off course with her story. "I was homesick, and when you told me your mom and sister were coming, I was so excited to see them."

As she went on with her story, the coil in my stomach wound tighter and tighter, and when she got to the part where Henry punched her, I put my mug down so hard it made her jump. I leaned forward and covered my mouth with my hand and waited for her to continue. I'd killed before, and the urge was strong in me now, but want and need were two very different things.

"I asked her to lie for me. What kind of a person does that? I just didn't want to lose you. I couldn't risk that again. I put Ellie in danger, but you have to understand, I love her like my own sister. I swear, John, I never would have brought your family into this if I thought for even a second that they would find me."

I could barely keep up it with her story. So many things raced through my head.

"When I got home, Doc Roberts seemed to know, and I needed something to clear my head. Mike had only ever taken me to the sixty-foot mark, but I wanted to keep going. It went okay, but then my foot slipped, and I lost my concentration and got stuck. I went through everything he taught me, but I was so confused inside I just couldn't get it back."

"Hold on." I held up my hand to stop her story and pushed to my feet. I moved to the table to lean against it while I processed what she was telling me. "Does Frank know any of this?"

She opened her mouth to speak but then closed it.

I shut my eyes and mustered through my frustration and anger. I wasn't angry so much with her, but the men she was dealing with were clearly a lot more dangerous than I'd realized.

"It didn't work the last time, so what makes you think he can fix it this time?" She looked at me in defeat.

"So, you were just going to, what? Ignore what happened and hope they'd go away?"

"It's the mob, John." She tossed her hands in the air with a heavy sigh. "They never go away. You need to know someone to make them stop. Right now, I don't. I just need some time to figure this out."

"I'm going to pretend you didn't just say that." I had to curb my temper. "You don't make deals with these people. They kill for pure enjoyment."

"Yes," her voice went hard, "and hit women without a care in the world." She moved to stand closer to the fire with her hands on her hips. "I've had some awful clients before, but none like them, and I made it clear that I didn't want their case. It was quite clear to me that they all knew Henry's son had pulled the trigger. But they wouldn't give up and insisted on me." She jabbed at her chest. "No isn't a word in their world."

I stared at her as something gnawed at the side of my brain. I tried to pull it forward, and as I did, it hit me.

"What?" She sensed my change in mood.

"I think I may have an idea." I checked the time and cursed. I put my hands on my hips and took a long breath. "Look, we have to be up at the house, ready to go for the party in one hour."

"Party?"

"Are you hurt? Other than your stomach?"

"No." She shook her head.

"I'll make some calls, and I need you to go get ready. I'll meet you up at the house in forty-five."

I went for the door when she called out. "John? What party?"

I had forgotten that she'd been gone for a while and wasn't in the know. "Family reunion-slash-we're happy to be alive party."

Before she could question me more, I raced out the door and up to the house.

"Where are you going?" Cole shot me a confused look.

"To pull a favor from a stranger."

"Is it smart?"

I paused on the stairs and couldn't make eye contact with my brother. "I hope so."

Once inside my room, I opened the closet and dug through my belongings. My special black gear that I wore while on our missions to Mexico was right where I left it.

I felt all around the top of the suit until I found it and pulled back the fabric over my left chest. I dug two fingers in and fingered the tiny business card and tugged it free. The three little letters above his name popped out from the fibers on the card.

I quickly dialed the number and waited for him to answer.

"FBI, Cooper Colins." His voice was all business.

"This is Recon John Black. We met in Mexico in a diner—"

"That's right." He cut me off. "How's your friend?"

"He's well, thanks. Look," I rubbed my head and looked out the window at the Tin House that blended with the trees, "you said if I ever needed some help, I could call you. Well, it turns out I need some help, if the offer still stands."

"It does."

"I have a problem with some members of the mafia in Washington."

There was a long pause, and I heard a door shut.

"The mafia?" He seemed confused. "How did a member of the US Army get tangled with a member of the mafia?" He chuckled like he was more entertained than shocked.

"My girlfriend is a lawyer, and she got stuck with a case she didn't want for some guy named Henry. Seems his son was found guilty, and now this Henry guy refuses to accept his son's fate. He's been roughing her up over it, and the last time things got a little out of control. I was hoping maybe you knew someone at the agency who could put an end to all of this."

"Mm," he mumbled, "I think I know someone who could make some calls."

I filled him in on the details, and to my surprise, he had gotten wind of that case several months ago. I guessed the news of Henry's son spread quickly and rattled some higher up family members. That was the mob for you; everyone seemed to know everything.

"I would really appreciate that."

"Give me a few days, and I'll be in touch."

"I can't thank you enough."

"Of course." He paused. "It's always good to have a soldier of your caliber in my debt." He chuckled once more.

I felt uneasy with his choice of words, but this needed to end now. "Talk to you soon."

I tucked his card away and headed for the shower.

By the time I was finished and was headed downstairs, the living room was in full-out party mode.

Mike and Keith were hugging their wives, and all the kids were playing together. Abby and June were gushing over Lexi's surprise, that she was very much pregnant. I had no clue how far along she was, but she seemed pretty big. Laughter and love filled the room and immediately lifted my mood.

"About time, hey?" Mark handed me a beer and smiled.

I searched the crowd and spotted Sloane with Savi and Mia. She was smiling and was telling a story about something. A tight coil formed in my chest with the realization that I could have lost her last week without even knowing it. The urge to call Trigger and have him handle it was on my mind, but I'd let the FBI agent give it a go first.

Cole joined my side and called over Mike and Keith. We stood in a horseshoe shape and admired the people and the lives we had made for ourselves. Whoever said it was impossible for an elite team to find love and have children had never met Blackstone.

We defied the odds.

"Welcome home, boys." Cole held his beer mug up and clinked his glass with Mike and then Keith. "I appreciate the two-year sacrifice it took to build Dusk. You did a hell of a job, but man, I'm glad you're back!"

"It's good to be home." Mike grinned at Keith, who happily agreed.

The plan always was for the guys to return to Shadows once the new house was up and running effectively, with the new team trained. Cole told me he was beyond impressed with how Mike and Keith had shaped the boys at Dusk into a younger version of ourselves.

Truth be told, we needed the help. The cartel were getting stronger, and they outnumbered us by the thousands. North Rock and Eagle Rock felt the same way and stepped up to train whenever they could. Whether it was Chamness over video phone or Waters in person, we trained those men to be the best of the best, nothing less.

"Do they know yet?" Mark asked, and I knew he was referring to who was going to be taking over Dusk.

Cole grinned around the mouth of his beer. "Nah, let's let them sweat it out a little longer."

"Are we just going to stand around?" Daniel stood on the stone hearth of the fireplace while he tried to hide a wince. "Or are we going to have a little fun?"

"Oh, Sue isn't going to like that." Mark shook his head with a laugh.

"Tonight," Daniel held up his beer and rolled his eyes at Scoot, who thought now would be the appropriate time to spread his legs and let his manhood out for some air in the middle of the room, "we leave our concern for North Rock at the door and we let loose. Tomorrow is another day, and who knows, it may be the day we get the green light to ship out and bring those boys home." We all cheered at that as Daniel eased himself to the floor.

Live music started to play from the corner of the room, and the energy in the house picked up.

As the night went on and the party was in full swing, the music suddenly slowed, and a familiar tune could be heard. I glanced across the room and found Sloane's sexy gaze already on me.

I nodded as if to tell her to come here.

She excused herself from Catalina and worked her way through the crowd, sending Doc Roberts and Abigail a shy smile.

I met her on the edge of the dance floor, and she stopped in front of me. I tilted her chin up with a finger and looked down at her for a moment, then slowly wrapped my arm around her waist and tugged her into me.

"Look, John, if you're upset with me, I completely understand. I just—"

"Hey," I cupped her face and rubbed my thumbs gently over her cheeks, "I'm not mad at you. I'm just sad that you didn't tell me." I let my mouth run because it was the only way the walls wouldn't shoot up. "I would have been there for you."

"You were supposed to be healing."

"Don't." I shook my head and let my hands fall. "Don't you get it? I want to be that person for you. I would have stayed up all night, talked until you fell asleep and still stayed on the line in case you woke." I paused to clear the emotions that apparently insisted on surfacing.

She sighed. "Everything I did that day and the next was wrong. When I got back to my room, I sat in the chair until it got light. My finger hovered over your number a billion times."

"Why didn't you call?"

Her brows pinched, and I saw the pain race across her frown. "I didn't want to lose you."

"Nope, I don't accept that."

"John."

"Sloane," I challenged.

"Because…" She paused. "Because I saw that look of doubt on your face when you thought I overstepped."

She held up a finger when I started to explain how I'd been wrong on that. "Please, hear me for a moment." I nodded for her to go on.

"That look killed me, and you turned off, and when I tried to explain, you blocked me out. And," she blinked a few times, "I'm just not sure I could handle that again."

She was right but wrong at the same time.

"Okay," I nodded, "I was wrong for doing that then, and you were wrong for not calling me the other night. Call it a truce? Learn from our mistakes?" I went for my best sexy smile.

Her mouth curved into a matching sexy but modest grin. "I can agree to that."

"Good," I smirked, "because if that ever happens again, I will chain you to me so you can never leave my protection."

Her eyes narrowed. "So, is that all it takes?"

We both twitched in the direction of the speakers before she stepped closer.

"It's our song," she whispered against my neck as she tucked herself in to mold to my body.

I loved that we had a song. "We'll always have the barn."

"And a scarred rooster."

She chuckled and held me tighter.

"But really, how are ya holding up?"

"I'm drained, but better now."

"Me too." I kissed the top of her head and appreciated her truth. I nodded at Cole, who was dancing with Savannah. If we could stay like this forever, I'd die a happy man.

TWENTY

"Wait." I blinked to clear the fog from my eyes and realized I was in the woods in my nightgown. "What the hell?"

I whirled around and tried to make sense of what was happening. Thick terrain blocked my view, but I spotted a path and rushed toward it. Wrapping my arms around my midsection, I made my way north…or was it west? I wasn't sure. I hadn't been here before. My bare feet fought with the uneven ground, and nasty twigs tore at me from every direction as I walked.

A bird landed in front of me, and I suddenly knew to look at a tree where a camera box was mounted.

"How did I know…" I trailed off and studied the

camouflaged box. "If that's there, then…" I looked over my shoulder and saw Blackstone running toward me.

"John!" I screamed, but they raced right past me like I was invisible. "John?"

Nothing.

As soon as I heard the hooting, I stepped back off the trail to hide behind a tree. I watched in fear as a couple of cartel guys charged after them.

"One, two, three," I counted, knowing two more had to pass. The last two were about thirty seconds behind. They stopped in front of me. One had a camera and was filming as the other held the rookie's radio. Something black was between his fingers, and it caught my attention.

What was that?

I stepped out and held my breath before I let it go in one shaky blow. "Hey," I whispered loudly. They didn't even budge.

Okay, so I *was* invisible. I pushed my panic aside and studied the black thing. It was the only thing that was blurry. No matter how many times I looked at it, my eyes couldn't focus in on it. Something told me it was important.

"*Santo Grial,*" the man in front of the camera said in Spanish.

"*Nosotros somos dioses,*" we both said together.

How did I know to say that?

Their voices faded out as a loud tapping noise took over my head, then a huge rush of adrenaline flooded my veins.

I covered my mouth to stop the scream before…

The wind blew hard against the tin roof and woke me from the nightmare that held me tight in its grip.

"Jesus," I panted and felt around my chest where my heart was trying to escape. "Where the hell did that come from?"

Another gust of wind had me pulling back the curtain. I squinted through the darkness to see hail and snow coming down like a cloak over the mountains. The howl of the wind through the trees was so eerie I leapt back under the covers to snuggle into the safety of John's warm body.

"Mm, mine," he muttered as he wrapped his arm around me to pull me in.

"Yours," I agreed as I lay there. My brain swirled with confusion, and my eyes stayed wide open until morning.

John's phone went off, and I felt him jerk up and snatch it from the night table.

"Yeah?" he answered and shifted to sit on the side of the bed. "Copy that."

I immediately felt the loss as soon as his weight was gone and the mattress lifted. I rolled over and watched him reach for his cargo pants. His body seemed charged with energy; it positively buzzed around his body. I knew it was something important.

"Everything okay?"

"We got the call." He cleared his throat and shrugged on a t-shirt. "We ship out in one hour."

My stomach dropped, and I tried to remember what Savannah taught me.

This is what they do. This is what they live for. They need us to be supportive when they leave. We can crumble once they're gone, then take our next deep breath when they return.

"Okay." I shifted to sit up on the headboard.

"I need to grab my gear and check my radio. Stupid piece of shit likes to crap out on me." Sweat broke out along my chest.

I can handle this.

"Okay." I wasn't sure what to say. Apparently, my brain was fixed on the only word it could come up with to get me through this.

Once he was dressed, he looked over at me, and I couldn't miss that flicker of excitement that glowed in his eyes whenever he was about to go on a mission. They all looked the same way, like kids who were handed BB guns and were told there were no rules.

"You okay?"

"Yeah." My shaky voice betrayed me.

He lifted my left hand and kissed my ring finger before he shifted and slowly pressed his lips to mine.

"You gave me a reason," he whispered, and I knew what he meant. I leaned forward and wrapped my arms around his neck.

"Please be careful."

"Remember, Sloane," he brushed my hair off my shoulder and let his fingers skim along my collarbone, "I want to come home just as much as you want me to." He kissed me one more time before he headed for the door. Just before he left, he turned back. "Hey?"

"Yeah?"

"I love you."

"I love you too."

He disappeared from my view, and I was left alone, feeling like the room was spinning.

By the time I dragged my zombie body from the shower and wiggled myself into something decent, I knew I had to hurry. I made it up to the house just in time to watch the chopper take off from the landing pad. The glare of the sun off the snow brought more tears to my eyes as I pressed my fingers to my lips and held it up to him. Maybe, just maybe, he could see or at least feel me.

"Please, someone watch over them," I whispered before the whirling blades dipped behind a mountain peak.

No matter how many times I tried to force the dream from last night from my head, I just couldn't. It was so persistent that I could feel a pain building in my head as though someone was constantly trying to get my attention.

"Morning," Abigail greeted from the living room. "You okay, dear?"

I smiled at her sympathetic tone and gave a nod even though I was far from okay. I wasn't about to bring up my fears about the team because we all felt it. What was more important for me to do was to concentrate on finding the truth about what was going on and not to burden the others with my mental state.

I forced my mind back to where it could be useful. I had never been so consumed by a dream before, and I decided I had to find a way to let it out. I went into the kitchen and poured my coffee then tossed the phone pad down in front of me and started to make a list of everything I could remember.

Location - Mexico

Time - Second to last mission

Pathway

Knew the words before they were said

Black rectangular blur

Invisible

Camouflaged video box on tree

Bird

Gods

I leaned over the table on one arm and studied the words in every different way.

"Morning." Dell rubbed his messy hair as he and Davie both went for the coffee pot.

"Mm," I muttered and tapped the pen on the marble countertop. The sound took me back to the sound of the boots on the pathway. *Tap, tap, tap.* My mind spun again, and I slipped back to the memory that wasn't mine.

I shoved the camera they used in the other guy's face, and the words "we are Gods" came out of my mouth like I was one of the men. Again, the black blur was raised, and my eyes locked on to it.

"We are Gods," I whispered, and the still of the room suddenly dawned on me.

"What did you say?" Dell's face was twisted.

"Huh?" I barely heard him.

"What did you say?"

"I…" I sat straighter and tried to recall my words. "I'm not sure."

Dell glanced at Davie, confused, and leaned on the counter and sipped his coffee.

I was so close to what it was I was discovering I could taste it.

"I need to go." I downed my coffee, ripped the piece of paper free, and rushed toward the door.

"Was it something I said?" Davie laughed behind me. "What's wrong with her?"

With Tripper by my side, I rushed back to the Tin House and pulled the box of files out on the conference table. One by one I lined up each guys' interview from the first day I arrived here. Using my teeth, I freed the highlighter and spat the cap on the floor. Every time the guys said the cartel were one step ahead of them, I crossed-refenced with the YouTube videos that came out just after.

I used the projector and kept the videos on a loop playing on the wall above the whiteboard. I numbered each cartel and started my own bio of each. Three and six were the camera operators, and eight was just ruthless. I didn't try to use names. They were trying to kill my family, so I stuck with numbers. Numbers kept me disconnected from my anger.

Three hours later, I knew I looked insane, with papers stuck to the walls because the whiteboards were too small, and each was filled to every corner. I could recite the videos by heart now, but there was one part I could never quite make out. Even the closed captioning failed to decipher the words. It was during the part of the mission where John got separated from the rest and ran into Brick. The cartel had popped up out of the bushes, and number six was speaking behind the camera to his leader. I could tell it was him from the tattoo of a weapon on his arm.

Suddenly, the leader stopped talking and leaned his head toward his shoulder as though he was listening to something, then he began to wave his arms around as he yelled at them.

What the hell happened then? What did he see or hear?

The heel of my shoe tapped as I swung my chair in a half moon, just needing to keep moving. My adrenaline was high, and my need to discover the something that gnawed at my insides made me feel about to burst.

Then it hit me, like a bright flash of light. I grabbed my phone and called Frank.

"Well, hello there," he started without waiting for me to speak. "You and I certainly need to have a chat."

"Yeah, for sure, but first—"

"Care to explain what the hell happened on your trip?"

Damn you, John.

"It wasn't John. It was Cole." He answered my unspoken mutter.

"Frank."

He immediately stopped talking when he heard my tone. "What is it?"

"Remember when Pix from Eagle Eye was in trouble, and there was that video of him at that bar, but no one could pull the audio mess on the witness?"

"Yes."

"They used something to retrieve it. Do you know what that was?"

"Um, yeah." He tapped on his keyboard. "the Army is now using it in court. I think it was turned into an," he paused, "yup, an app. It's called Static Retriever."

"Thanks. I'll call you later." Before he could argue, I hung up and tapped on the app icon on my phone and quickly downloaded the handy little tool.

"Please work," I pleaded out loud.

Turning the volume up and placing my phone a few inches from the speaker, I pressed play. The words popped up over the screen, and sure as anything, the moment it got to the part I needed, I read those four little missing words.

What the hell does that mean?

I grabbed my coat, called Tripper, and raced back up to the house.

"Doc," I closed the door behind me, "I need to talk to someone on the team. Is Daniel, Dell, or Davie around?"

His brows pinched together above his glasses, no doubt once again trying to read my mind.

"Davie is in the kitchen with Savi. I haven't seen the others yet today."

"Thank you." I rushed by him and across the living room. Savannah and Olivia were watching TV, and the babies were playing near them on the floor.

"Hey, girl," she called, and I waved but didn't stop. I could hear his voice, and as I whirled around the doorway, he looked up from his laptop.

"Hey," he stood slowly, "everything okay?"

I heard footsteps behind me, but I didn't take the time to look.

"Twenty-nine red fires," I blurted, and his face dropped. "Does that mean anything to you?"

"Where did you hear that?"

"Davie," I took a step toward him, "I'm vetted, and this is my job. What does it mean?"

"It's one of Blackstone's code terms," Dell chimed in from behind me. I didn't even turn; I just kept my eyes on Davie. "We use them, like, when we're talking to North Rock."

"They change them up." Davie spoke up now, knowing it was okay to do so. "Each day is a little different. That's a Tuesday term."

"But it's impossible." Dell rubbed his head. "No one knows this stuff but us. It's our only form of protection." He pulled out his phone and went to make a call.

"I need a radio. I need to reach the guys, right now."

"Um," Davie hesitated, "Sloane, you can't just—"

"Here." Savi was by my side with a huge satellite radio, already pushing some buttons on the face of it.

I gave her a nod of thanks and held on to her arm while it rang.

"Black." John's voice burst over the air waves.

"John." I took a moment to get my words in order.

"Sloane?" He sounded completely different. "Why are you calling me here? What's happened?"

"John, I need you to hear me." My heartbeat raced at the sound of the propellers. "Twenty-nine red fires."

Silence.

"John, they know your codes!"

"Sloane," his voice lowered, "that doesn't surprise me. They have one of our radios, so they are bound to hear our code words. They can say them, but they'd have no idea what they mean."

"Don't they? Then how do you explain them being one step ahead of you? How do you explain that when Cole gave the order over the radio on that mission where you ran into Brick, they knew to spread out and do exactly what you did? It's all on the video. Somehow, they know and understand what you're saying! What your plan is!"

I reached forward and handed Daniel, now in the kitchen, my cell phone and watched as he and Dell witnessed what I did.

"Please, John, I know this is crazy, but listen to *my* gut on this." I took a breath and glanced at Savannah's red eyes. "I would bet my life with you on this. They know. They *know*."

Daniel came to my side and reached for the phone.

"She's right, John. I just saw the video. Esteben gave the order to circle around you right after Cole gave the code. You need to contact Chamness now, because you all are heading into an ambush."

"Copy that." Cole's voice crackled through loud enough for me to hear it. "Tell Sloane…" I couldn't hear the rest.

"Tell Sloane what?" Savi asked before I could.

Daniel held on to the island while he muttered a prayer for the boys. Their mission just went from bad to worse, but at least now they had a fighting chance.

He turned to us. His face was drained of color, but a little relief showed in his eyes. "That you're now fifty-eight."

"What does that mean?"

Savannah broke out in a smile. "It means you're one of us, and you can't leave."

I let out the air I had been holding in one big rush and let Cole's kindness that I did have a place here wash over me, even if it was just for a moment.

Daniel pulled up Frank's name in his contacts. "Now we just need to figure out how the hell they've cracked our codes."

TWENTY-ONE

JOHN

Our entire team stood motionless, each lost in our thoughts. The only thing that proved our existence was the fact that we would catch our balance whenever the chopper took on turbulence.

It was difficult to process that the enemy could *speak* our language, that they knew our secrets, that they could open us up, leaving our belly exposed to attack. It explained so much, but it brought even more questions.

"All right." Cole slipped into colonel mode, and I knew we were back on track. We spent the next forty-five minutes listening to his new plan of action. It was intense and quite possibly would be the wildest, most unrehearsed attack we'd ever tried.

But this was what we did. We planned for the unexpected, got in and got out by any means possible.

Cole didn't switch channels when he placed a satellite call to Chamness, and I could only imagine the thoughts running through Chamness's head when he saw his phone light up and heard those two simple words, words that would make any commander freeze on the spot.

"Black Mirror."

We have been compromised.

We all watched as Cole's eyes stayed locked on the bar across from him. If one of the cartel knew what that meant, we'd know Chamness was a mole. There was a missed beat or two of silence, then his words came back over the radio.

"Copy that."

Cole ended the call and continued to explain the plan. We would attack backward and work our way toward the start.

Once we were briefed, we each replayed our parts over and over again until no uncertainty was left. Sometimes we'd sign each other questions about who was where and when instead of breaking each other's concentration with the use of the radios.

We had made good progress into Mexico, and I used the drone of the chopper's engines to focus my thoughts. I turned to Cole and switched to a private channel.

"I never shared my sister's recovery with you guys because I didn't want you to have to carry it." I had no idea why I was bringing it up right now. I guessed I just wanted to go into this war with a clear head.

Cole slowly turned to look at me. His face carried a level of stress that was to be expected from a leader.

"I think it's fair to say we all would have done the same thing."

"All right." I gave a tight nod and went to switch the channel back when he held up a hand.

"What you carry on your back, we can carry together."

Mark, who must have been reading our lips, gave a nod in agreement. I knew they were right, but I was my own worst enemy, and guilt was rooted so deep I couldn't see past it until now.

The hum of the chopper settled back over us as we waited for the command to drop.

When the engine throttled back, we moved to stand in line, and Mark's hand landed on my shoulder, and I did the same to Mike in front of me, until we were all connected as one.

In as one, out as one. No one left behind.

I watched as my brothers disappeared into the unknown below the belly of the beast. We never knew what awaited us on these missions, and for sure no one knew what awaited us this trip. All we could do was keep to our training and not get killed. It was times like this that made you realize just how important our training really was. It was the only thing that kept you alive—that and complete faith that your brothers would do the same.

I checked the satellite phone that was tucked into the side pocket of my gear. Cole told me to take it since our radios were unreliable at the best of times. This was a trip where no errors could afford to happen.

Just before I went for the rope, I clicked on my music, and *Backbone* by Kaleo poured through my radio. I knew it wasn't the smartest thing to play music, as it would hinder one of my senses, but I knew I needed to be hyper-focused, and I needed this to settle my adrenaline. I loved the last three minutes of the song, and I listened to that as I watched the chopper disappear in the blackness above me.

My knees absorbed the impact, and I made quick work to find cover. Mike signaled, and I returned an affirmative, and we raced together down the pathway to our second point. Dawn would be on us soon, and that meant we were going to be easy to spot. I thought about each of my steps, careful not to step on any branches or twigs. As I pressed forward, I would pull back each branch and press it behind me for Mike to take hold. When I let go, I knew he would do the same and ease each branch back to its original place behind him. We worked well as a team. I led, and he trusted my actions.

We hit an area where we had to run flat-out for quite a distance before we came to the base of a cliff, our next challenge.

"Time?" Mike asked as we each filled an old t-shirt full of rocks and flung it on our backs. People might think we were crazy for adding more weight on such a steep climb, but we were about to climb a hundred-foot cliff that jutted out over water. We all knew from the pain of training in the past that if you fell, it was like hitting cement. If we dropped the t-shirt before we hit the water, it would break the impact for us. It gave us at least a hope in hell of not landing on solid concrete water.

"We're under." I grinned, holding my wrist up to show him my watch, and went for the first ledge to haul myself up off the ground. "Let's shave more time off."

"Ten-four." Mike chuckled next to me. He and I took pride in the fact that we were fast.

Just like on the path we had taken to get here, every move was thought out before we went on to the next.

It wasn't lost on me that we were now chasing the sunrise, and we were about to be targets on the side of a mountain, so we had to move as fast as we possibly could. Anything metal was tucked away so light couldn't reflect off it and give away our location.

The sun soon found us, and two hours into the climb, that same cold prickle inched its way up my back, in spite of the sweat that ran freely down through the goose-bumps. Something told me we weren't going to be alone for much longer.

"What?" Mike looked up at me. "I know that face."

"I'm not," I looked around the best I could, "sure."

"Dammit, you and Trigger have that same spider sense when shit is about to get real." He moved up to my level, and once he got his footing right, he used his shoulder to push his sunglasses up on his forehead to eye me better. "Okay, do your one with nature thing and tell me if we're about to get—"

Zip! Zip! Zip!

Suddenly, bullets sprayed down all around us, echoing off the adjacent mountain. Rock dust created a momentary protective screen, just long enough for Mike and me to know what we needed to do. He used all his strength to push off from the rock and leaned into the fall.

I'd dropped from worse heights, but staring down at a gun barrel within a sniper's range was slightly different.

My fingertips scraped the ledge as I let go. I used my feet and pushed myself farther out. Somehow, my mind went back to my music, and that wonderful sad loop of instruments seemed incredibly fitting as I watched the flashes of orange light above me like a spectacular lightning show.

As I dropped lower, I turned my head to the rock to watch for the scrape mark we'd made so if the unthinkable did happen, we knew when to...

I twisted, reached for the knot that held my rocks, and let them tumble ahead of me. Using all my muscles, I prepared for the impact. My heels took the brunt of the hit, and I kept my arms tucked in tightly, but my elbows still got a blow. Bones could be healed, but the phone was our only reliable resource, for us and our team.

Water rushed in my nose and tried to haul me down to the bottom. Every single instinct I had told me to hold my breath and swim forward.

I kicked hard and beat my arms through the adrenaline that coursed through me. As much as I wanted to surface to find Mike, I was just happy all my limbs were still intact, and my lungs still held life-giving air.

When I started to see black spots, I pushed to the surface, and the moment my head broke through, I did a quick sweep of the shoreline.

A familiar quiet bird sound caught my attention, and I squinted to see Mike embedded in some shrubs at the bottom of the cliff. I gave him my own quiet tweet back before I ducked under and swam over.

"You good?" I asked softly as I tugged the satellite phone out and breathed a sigh of relief to find it intact.

"Yeah. You?"

"Better now." I belly crawled up into the shrubs next to him to catch my breath. "Well, that was a waste of a climb."

"Never a waste." We chuckled like the adrenaline junkies we were. "The others made it to the rendezvous point and, since he's scratched the idea of us ever getting up to the lookout point, Cole wants us to join them."

"Glad to know the radios are working."

Mike grunted in agreement as we started yet another long journey to meet up with the rest of our unit. I didn't like being on low ground. I was wired to be up on a ledge somewhere looking down. It unsettled me not being able to see what was around me.

"How's the family settling in to the mountain?" I whispered to Mike, needing the distraction as we hit our rhythm in a slow, careful jog. We both dodged a makeshift trap the cartel had set in hopes someone would fall through into the barbed wire below, and we both kept our eyes on where we were putting each step as we went.

"Couldn't be happier." He let out a long sigh. "I loved being home, but man, I didn't miss the humidity."

"How's Keith with leaving Nan?"

"Leaving?" He tossed a smirk back at me. "When she heard Keith was moving and the baby wasn't going to be born here, she got hold of Frank and arranged to have her stuff moved to a place just down from Dan and Sue's. Said something to him like, 'What's a little old lady going to do? Give up the location of her grandson and great-granddaughter?'"

"What?" This was the first time I'd heard about that.

"Oh, yeah, I believe the next thing she said was, 'Besides, ski asses are the best to gawk at.'"

I had to fight the laugh that wanted to escape my throat.

"She's pure comedy. What did Keith have to say about that?"

Mike slowed slightly to avoid another hole, and I cursed as I jumped around it.

"He was all for it. He can't get enough of Nan. Guess he recovered from that texting hiccup a while ago." He chuckled. "He was more than happy to have her come along."

I laughed harder at the memory of Nan sexting her grandson accidentally and the pure horror that Keith went through. Mark even got Doc Roberts in on the fun, and he made him agree to a mandatory psych meeting.

"Oh, did Mark ever have a—" My sixth sense had me reach forward to grab Mike's arm, and we both ducked, as he had caught sight of something too. He turned slowly to sign, and I motioned for him to veer off in the opposite direction while I stayed low and slowly made my way deeper into the forest. I crawled forward silently. Every sound was heightened inside my head as my body wove in and out of the brush and grass until I reached a hollowed-out tree trunk and I pressed my back up against it.

Click, click, click. I sent the others a message via our version of Morse code. Three quick clicks and two short told me Cole understood.

With my entire body hidden from view, I stayed put for hours, hyperaware of the cartel as they ran by the path that was only about ten feet from me. We must have stumbled on to their main route, and I knew better than to try to budge from my position while they were on the move. Each time I even thought about it, another cartel would come racing by. Mike had checked in and said he was taking cover not far from me. He was stuck in the same shit luck situation I was. By the time the sun had moved across the tree line, we were still holed up tight.

"Country?" Mike's nickname for me whispered over the radio just as I had done another sweep of the path in a vain effort to find any escape.

"Yeah?" I whispered.

I closed my eyes, pissed I stumbled into their territory and hadn't seen the signs.

"I have Tripper in my sights. At nightfall, he'll head toward your room."

A sense of relief rolled over me. Mike could see me, and I was to head east at nightfall. Okay.

"Ten-four." I lifted my rifle and scanned the horizon until I heard the triple click on the radio to show Mike's position.

Darkness swept its cover over us, and I checked my watch. I'd wasted thirteen hours sitting here, and it was time I moved.

Voices suddenly found their way to me, and I desperately scanned the area for the thousandth time. Bullets sprayed across the ground, kicking up bits of dirt. Some came so close to my knee it spasmed, and I nearly bolted. Only my training held me in place as I tried to figure out how they knew I was there. I desperately scanned the trees around me and, sure enough, spotted a camera. *Shit!* There was one high above me a few yards away. I never would have seen it, except in the dark I could see a small light glint from it. Squinting, I wondered if there was a live feed attached to it or if it was one they would have to revisit later. If so, I wondered just when that visit would come.

Shit! I tried to become as small as possible and held my gun close to my chest.

"I can hear your heartbeat, soldier," a voice said nearby through his thick accent.

Slowly, I clicked my radio to put the word out to Mike that I was okay.

"That's fine," he called out. "We can wait. We are very patient men. We will do just like before and remove you each one by one."

I could hear laughter from some other men, and I felt my fingers get twitchy against my gun. I knew better than to move. They fired more shots in the opposite direction from where Mike and I were, and I began to realize they couldn't know exactly where we were or even if we were there. Two more hours they taunted with stories of how they'd killed some of my North Rock family. Maybe it was true and maybe it wasn't, but regardless, it ate away at my soul, and I longed to jump up and blast the smiles right off their faces.

Many scenarios went through my mind about how we could get out of this, but their camp just continued to grow. As more cartel arrived, our situation worsened by the minute. A few started to horse around, and one guy practically fell inches from my boot. Like the classic scum they were, meth lined their veins, and discipline was nonexistent. The sound of a flint striking, and the distinct smell of cheap cigarette smoke filled my nostrils. *Holy shit.* I didn't have to see him to know he was there. My fingers tightened on the trigger, and just as I was about to make my move, Chamness's voice called out over his radio.

"Back Mirror, Black Mirror."

The man beside me froze, fiddled with something,

then turned and shouted to his men to move, and just like that, they all headed out.

I took a moment to settle my heartbeat and eased up to my feet. I stayed glued to the tree and listened for any sound. I pulled up the radio and clicked it to let Mike know I was ready to move out.

The cold steel cut into my flesh right below my hairline. Blood ran down my brow and dripped from my lashes.

"I smelled you, *gringo*. Your stink gave you away."

A blow to my knees had me face down on the ground. His hand grabbed a fistful of my hair and hauled me back up to my knees, and the blade found its way into the groove of the cut. Another two men appeared. One looked totally strung out, and one stepped up to me.

"You thought you could outsmart us, but we outsmarted you. He was right to go for the young blood."

Who?

The junkie scratched his neck wildly as his eyes shifted around, no doubt waiting for the rest of my team to emerge.

"Scalp him already," he hissed, and I noticed most of his teeth were missing. I tried to think of a way to escape, but I couldn't see a good outcome.

The one in command smiled at the junkie before he pulled out a GoPro camera and aimed it at himself. Then he rolled up his shirt and showed off his spiderweb tat with the seven in the middle of it to the camera. He then made a strange motion with his hands like a variation on how a Catholic would cross himself, then he turned the camera on me.

"This is for you, Denton."

The shock of The American's name blinded me momentarily as…*zip, zip!* A warm spray shot over my face, and the machete lost its pressure and tumbled to the ground along with its owner. I jumped to my feet and kicked the guy with the camera in the gut just as another bullet lodged into his skull. The junkie cowered on the ground, and I drilled my fist into his face and sent him backward and into the hot coals of the fire. I frantically felt my head to make sure I still had hair and breathed a sigh of relief.

"I wish Trigger was here to see that." Mike emerged quietly from the bushes. "You good?"

I nodded, wiped some blood from my eyes, and shook off the last few moments. I wished I had time to process it all, but I knew we needed to get the hell out of there fast. Using the butt of my gun, I removed the camera and tucked the piece of technology in my side pocket. I scooped up my gun and headed out with Mike on my heels.

Thirty minutes into the jog, my mind still spun in about a billion and one different directions. It wasn't until Mike's fist hit my shoulder to get my attention that I jumped back into the present.

"Clear that shit out of your head before we get there, Black. Whatever it takes, just do it."

I stopped and closed my eyes for a second and felt the gash that stung like a bitch whenever I moved my face.

Mike took a seat on the ground with his weapon raised, ready to fire. He was giving me my moment.

With an unsteady breath, I did the forbidden and pulled out the satellite phone and called home.

"Logan," Daniel's voice rasped over the phone. No doubt he hadn't left his son's office since we'd left.

"It's Black." I tried to keep my voice even, but it was a task.

"What's wrong?"

"I'm breaking protocol to clear my head." I went with the truth. He knew I would never do that without good reason.

"Okay," he cleared his throat, "what do you need, son?"

I wiped the blood from my eyes and let out another uneven breath.

"I'll go get her." He read my thoughts.

I glanced at Mike, who kept his gaze fixed on our surroundings.

"John?" Sloane's voice nearly brought me to my knees, and I wanted to grab her and use her body to anchor me. "John, are you there?" I heard her whispered concern to Daniel, and he told her to give me a second. "Okay, I'm here." She was close to tears, and I fought to know what to say.

"Marry me, Sloane," I blurted. "I need you to say yes." I choked back the rush of emotion that I never even knew I had inside of me. "Marry me," I whispered again.

"John," she started to cry, "what is going on? You're scaring me."

"Say it, Sloane. Please." I just needed those three little letters to string together.

She sniffed and gave me a happy laugh. "Under one condition?"

"Which is?"

"You come home in one piece, no dents, holes, or scary scratches."

I stared down at my bloodstained hands and let the pain of the day drain from me.

"Deal." It was that very moment that proved to me that Sloane was my other half in this life. I would take whatever punishment came along with making that call. I knew I needed it.

"Then yes, Mr. Black, I would love to marry you."

"Good." I sighed with relief and glanced my watch. "I have to go."

"Wait. John?"

"Yeah?"

"You have to keep your promise to me."

"You have my word. I love you." I hung up and headed back toward Mike with a clear head and a promise to keep.

"Better?" I helped him to his feet.

"Yeah." I nodded, and we continued our hike toward our brothers.

As a soldier, we were trained to be aware of every single thing that moved, made a sound, or even what didn't. Our instincts were always on high alert, so when we grew closer to our checkpoint, we both tuned in to something dark, a feeling that warned us we were once again walking into the lion's den. Mike's tense body language told me he definitely felt it too. They were close.

"Behind you!" Mike hissed, and I swiveled to block his swing, then wrapped my arms around the fucker's neck and twisted him with such force his neck snapped in two places.

"Never mind." Mike chuckled and flung the extra gun over his shoulder.

Cole's voice came over the radio; he was using our old codes. We listened as we hunkered down just off the beaten path. His plan was to lure them to an area where we had the advantage. It seemed to work, as I could see movement and hear their progress. Now it was time to take out as many of these assholes as possible.

"Three over there." Mike pointed and further justified our haunted feeling. "Looks like seven there."

"Eight." I pointed at one of the cartel, who about fifteen feet back, trying to sneak up on Keith's blind spot.

"Ready?" Mike's gun rose as I followed suit. For once, we had the element of surprise.

"Let's light 'em up."

We used our ammo wisely, only firing when we knew we had the shot. Chamness screamed over the radio, shouting orders from his location. We consistently decoded what was being said to us and what was being said to the cartel. If this was the sixties, you would have thought it was something out of Vietnam. Bodies and blood everywhere, coating the forest and draping the leaves in their sins.

I caught Cole's eye, and he signaled for me to make the call. For the second time tonight, I made a satellite call that would seriously impact our lives.

"The Eagle is fifteen minutes out," I shouted, not wanting to risk the radios.

"Copy that," Keith shouted and sprayed bullets into a group of cartel who appeared suddenly.

"I'm out!" Chamness called from behind me. I tossed him a clip and went back to providing him cover.

"No matter what," he coughed through the gunpowder that hung heavy in the air, "I want the leader."

"Ten-four, Chamness. You better make your move before the Eagle hits."

"I have a twenty," Mike called. "He's to your eleven."

"Go." I raced through the trees and took cover behind a fallen trunk. I watched as Chamness dropped his weapon and went in for hand-to-hand combat with the man who had killed off more than half his team.

We held the cartel off, killing any of them we could see, until we heard the beloved sound of the chopper.

"Move out!" Cole ordered, and we started to retreat, but I noticed Chamness wasn't about to leave, and I wasn't about to go back to the United States down another North Rock. I raced back toward him just as the first bomb hit and fire blasted through the trees. I grabbed Chamness around the vest and yanked him backward, my gun on the now bloody cartel leader.

"Time to move!"

"No!" he shouted and turned back to fight.

Bomb! Another bomb hit, and this time it shook the earth below us, knocking us all to the ground.

"Then finish him!" I shoved his weapon into his hands and watched as the cartel leader reached his arms out wide and laughed hysterically. Chamness planted a bullet directly into his mouth, and all laughter ceased. I grabbed his vest again and hauled him toward cover before the next drop.

Screams filled the forest as we sat in cover a few yards back. I felt no pity; they deserved all they got and more. It was our turn. We were battered, bloody, and beyond exhausted, but we came to do a job, and that was just what we did.

Though we had caught this group, we knew many more would take their place. They were vast and had endless money. We only hoped it would send a message that we would keep coming for them, and we would not be stopped. Not by anyone.

———

I breathed a deep sigh of relief when we finally touched back on US soil. When I stepped out of the chopper on top of our mountain, I fell back and let the others go on without me. My phone alerted me that a message had come through, and I took a quick glance at the screen.

> Agent Colins: The situation has been handled. Your girl is now safe.

Jesus, thank God. As much as I was relieved, there still was an unsettled feeling in my gut. Maybe it was nothing. I was just coming off the high of the mission. Either way, I decided I would conduct any further business through the Devil's Reach from now on.

> John: As in, I'll be hearing about it on the news?

> Agent Colins: Some things are better left unsaid.

I pictured a hole dug in the middle of the desert and a pile of bodies left for the vultures. It wasn't the most ethical move, but when it came to Sloane, I didn't care.

I quickly voiced my thanks and stepped away to intercept Cole.

"Cole," I stopped him, "we should talk."

"All right." He dropped his duffle bag and folded his arms.

"I know why we are being targeted. Well, rather who is targeting us."

"Who?" His eyebrow raised as he waited for my answer.

"Denton Barlow, The American."

Cole's whole body turned to stone, and I knew I had

about five more seconds before he'd lose his shit—well, internally.

"Just before this happened," I pointed to my forehead, "the guy pulled out his camera, did some stupid pledge, and said, 'This is for you, Denton.'"

Cole shook his head slowly a few times as he digested the information then snatched up his bag and headed down the hill.

"Black," he stopped and looked back at me, "not a word to anyone."

"You have my word."

I took a long breath and tried not to show my concern to Cole. If Savannah ever got wind that The American was involved, I wasn't sure what old wounds would surface and where they would take her.

I followed Cole down the path to home.

TWENTY-TWO

While everyone rushed to meet their loved ones outside, I held back a bit, unsure how I felt. True, they hadn't called in that anyone was hurt, but I was still mentally scarred after what happened the last time they returned from a mission.

I stood by the window and pulled back the curtain and watched as Savannah jumped into Cole's arms. He buried his face into her neck then reached out to Livi, whose high-pitched squeals of "Daddy! Daddy!" as she ran from the porch blew her lad-like image right out the window.

Lexi had Keith in quite the kiss, Mia was battling the boys to hug Mark, and Mike and Catalina had already disappeared down the path, but her giggles as they went made me smile.

Though the pain and worry were terrible when the guys left, their reunion when they got home was something spectacular.

The bonds of love and family could be felt for miles around, and the house would be full of it tonight.

"You all right, dear?" Sue found me by the window in the living room. She was so kind and mothering at the best of times.

"Yes," I wiped my wet cheeks dry, "just watching."

"You shouldn't be watching. You should be out there."

"Yeah," my legs were a bit shaky as I moved toward her, "I guess I should be."

"Sloane," she held on to my shoulders as I got closer, "the truth is, that anxiety you feel never really goes away, so the best way to deal with it is by embracing all the times you have them in one piece in front of you. I see how happy you make my boy," she smiled like she did whenever anyone brought up her Blackstone boys, "and I see how happy he makes you. Go, greet him, and remind him what he has waiting for him at home." She leaned in and hugged me tightly.

"Thank you, Sue."

She nodded toward the door, and I hurried to the front porch and stopped at the top of the stairs when I saw him. He looked worn out by the way his body moved coming down the hill.

His eyes searched for me, and when they met mine,

he looked directly at me, and his whole face broken into one of his famous John Black smiles. His dirty black t-shirt clung to his body, and his Army pants and boots looked incredibly sexy as he came closer. He stopped a few steps away and dropped his bag to study me then took a step closer.

"Come here, baby." He barely got the words out as I jumped into his arms. He held me while I let out a huge sigh of relief that he really was okay. "Yesss."

"Are you okay?" I kissed his neck and then his jaw but pulled back when I felt the bandage along his forehead. *How had I not registered that?*

"I made the promise after it happened." He chuckled lightly but stopped when he saw my worry. "I'm okay."

I shook my head, unsure of what to say. With one hand, he held me to him, and with the other he covered my hand that pressed to his face. "I'm..." His face suddenly lit up when he felt the diamond on my finger.

He lowered me to the ground but kept our fingers entwined as he inspected the ring.

"Livi found it. She insisted I put it on." I tried to hide my smile. "You know she knows everything that goes on in this house."

"Yes, I'm very much aware." He chuckled. "But, actually, I was in on this one."

"What?"

"This was one of the worst trips I'd been on yet." He breathed deeply, and I saw the weight he carried home with him. "I needed to know I had a plan in case something happened out there. Livi knew if it did, if something went badly, she was instructed to give it to you. I trusted her to know if the time was right. That girl always has her thumb on the pulse of the house."

I swallowed back the thought that something had gone badly. It wasn't what he or I needed to think about right now.

"So, how did she know to give it to me?"

He nodded over my head, and I slowly turned to see Daniel grinning from the doorway.

"Thanks, Daniel."

"Of course, son." He gave me a wave before he wrapped his arm around his wife and closed the door.

"Okay, so, I'm impressed." My words trailed off when I heard the familiar huff of the fur ball. I stepped back just in time for Tripper to slam his body into John.

To my shock and amusement, he fell backward and wrestled with the giant Shepherd, who growled and whined like he hadn't seen John in a month.

My heart swelled. I understood that need to love the people around you with all your heart and soul and to hold them tight with all your might. Once the reunion was over and John was able to get to his feet, he grabbed his bag, wrapped an arm around me, and walked us down to the little Tin House.

"Your turn…" He winked at me as we headed inside.

We were tearing off each other's clothes before we made it to the bottom of the loft stairs. John grabbed for my waist and turned me around and held my flushed face while I huffed out a hot breath of air. My wild hair covered half my face, and I flexed my legs instinctively.

"You…" He paused like he couldn't get his thoughts in order. "You got me out of there."

His eyes held the depth of the fear the mission had left lurking there. The mission was unlike most, as they were looking for their own, and there were still unanswered questions that may or may not haunt both of us for life.

"You deserve better than…"

"What?" My mouth dropped open at his sudden turn in conversation. "Don't you dare finish that sentence, Black."

He grabbed my hand and held it up, and the white gold three-carat pear-shaped halo engagement ring glinted its promise.

"You deserve a better engagement story to tell our kids than me calling you over the radio from the armpit of hell."

Kids…and there went my stomach.

"How deep *is* that cut?" I joked as beads of sweat broke out across my neck.

He bent down on the bottom step and hiked me over his shoulder. "I'll make it up to you, but first," he slapped my ass, "we need to practice makin' some kids."

"*Practice* is the key word, here."

I was swung around and tossed onto the mattress, and I waited for his body to cover mine, but it never came. When my eyes opened, the room was black, and the click of a remote brought my attention to the opposite side of the room.

Stone Temple Pilots poured through the surround speakers. A strike of a match gave up his location as he lit a candle and set it on the dresser. As the flame moved down the wick, the light became brighter, leaving a perfect circle on the ceiling and casting shadows in all the right places on John's lean body as he slowly removed his shirt.

In a smooth motion, I unclipped my bra and tossed it to the floor and shimmied out of my pants.

He stood at the edge of the bed and crooked his finger at me to come to him. I raised myself up to my hands and knees and slowly crawled along the mattress, looking up at him with hungry eyes. As soon as I was within reach, I stopped and devoured him as the flickering candlelight played with his muscles.

His hands were suddenly in my hair, and he pulled me up to him and took over my mouth. I could tell he was in the mood for control, and I found I wanted to give it to him, but I also wanted to play a little.

I moved my fingers to his stomach and fiddled with the clip on his Army pants. Once they were open, I pushed them down past his hips and leaned back on my hands, arching my back, my nipples erect in an invitation to show him how much I missed him too. He leaned forward and reached around and pulled my wrists outward to release my weight, and I lay flat, my breasts screaming for his touch.

Bending down, he hooked his arms under my legs and slid them out from under me as he pulled me tightly to him. I didn't get a chance to think before he dove straight in.

"Jesus." His neck contracted, and his stomach muscles flexed, granting me a show as I adjusted to the invasion. "I will never tire of this feeling right here."

I wiggled to make more room, and he slipped in farther. My back bowed, and his hands were all over me again.

He rocked back and forth and took his time dragging in and out. His mouth moved like he was talking, but the music drowned out his words. He was thoroughly enjoying his moment…while I, on the other hand, needed some kind of release before my blood got any hotter and my heart beat right out of my chest. It had been a long, stressful time since he'd left, and all that pent-up emotion needed to be torn from my core.

He changed angles and hooked my left leg over his shoulder and picked up the pace. My head whipped back and forth, and my hands clawed at the sheets. I wanted to cry and scream at the same time. Finally, when the buildup became too much, I pushed on his shoulders, making him fall backward with my sudden show of strength.

"No." I batted his hands away as I crawled onto his erection.

"What?" He smirked.

"No more touching unless you're making me come."

"Aww." His smirk became wider, and I wanted to smack him. A woman in need was not someone to mess with.

I slid up and down and started my build-up again, but my way. I rode his tip and used his arousal to coat my already slick opening.

"Sloane," John's neck strained again as I relished the control, "let me touch you."

"No," I panted and ran my hands through my hair, giving him a good show. My breasts bounced around as I grew closer to my bliss.

Oh, so close…

Whoosh!

John somehow was now on top and was pumping himself into me at a maddening speed. I screamed and bucked, and just as I was about to find that place inside that let all my worries fade away like mist on a lake, he leaned in and spoke.

"There's nothing I love more about you than when you're wild with need."

His hips flicked hard, and I burst upward like a confetti popper, colors exploding in my head.

I had no idea when I came down from my high, or when morning decided to show itself, but all that mattered was that I woke to John Black wrapped around me like a warm rug. I snuggled in and went back to sleep.

I vaguely remembered the bed dipping and some movement in the bathroom, but I was just too tired to pry my eyes open.

When I woke for the second time that morning, John was gone, and the urge to throw myself back into my work was strong. For the next four days, I hibernated in my Tin House, desperately going through everything over and over. I needed to figure it out; I needed to find the link that hovered just out of reach.

How were the cartel able to figure out Blackstone's movements when they were speaking in code? How the hell did they know what the codes meant? I was exhausted and knew I needed a break soon. I stood and put my hands on my hips and leaned back, trying to alleviate the ache in my spine.

I hadn't seen John or the guys much, as they were closeted with Frank being debriefed on the mission and going through every detail, as I was.

Savannah poked her head in the door and held up a bottle of red. "Dinner's in ten, and this time don't miss it. You've been hiding away in here way too long. Besides, I have a bottle of Hess here with your name on it."

"You had me at bottle." I laughed. "I'll be right up." For the fourth or fifth time this week, I closed the file that had haunted me since we'd discovered the cartel knew the codes.

The smell of warm bread hit my nose as a Marcus Martini was shoved in my hand. The guys were standing around with drinks, a typical Friday evening at Shadows.

"You've been MIA lately." I turned my attention to Mark.

"I could say the same for you."

"Meh, it's all part of the job." I wanted to ask him how it was going, but Liam raced by with a water gun, and Mark was soon hard on his heels. Shrieks of laughter came from the kitchen as the two of them ran through. Daniel and Sue had their heads together and were whispering over something that had Sue giggling with excitement.

As I went to join them, a loud shriek came from the kitchen. Savannah ran into the room and turned on the TV. She shouted for everyone to come and listen. Cole stood behind her and rested his hands on her shoulders as they looked at the TV. We all tuned in to what the newscaster was saying.

Erin Kitley, from Channel 5 News, pointed over her shoulder at the activity that was taking place behind her as she spoke. "At 3:46 p.m. today, the Montana Federal Prison broke out in a riot. Four inmates have been killed." As the pictures flashed up on the screen, the entire room went still. "Denton Barlow, who was well known to have strong ties with the Mexican cartel, was among those killed." I quickly glanced up and noticed a look pass between Cole and John.

"Oh, my God, is it really over?" Savannah couldn't contain her excitement, and Cole spun her around and pulled her into his arms as a champagne bottle popped. I couldn't help but smile. John had shared part of Savi's story with me, so I knew this was big.

"If there was ever a time to celebrate…" Daniel laughed as he poured the bubbly into several glasses, and the dinner that followed was filled with laughter and good old-fashioned storytelling.

"There you are." Savannah found me on the back deck looking out over the frosty lake, and her eyes literally sparkled with happiness. It seemed as though a weight had been lifted from her shoulders. "We voted, and we are having girls' night at your place tonight, so come on. We can't be there without you."

The five of us girls headed down the path, bottles of red and sparkly tucked under our arms. Of course, Lexi had sparkling water, but she was a good sport about it all. We took a moment to watch the guys, who had the kids sitting in the snow listening to instructions. Mark, John, Cole, Mike, and Keith all held Nerf guns as if they were heading into battle. Cole's voice could be heard as he laid down the rules of the game. We had to laugh at how serious they all were. B insisted on being glued to Olivia's side as she tried to listen. As we watched, one of the twins slowly slid an extra Nerf gun behind him and was reaching for another.

Mia raised her eyebrow at me. "And that's why I drink." She raised her bottle of red.

As I sat back and watched my new family around me, I realized I was happy to be here. I was glad I was a part of it all when Savannah got such life-altering news. I noticed Lexi and Catalina had become quite close. It didn't surprise me, as they had both come from such violent backgrounds and had been living at Dusk together before they moved here. Mia and Savannah seemed to be much more approachable. They both wore their hearts on their sleeves and seemed to adjust easily to whoever they were with.

Later that evening, with the kids all in bed, shouting and cheering from the guys brought us to the window to see was happening.

Catalina flopped back down in her seat. "I guess more good news was shared tonight. Davie and Dell will be taking over Mike's and Keith's positions at Dusk."

"Fine by me. I'm just happy we are all together." Catalina smiled. "Mike seems a lot happier to be back here, and I know he's happy to be closer to California."

"Why does that guy scare me in all the right ways?" Savannah laughed.

"Who?" I questioned, looking around at their pink cheeks. "What?"

"Oh, wait, you haven't met Trigger." Savannah fanned herself.

"That's a damn shame." Mia snorted, and the other girls hooted with laughter.

"I guess I have some catching up to do!" I leaned forward and cheered the girls' glasses.

By midnight, Savannah and I were the only ones left standing. The others went to bed, knowing they had to get up early with their little ones. With a glass of water in her hand, Savannah stood and studied my wall of pictures and diagrams of the all the possible scenarios I had sketched and glued everywhere.

She pulled the rookie's photo down and with her back

to me muttered, "He was so young. As much as I respect and understand what Cole and the guys do, it's not for everyone, and definitely not for someone this young."

I moved to join her and sat at the conference table. I rubbed my head in frustration. "He may have been young, but his family pulled many strings to get him into North Rock. He had quite the reputation for cheating."

"What do you mean?"

"I guess he had a terrible memory. He failed the first test, and then his family paid off a general to get him back in to write it a second time. Don't worry," I held up a hand, "the guys figured out which general it was. He was just some ass with too much power. From what I hear, the rookie probably had a cheat sheet in order to pass the test. His classmates certainly weren't very fond of him. They all knew he had someone from way up giving him freebies."

Savannah turned toward me as she pointed to a position on the map. "So, the rookie was killed, stripped of his radio and all his belongings, so how do we know he hadn't written them down? If he had that bad of a memory, he may have written the codes down too. It would have been pretty stupid, but that could be a possible theory, right?"

It was as if someone had cleared the fog away, I grabbed my laptop and opened it to play the one YouTube video that had always bothered me. I fast forwarded to the part where the leader had the radio, and the small black thing he held in his hand suddenly became clear to me. I watched as the leader listened to something on the radio then looked down at it as he gave orders to his men to move out. "Holy shit, how could I have missed it?"

I raced around the table and grabbed Savannah and hugged her so hard I nearly knocked her off her feet. "Thank you! Thank you so much!"

I grabbed my laptop, and we both ran up to the house. "John," I called as we raced into the living room.

"Out on the deck," Abigail said as she pointed to the door.

All the guys were around the firepit with cigars and brandy and looked up in surprise as we burst through the door.

"We got it. We figured it out. Look!" I opened my laptop and showed them the YouTube video once again, only this time I pointed at the object in the leader's hand. "He must have written the codes down. Nick Stewart always wrote everything down."

"That's suicide." John moved to see the screen better. "How sure are you?"

"I would bet my career on it." I just knew in my heart I was right.

"That's good enough for me." Cole granted me a small but worried smile.

"What an asshole thing to do." Mark shook his head.

"You took the words right out of my mouth," Cole muttered in disbelief.

"What a way to lose such good men. There's protocol and training put in place for a reason," John said as he pulled me onto his lap. "Thank you for figuring this out." He kissed me.

"Actually, it was Savannah who made the connection."

"It was all right there, Sloane. It just took a fresh set of eyes to see it."

"Regardless of who found what, we have the answer now. Good job, girls. I'm taking this to Frank." Cole had his phone to his ear as he hurried inside.

"Score one for the girls," Savannah cheered with her hands in the air.

"Yeah, it's always bittersweet when you learn the answers and it's not what you want to hear. I know that Chamness will take this hard, but at least the remaining members of North Rock will get some closure and rest easier tonight." I reached for John, and he wrapped his arms around me, and his lips found my neck.

TWENTY-THREE

JOHN

I glanced at my watch then went back to reading the news on the iPad. I had fifteen minutes before we gathered downstairs to discuss how the last mission went and to hear what Frank had to say about Washington's reaction to what we had discovered.

My phone buzzed on the counter, and I glanced at the screen.

Huh.

"Black," I answered.

"Hey, man." Brick took a moment to inhale. "Got a second?"

"I do." I turned off the iPad and replaced it in its docking station.

"Your team that you had in Mexico, are they still there?"

"No." I leaned against the counter, curious where the conversation was heading.

"Shit, okay."

"Why?"

"I don't know, maybe it's nuthin', but you know I was following the Stripe Backs. After we hopped the border from Texas, they stopped to meet some guys in suits. I didn't recognize any of them, but one had a nasty scar up his neck." He made a disgusted noise. "The meeting took forever, so I hunkered down and had a few too many shots of whiskey." He took another drag of what I assumed was his joint. "Suddenly, some men decked out in masks and black military pants came in, took a seat, and started talking to them."

"As in feds?"

"What feds do you know would walk into a house with a bunch a lowlifes, pull up a chair, share a drink, and chat?"

I smirked. He was right on that one.

"One thing led to another, and someone starting shouting. When I jumped back up to look, bullets were flying."

"Shit." I'd been there, and I knew how things could change in a blink of an eye. "Anyone make it out alive?"

"One did for sure." He paused. "I didn't stick around to find out about the rest. The Stripe Backs' pres bolted, and I followed. He was my mark, so, yeah, I moved on to stay on his ass."

"Right." I nodded, understanding that statement, and

brushed a hand through my hair. "Well, I can assure you our brother team is not there right now. We pulled the rest and are waiting to rebuild and relocate."

"Yeah, sorry about that." He lowered his voice. Despite the life Brick lived, he had a good heart, and from what I understood from Mike, he was a damn good friend to his guys and to Tess. "Never easy to lose a family member."

"No, it's not." I closed my eyes and mourned my friends for a moment.

"All right, well, I just had to ask."

"No problem, man. Anytime."

"Thanks." The line went dead, and I found myself wondering who the hell the masked men were, and if they were law enforcement, why in the hell they'd sit and have a conversation and not just storm the place.

"Black." Mike tapped his watch to tell me to get moving. "You good?"

"Yeah." I shook my head and followed him downstairs to take my seat at the table. Cole didn't waste any time and jumped right in.

Two hours later and a great job from the boys in Washington, the meeting ended.

I waited for everyone to leave the meeting then leaned against the table and watched Cole tuck his files away.

"How did Frank take the news?" I broke the silence, curious to see were his head was.

"After presenting the evidence Sloane emailed me last night, he and Chamness agreed that the rookie did put the codes on paper. Frank is just as dumbfounded as we were. How any soldier, especially one who went through the training program, could be so reckless just shows how much more we need to screen the men we select."

"And those involved in the process." I let that one sink in for a few seconds. "So, what happens to the general?"

"His ass will be relieved of duty, and he'll face an inquiry sometime at the end of the month."

"Great." I was pleased to hear Frank took it as seriously as we all did.

Cole tossed the last file on the desk and rubbed his face like he was struggling with something. I couldn't tell what was up, so I figured it was best to leave him be with his thoughts.

"Black," he called as I opened the door, "the video camera you retrieved was blank, although Davie does feel he might be able to pull some data. Time will tell." I gave him a tired nod before Cole rubbed his head. "And thank you."

"For?" I closed the door behind me and turned back to him.

His jaw ticked, and I could tell he struggled with what he had to say.

"For giving me a reason to kill that son-of-a-bitch."

We all had been waiting for the moment we could alert the CIA that Denton needed to be taken out. They just needed proof he was still working with the cartel, and they'd do what they did. Remove the problem in a roundabout way, and none of us would have the blood on our hands. Nice and clean.

"It needed to happen."

He nodded and glanced at the phone that buzzed beside him.

"I guess he had some cult following in prison, called himself Seven Webs." Cole chuckled while I shook my head.

"That explains the lame tattoos, then."

"He was relentless, though. He couldn't stop until he got what was mine." His eyes darkened while he flicked a pen through his fingertips. "Chamness and BT have decided to move to Dusk," he switched gears, "and I think we'll hold off putting another team in Mexico right now."

"Smart." I nodded. "We need to change things up, and until we know who is a good fit, it's best to start slow."

"I think I might build a new team, take them directly from Camp Green. Groom them myself. It will be a lot of work, but it's the right call."

"Agreed."

Cole sank back in his chair with a heavy sigh. We both stayed silent while we mulled over how quickly our lives were changing. "When did this happen? It used to be so simple, and now there's all this entwined with the job."

He looked so stressed I had to smile, but what I was about to say was cut short as we both looked at the door at the sound of the twins running down the hallway while Mia huffed threats after them.

I stood and opened the door then pointed down the hall with my chin. "When we all found someone." I shrugged. "It's not just the five of us anymore. We have more to protect, more of a reason to come home." I chuckled lightly, loving how this conversation finally included me. "Our days of playing reckless heroes are long gone, my friend."

"I suppose you're right." The lines around his eyes softened and lit up when Olivia appeared outside the door holding Ethan's Nerf gun with pride. She held a finger to her lips to hush us and giggled when Cole gave her a high five in the air.

"God, I love that kid." I gave her a thumbs up. "Can you imagine that little lady running this house someday?"

"And that reason right there is why you need to have a kid or two of your own. You can't leave her alone with the twins." He laughed as foam bullets sprayed down the hallway.

"I think she'll be just fine." I was happy to see the stress leave Cole's shoulders. He carried a lot these days, and it was important for us to remember to enjoy the times we had before we couldn't anymore. Kids were not at the top of my list right now, and I knew Sloane felt the same. We were more interested in spending time alone together. There were lots of kids for us to enjoy right here. The pure joy I got at being able to hype Mark's twins up on sugar and then send them back right at bedtime like wound-up cats on catnip was awesome.

"Babe?" Savi called from the other side of the glass

door. "We'll need to knock out the wall in the playroom." She smiled as she held up a pregnancy stick that read positive.

"Holy shit!" Cole jumped up from his chair and raced out to wrap Savi in a huge hug.

"See, you just evened out the score." I slapped Cole on the shoulder and kissed Savi on the cheek. "Congratulations, guys. I'm so excited for you both."

"Thanks, John." She wiped her cheeks dry and beamed up at Cole. "Wow."

"Wow." He mirrored her excitement. Cole really needed that right now.

"Oh," I turned around, "and before Mark gets his bets in, I'm calling it now. It's a girl."

Savi laughed and buried her head into Cole's chest.

"All right, I'm out." I waved at them to give them their moment and blocked Ethan's path when he tried to race by.

"Uncle John!" he shouted, and I laughed all the way outside.

———

The warm morning sun beat down on our backs as we climbed the mountain for the twenty-some odd time this year. I was proud and honored Sloane took such an interest in something I loved to do. She probably would never climb without ropes or a helmet, but the fact that she'd been pushing her limits since Christmas was impressive. She wasn't going to let this cliff beat her.

"You think you have enough in you to keep going?" I asked when we were about three-quarters of the way up. We had yet to reach the top of the peak in any of our climbs, but I knew that was her goal for today.

"Why? Are you tired, Black?" She beamed at me, and I saw her determination to make it. That was good, because I needed her to.

"Just making sure." I motioned with my head for her to keep going. Just like Mike and I had taught her, she went slowly and made sure every move was calculated and well thought out.

"Oh, your brother called yesterday. Said he and your parents are coming in tomorrow morning. I thought I'd bring Mark, and we'd grab them on the way through town."

She laughed and hooked her rope through the next loop. "Poor Mark. You just like to see my father make him sweat."

"That's exactly why," I answered without an ounce of shame. "Besides, he's a charmer and gets your mother all flustered."

"That is pretty funny to watch." She paused when her hand suddenly reached the top of the ledge. "Oh, my God," she whispered through a smile, and her eyes sparkled with excitement.

"Use your arms to hike yourself over and hook your leg," I started to direct her, but I might as well have saved my breath as I saw her adorable ass disappear above me, and I quickly followed suit.

"John?" She stood a few feet from the edge while I hopped to my feet. "What is this?" She stood, holding a small box of tiny heart-shaped cookies I had placed there for her.

"This…" I brushed the rock dust from my hands and wrapped an arm around her and turned her to face back out over the house. "This is me making something right."

"What do you mean?"

I rested my chin on her shoulder and kissed her slender neck. "See, right there," I pointed to the lake by the house, "this view is my most favorite place in the world. It's where I come to think, where I shake off the stress of a mission, or just to get away. I've only ever shared it with Mike, but now…" I held her tight to my chest. "Now I get to share it with you."

"I love that." She kissed the side of my jaw. "Thank you."

"No, Sloane, thank you." I hated how my emotions were all over the place lately. Though life had settled back into a rhythm, the aftermath of losing most of North Rock still lay heavily on our souls. We just needed time. "So, let's go through the checklist. One, you made it here. Two, it is my absolute favorite spot to be. Three, we have cookies Savannah made, and Keith didn't get a single one. And four, what's four again…?" I teased as she turned in my arms to look up at me, no doubt confused. "Oh, yes, of course." I slowly lowered onto one knee. "A proper proposal."

"John, you don't have—"

"But I do. You deserve not to be pushed into a marriage with the fear I brought you that day. No, you, Sloane," I took her hand in mine, "deserve the world, and I intend to give that to you." Her free hand flew to her mouth as her eyes got glossy.

"Sloane Harlow, you came into my life, and I made it nearly impossible to be around me. I didn't understand how the wall I built up for years could crumble with a single look from you, my beautiful woman. You are smart, quick, and strong. My life isn't like most. It will test you; it will hurt you and stress you out to no end." I took a moment to get my words in order. "I promise you, if you choose me, I will make it my life's mission to always come back in one piece." I gave her a wink, and she laughed a little. "And that I will love you with all my heart. So," I pulled the diamond from my pocket that she had taken off to prepare for her climb and left at the Tin House and held it up for her to see. "Sloane Harlow, in front of every living creature watching us with curiosity and right here above the world, will you marry me?"

Her lips pressed together as tears leaked down her pink cheeks. "Yes, John Black, I will marry you." When the ring slipped over her finger, she dove into my arms and kissed me with all her might. We spent the rest of the morning eating our treats before we headed back down to the house to get ready for tomorrow.

———

"Well? What do you think?" My father stood next to me at the back of the barn as we looked around at his temporarily transformed ten thousand square foot barn. The old wooden structure looked pretty damn perfect to me.

"I think Savannah missed her calling," I joked and tugged at my tie and fiddled with Paul's pin that he was given when he started with Blackstone. I missed my best friend every day, but I knew he was here with me right now smiling down.

It had taken Savi three months to plan and direct everyone to put together the perfect wedding for us. We wanted simple, elegant, and rustic for our theme, and that was just want we got. Plus, the weather was cool enough that my dress blues weren't suffocating me.

White chairs were five people deep on each side of the aisle. White flower petals were strewn along the pathway for her to follow to me. White lights and long lengths of white silk fabric were draped through the beams in the rafters above. Small half barrels filled with light pink roses were strategically placed throughout the old barn. I smiled at the rusty old Chevrolet truck Ellie and I used to play in. It was backed up to the edge of the barn, and inside its flatbed was a mountain of ice loaded with beer and white wine for the guests.

"Did you see these?" My mother held up one of the metal horseshoes from a basket that sat on the table outside. "They're placeholders!" Her excitement mirrored mine. It was all pretty damn impressive. More twinkle lights were woven into the trees, and about a billion candles in jars were strategically placed to give more depth to the property. They flickered in the early evening, and I knew they would look pretty cool as the sun went down. Mom held up the tag that read *Luck found us, and we are hoping it finds you too.* "Sloane wasn't just lucky for you, son. She was for the whole family."

"And team," Mike chimed in from somewhere then chuckled about how his sister's heart would be broken after this.

"Agreed about the team," I called, ignoring his comment about his little sister, and then addressed my mother. "I can't believe Ellie." I thought about how my sister's fate had looked so bleak, but now she was showing more progress than we could have ever hoped for. It gave me such a rush when I first realized she had retained who Sloane was. She seemed a lot happier and was using the tools she'd learned in therapy, so her meltdowns were now few and far between. None of that would have happened if it wasn't for Sloane showing us how to live again.

"We've gained a part of her back." Mom sniffed and tried to keep it together as the rest of the guys joined us.

"Last one to get hitched. Not having second thoughts, are you?" Keith joked as he helped his Nan into a seat then fixed her sweater to cover her bare shoulders. The moment his back turned, she let the fabric drop and eyed my uncle when he came in. I hid my smirk from Keith.

"None." I glanced at the time. "Just want to seal the deal so she's mine."

"I know that one," Cole muttered as he looked around for his wife.

When the minister came in and gave us the cue that they were about to let the guests in, I slipped out back and waited. I couldn't choose a best man. That would have been like choosing a favorite kid.

Olivia.

So instead I asked my father, the one who showed me how to be a man and how to love through thick and thin. Though my father had lost his way when Ellie got hurt, I was able to show him the light without even knowing it.

The music started, and my father and I moved to stand in front of all our family and friends. Olivia made an adorable flower girl, and Baby B who was glued to her side once again as the ringbearer. Against Sloane's protests, Mia did not want her twins in the wedding. In fact, I heard a rumor that Mark was going to tie them to a tree during the ceremony.

My heart almost stopped when I saw my twin standing with a bouquet of pink flowers between her hands. She smiled when she spotted me and started to walk forward. I could tell she was nervous, but having Dad and me in her sights helped.

Sloane had made my sister her maid of honor. *Holy shit.* The thought of that made me fall in love with her all over again.

"Hi, little brother," she whispered as Mom pointed to

where she needed to stand. "I hope you and Sloane will be very happy together."

I blinked back the pesky tears that broke through my dam. My sister was able to remember my soon-to-be bride's name. That was the best gift I could have received.

"Twins before anyone else." I winked, and I saw her face light up. "I love you, Elle."

"I love you too."

I heard my father sniff, and I kept my eyes on the floor as I reined in my own emotions. I never thought I'd have such a moment with my sister again, let alone in a public setting.

A sudden silence, then the gasps and my father shifting to stand a little straighter. I savored the moment, waiting for the perfect time to look up and see my future wife.

One, two, three.

There she was, in a form-fitting white lace dress, hair down in big curls but pinned up on one side, and her light pink lipstick matched the color of the flowers. And when her deep blue eyes latched on to mine, I knew we were meant to be here, right here, right now. This moment in time was written for us.

I barely recalled holding her hand, listening to the minister, and saying our vows. When I did snap back to the present, it was when he finally said I could kiss my wife. Just as I was about to lean in, I felt a peck on my shoe and looked down at Doug, who was making his silly chicken noise. Sloane laughed and scooped him up before

I could react, then she grabbed me with her free hand and kissed my open mouth madly while the entire place roared with happy laughter and cheers. I grinned like an idiot, taking Doug from Sloane before he could do any damage to her lovely lace dress.

"Well, Doug, it is your house, after all," Sloane laughed, "and you are his best friend. Glad you could join us."

I took her hand, and we walked down the aisle together while thousands of white petals floated around us like butterflies. We took our place at the table and spent the next two hours listening to funny stories and laughing with friends.

"I don't think I can look at another piece of cake for as long as I live." Catalina flopped her head onto Mike's shoulder. Dinner was impressive, and so was Savannah. She had listened to both of our wishes on how we wanted the wedding to be, and she never once went overboard. The barbeque dinner was perfect and the cake simple.

After the party started, we headed for the spot where bales of hay were pushed together to form a circle of couches with blankets draped for comfort. Savannah said she'd made this place for us, so we could escape all the people and be with our loved ones.

I sat back and took in the scene. I watched my brothers with their wives, I watched the kids playing with little battery-operated lanterns throughout the fields, and I spotted my parents on the dance floor holding one another and my sister coloring a picture with my aunt. I suddenly felt at peace.

Somehow, I had found the courage not only to live again but to love.

"How are Davie and Dell working out at Dusk?" I asked Chamness as he leaned into the doorway that looked out over the party.

"I'm pretty impressed, actually." He sighed, and I saw the weight of his family's loss hanging over him like a dark cloud. "I think I might stick around and do a few missions with them. Teach them what I know."

"I'd appreciate that." Cole raised a beer to him.

"Make sure they aren't using those shit neck radios." He smirked at me. We'd had many debates over which radios were the best, and it took years for Frank to change them up.

"Touché." I chuckled, happy that his sense of humor hadn't disappeared completely.

Sloane squeezed my leg to grab my attention as she unlinked our hands and pulled my arm around her shoulders.

"This was pretty perfect."

"It was." I kissed her softly and drank in her scent.

Cole shifted Savi from his lap to retrieve his phone. He looked at it and then at me.

"Logan," he answered as a greeting. "Now is not the —" He paused, and I saw his face tighten, and we all tuned quickly in to his mood.

"All right, boys." He stood and kissed his wife.

"Wait, what?" Sloane looked around, confused, while I shot up and tugged at my collar.

"We gotta go." I felt the rush that always came with our missions.

"What?" She shook her head, but instead of getting upset, I saw she understood. There were no days off when it came to our job. This was what we did.

I wrapped my arms around her and kissed her hard before I whispered, "Be naked when I get home. I'll meet you at the peak." I growled, wanting her right then.

"Well, that's a promise I can look forward to." She laughed as I walked backward with a dirty grin full of promises about just what peaks we could reach together.

"Welcome to Blackstone, baby."

EPILOGUE

"All right, ladies." I turned my back to the guys and inspected my team. Our uniform consisted of white knee socks, tight black shorts, and deep blue t-shirts that read "Ladies of Blackstone." Eye grease lined the tops of our cheekbones to cut down the glare from the summer sun. Today, we were not the wives of our beloved husbands. No, today, we were here for war. We were here to beat the boys at their own game.

"You look cute." John came over and tried to wrap me in his arms.

"Oh, no." Savannah held her hand up and pushed John backward. "This," she pointed to the rest of the guys, "is because of what you all did. No touching until after we kick your asses."

"Your wife is scrappy, Logan!" John called over his shoulder.

"But she's so cute when she's scrappy," he said and laughed back.

"Save it for the bedroom." Savannah smirked and pulled me back toward the girls. Her son Easton sat snug as a bug in his grandmother's arms. June held Reagan, Lexi's daughter, who was now nine months old. She was the perfect mixture of Lexi and Keith.

Daniel walked to the center of the lawn and held up a megaphone. Then, in a very important voice, he directed us to move into place.

"Hands in, ladies." Lexi put her hand out, and we all joined in. "Lips, bits, and tits, hoorah!"

One by one, my sisters took their turn racing against the guys. We might not have had their training, but we were small, agile, and very determined.

Savannah tapped in Catalina before she dropped to my feet gasping for air.

"You would think the workout my husband gives me every morning would prepare me for anything, but apparently, that's not the case."

With a laugh, I hauled her to her feet and handed her a bottle of water.

"You did good." I tried to keep my head in the game. "We need to win, or we'll never get rid of that rodent."

"Heads up." Savannah nodded over my shoulder. "You're our last hope!"

"You know what to do." Catalina winked as the rest

of them stepped back, and I moved to stand at the starting line. I glanced over at John, who was very much enjoying my outfit. So, I used what I had and bent over dramatically to stretch down low, and I heard him chuckle.

"You can play dirty all you want, baby." He blew me a kiss.

"Ready, set, go!" Daniel shot a blank into the air, and I took off running.

I didn't waste any time as I jumped up high, grabbed the rope, and started to shimmy up to the top of the first obstacle of the course. It wasn't easy, but I had worked on my arms for the past few weeks with the girls. Next, I wrapped my arms around the line and hung out over a twenty-foot ridge and inched my way down using my bodyweight for speed.

Once my feet touched the ground, I raced across the lawn and dove like a champ into the mud and Army-crawled under the netting. Mud eased its way into every nook of my body, but I didn't care. I used the sides of my shoes for grip and hauled myself through the thick sludge. Mia screamed my name and kept me aware of how much time was left on the clock.

Livi and Baby B were racing around, cheering me on, while the twins were on the other side for their uncle John. Abigail, Sue, and Doc Roberts were like balls of nerves vibrating as they stood at the finish line. They were on our side. *It* had to go, despite how much the guys loved it.

I glanced over and saw John seconds behind me, battling with his size under the nets.

With a huge effort, I kicked out with all my might and was able to bring myself up out of the mud. My legs were on fire as I jumped to my feet and ran across the finish line, beating John by a fraction of a second.

The girls raced across the yard screaming. Lexi slammed into me with a hug, and the rest of the girls followed suit.

"Whooo!" Savannah cheered while the high of what we just did settled in.

The relief that spread through all of us was just what we needed. We Blackstone Ladies finally beat the guys at something, and oh, boy, was the prize the best gift of all.

Daniel walked toward us slowly. "Well, here you are." He handed me the monster, and I glanced at the girls.

"Ready?"

"Hell, yeah!" Catalina laughed before we all took off toward the dock. One by one, we all jumped into the warm lake water.

I popped up and treaded water while the guys came down to the dock. Their long faces did not conjure up even an ounce of sympathy in any of us.

"I feel like I didn't get to say goodbye." Mark folded his arms. "Like we didn't have enough time together."

"Time," I blurted. "This monster has been around way too long. It's the worst thing in the house."

"It's not the worst." Mark fudged a pissy face.

"It's the worst, babe." Mia nodded. "Sloane, do it."

"All right." I held up the miserable little Furby that had been used to scare us too many times, far more than I could count. "Time to go." I tossed the toy as far as I could toward the middle of the lake, and we all let out a sigh of relief. "Good riddance, you little monster."

"Monster," Mike hissed as he dabbed at his eyes. "That thing was like family."

Catalina rolled her eyes at the guys as they sadly headed back up toward the house. We spent the rest of the day in the water, thoroughly enjoying our win.

The firepit party was in full swing that evening. We were all still bragging about beating the guys and decided we should do it every year. We even designed a trophy.

"You warm enough?" John handed me a coffee.

"I am," I answered as he bent down and kissed me softly. "Well, actually, maybe I am a little cold. Could you grab me a blanket?"

"Of course." He kissed me one last time and caught up to Mark, who was heading in for another beer.

Savannah caught my eye and shot me a devilish smile. I matched her humor and…

"Son-of-a-bitch!" John yelped, and Mark came running out of the house like he just got stung.

"What the hell?"

"Cheers, ladies." I smirked. "*Welcome to Blackstone, baby!*"

The End

For anyone who has a loved one who has experienced a brain injury, here is a wonderful resource.

www.craighospital.org

Remember, you're never alone.

ACKNOWLEDGMENTS

To my mother, who worked so closely on this story
with me.

To my daughter Brooke, who helped me with story ideas,
research, and Tripper moments.

To my dear friends, Jill and Steve Chamness, for once
again letting me dive into both of your professions and
pick away at the details.

To my girls, Kim, Vanessa, Veronica, Elizabeth, Jamie,
Jaci, and Lisa for helping me keep all the stories straight
and your wonderful input along the way.

To my beloved editor Lori Whitwam, for all your input.
Cheers to book 14!

To Lydia Harbaugh, for being such a great marketing
director. I appreciate you so much.

To my reader group and street team for believing in me.

To my readers for following through these stories from the very start.

I, and the Blackstone families, thank you.

J.L. Drake, born and raised in Nova Scotia, Canada, later moving to Southern California. Though she loves the weather in Cali, she would sell her left kidney for a good rainstorm. Jodi's love of the seasons back home in Canada definitely appear in her books.

When she's not writing, you can often find her sitting somewhere along the coast of Huntington Beach, reading, or at home curled up on a couch with her two children and husband, binge watching a good movie.

AUTHORJLDRAKE.COM

FOLLOW ME ON SOCIAL MEDIA

facebook.com/JLDrakeauthor

x.com/jodildrake_j

instagram.com/j.l.drake

tiktok.com/@authorjldrake

bookbub.com/profile/j-l-drake

BROKEN TRILOGY

Broken

Shattered

Mended

BLACKSTONE SERIES

Honor

Escape

Freedom

Courage

DEVIL'S REACH TRILOGY

Trigger

Demons

Unleashed

QUIET MAFIA SERIES

Quiet Wealth

Quiet Secrets

Quiet Power

Quiet Empire

DARK WATER SERIES

Shadows

Whiskey

Alpha

Tango

<u>HAVOC OF SINS</u>

Grim

Havoc

Sins

<u>DARKNESS SERIES</u>

Darkness Lurks

Darkness Follows

Darkness Falls

<u>STANDALONE BOOKS</u>

Behind My Words

Christmas At The Cabin

Omerta

For the suggested reading order, please scan the QR code: